DANCE OF LIFE

Barbara Blythe

DANCE OF LIFE

COPYRIGHT 2013 by BARBARA BLYTHE

Contact Information: titleadmin@pelicanbookgroup.com

Scripture quotations, unless otherwise indicated are taken from the King James translation, public domain.

Cover Art by *Nicola Martinez*

White Rose Publishing, a division of Pelican Ventures, LLC
www.pelicanbookgroup.com PO Box 1738 *Aztec, NM * 87410

White Rose Publishing Circle and Rosebud logo is a trademark of Pelican Ventures, LLC

Publishing History
First White Rose Edition, 2014
Paperback Edition ISBN 978-1-61116-316-2
Electronic Edition ISBN 978-1-61116-315-5
Published in the United States of America

Dedication

To Mom— thank you for giving me a love of dance; to Dad— thank you for giving me a love of history. And to my Lord and Savior who gave me parents who have always been there for me.

Praise

Fire Dragon's Angel

"A charming tale of adventure and love in colonial times...well worth the read. I highly recommend this book. ~ Pegg Thomas

Ransom for Many

"The book will keep you on the end of your seat (pirates, passion, et al). The story was intriguing and...had charm." ~ Review by "Elizabeth" at Book Collector

1

Paris
October, 1845
Le Théâtre de la Mondé

Rosin, sweat, and gas permeated the charged air, thick with discord and the Russian rants of Nicolai Rubenevski.

Feet aching and head pounding, Charice Marin wondered how much longer she could put up with this.

Poor Mira stood before Rubenevski, head hanging as she bore the brunt of the man's tirade.

Didn't the man realize he was wasting his breath chastising Mira in Russian when she spoke only French? He'd been shouting nonstop for thirty minutes because Mira's slipper ribbons had loosened during the rehearsal of the opening act.

Charice feared the girl now wished she'd remained in her village and married the neighboring sheepherder her parents had favored instead of running away to Paris to become a ballerina.

Releasing a sigh while summoning her nerve, she prepared to present herself on stage and end Rubenevski's tirade. There'd be no practice if she didn't. The man had been known to shout and yell for hours. Lifting her chin and stretching her neck to regal lengths, as her mother did when portraying a woman who would not be denied, Charice darted out of the shadows. And slammed into the broad back of a man.

Inconsiderate oaf. Couldn't he see me? He stepped right in front of me.

Pivoting, the man's emerald green gaze slammed into Charie's and flared. A shock of nearly black hair fell over his brow. Lips twitched, and a scar leaped at her. *"Pardon moi."*

A sense of familiarity settled as the deep timbre of his voice vibrated within her.

Broad shoulders were defined by the taut linen of his pristine white shirt. Trousers hugged corded thighs while his scuffed boots outlined muscular calves. He had the look of a *danseur*. With his towering height, he was almost intimidating.

But Charie would not be intimidated—not by this man who seemed far too certain of himself. *"Aucun préjudice causé." No harm done.* Averting her gaze, she hurried past. Was that a soft chuckle that floated behind her?

"You are a thoughtless, witless girl," Rubenevski barked, his volume shaking the rafters.

Charie cringed, thankful that Mira couldn't understand his words. She wished she couldn't.

Behind Rubenevski stood Antoine, shifting from one foot to the other while exuding indifference. The egotistical danseur had no care that a member of the company suffered humiliation. Charie noticed his shoulders lacked the breadth of the man's who'd bumped her. Banishing the unwarranted comparison, she cleared her throat.

"Gospodin Rubenevski, if I could have a word." Charie's flawless Russian caught the man's attention, and he fell silent. Swallowing hard, she met his

enraged glare and stopped before him.

"What do you want?"

"I want to practice, and I can't if you continue bellowing. You are wasting time and the count's money. What will you say when he arrives and finds you badgering a dancer?"

Intakes of breath occurred simultaneously, and the ensuing silence deafened as all awaited Rubenevski's response.

Charie wasn't sure she was breathing.

"I am the choreographer, *baryshnya*, and you would do well to remember that. Your *prima danseuse* status does not allow you to dictate. And though I planned to tell you after rehearsal—as you've chosen to interrupt—I think it only fair to let you know I am in agreement with *gospodin* Phillipe. Roberto Capretti will partner you in *Long Ago in Bethlehem*."

"What? You can't be serious. Surely you remember his behavior last year in *Marionette?* When he managed to present himself sober, he was disagreeable—when drunk, he was disgusting. *Monsieur* Phillipe might admire his skill, but he's a disruption to any troupe. I have ethics and principles. God would not want me to dance with him."

"I don't believe Phillipe has consulted God. He wants to draw an audience. Women enjoy Capretti's dancing. Women bring their husbands and paramours who spend lavishly to keep those women happy. Do you understand?"

Charie felt faint from a suffocating heat. An overwhelming need to escape took hold while tears burned behind her eyes. Her breathing dissolved to short, angry gasps.

A movement near the curtain ropes caught her

eye. It was the annoyingly handsome man who seemed to enjoy the unfolding drama. At her expense. Elevating her chin, she met Rubenevski's livid gaze.

"This will not be."

"Do you plan to run to the count and complain?"

Charie had never resorted to tactics of that nature. *Monsieur* Rubenevski knew she wasn't one to take advantage of her fatherly relationship with Count Stanislov. She wouldn't do so now. "No. But I will not partner with a man who is vile and immoral."

"See how far your 'ethics' and 'principles' take you in this business, *gospoja* Marin."

Something deep within her exploded, and aware she was about to either burst into tears or slap *Monsieur* Rubenevski, she whirled around and retreated. As she passed the annoying stranger, he reached out as though to stop her, sympathy spread across his rugged features.

Shaking her head, she surged forward, pausing only long enough to retrieve her cloak from her dressing room. Throwing it about her shoulders, she fled the backstage area, flew down the stairs, and exited through a rear door. A blast of cold October air enveloped, while a steady mist and red-gold leaves coated her. Lowering her head, she pushed into the wind, her steps automatically taking her towards the *Théâtre Impérial*.

****

Charie had just divested her wet cloak, and commenced pacing when commotion in the hallway signaled the advent of her mother.

Which meant the final curtain had fallen on the

Thursday matinee of *The Misadventures of Sally*.

Charie hurriedly smoothed the tendrils of her curling, auburn hair that had loosened during practice and her recent dash though the wind and rain.

Her mother always looked elegant, perfectly attired, and every hair in place. No torn stockings and worn tutu for Matilda Marin.

The door of the dressing room burst open, and her mother swept within, her arms laden with roses and lilies, while her dresser, the ever patient and mothering Swede, Lizbet Borgensen, shooed the lauding throng away. Order was immediately restored as Lizzie slammed the door in the face of a balding, rotund, mustachioed man.

The flowers perfumed the air, so much so that her mother cracked a window. As soon as she turned towards Charie, concern clouded her crystal blue eyes.

"This can't be good. I've never known you to visit me in the middle of the day." Her mother spoke English, her slight drawl marking her as a Virginia native.

"Oh, *Maman*, everything is all wrong." Releasing a sob, Charie moved towards her mother, warmth enfolding as Matilda wrapped her in her arms.

"You're not ill, are you?"

"No." Charie pushed away. Folding her hands, she paced. "I need your advice. *Monsieur* Rubenevski spent all morning and part of the afternoon shouting in Russian, and then informed me *Monsieur* Phillipe has decided I will dance with Roberto Capretti in the company's performance of *Long Ago in Bethlehem*. You know how I feel about the man. I've a good mind to quit the ballet, *Maman*.

"*Monsieur* Rubenevski said I shouldn't worry so

5

much about ethics or principles. It's bad enough that people accuse us of immorality because we are performers. If I dance with Capretti, there are those who will think, 'birds of a feather—'" Charie shuddered.

Matilda grasped her hand and led her to the divan. They sat down and her mother gathered her close as she had when Charie was a child.

And as though she was, Charie laid her head on her mother's shoulder.

"I told you long ago we don't fit society's idea of a lady. But in God's eyes, we're just as much a lady as— and maybe more so than—some tongue wagging, tongue lashing, hoity-toity socially acceptable female. When I decided to become an actress, most of my kin nearly died, including Ma and Pa." Matilda now sounded like the simple southern girl she'd been at the age of seventeen when her love of performing had drawn her to New York City.

Gone was the cultured, refined voice of the stage actress. "But I'm not one bit sorry. And you're not to be, either. As long as you love the ballet, dance. When it becomes burdensome, quit. But while you're dancing, don't compromise. I agree with your opinion of Roberto Capretti, so tell *Monsieur* Phillipe. If he won't listen, I'll speak to Olar."

"I wouldn't want you to do that."

Her mother shared a strained relationship with the Russian noble who was the patron of the Ballet Eleganté.

The two never saw eye to eye on anything, and sometimes Charie felt like a rope tugged back and forth between them.

Their on-going battle had waged for nearly four

years, ever since Count Olar Stanislov had taken the *corp de ballet*, bordering on bankruptcy and on the verge of disbanding, under his wing, physically and financially.

"I will, if it would help."

Charie would rather be dragged through a re-staging of the battle of Waterloo than have her mother "speak" with the count. "No, I'll tell *Monsieur* Phillipe how I feel. Immediately, because you need to change, and I should return to the rehearsal."

Lizzie, who'd remained silent during their discussion, shuffled the gowns in her mother's armoire, an indication that she was ready to help Matilda out of the costume she wore in her portrayal of Sally Sharp, a feather-brained beauty with romantic troubles that somehow resolved themselves humorously.

If only Charie could resolve hers in the same manner.

"Stay as long as you like." Her mother gave her one of those "everything's going to be fine" smiles.

"I can't. I threw a tantrum for the first time in my life and then stormed off the stage. I didn't know what else to do when *Monsieur* Rubenevski said I was to dance with Capretti. And Rubenevski had already angered me by treating Mira abominably."

"When you return, tell Phillipe exactly how you feel." Matilda kissed her cheek. "Now, you're to be punctual for dinner."

"I will," Charie promised sheepishly. She was notorious for remaining at the theatre long after the others had left, practicing alone and so absorbed, she'd forget about eating and everything else. "Thank you."

"Don't thank me. I'm your mother, the most

important role I've ever played or will ever play. I hope you never decide you don't need me." Matilda looked at her closely. "Are you certain you're not taking ill?"

Charie shook her head. "I'm certain. Sometimes I wonder if my father is sorry he left you."

A troubled light clouded her mother's eyes.

Charie stood, reaching out to clasp her mother's hand. "You've worked so hard over the years to make a good life for me. And you had not one bit of help from him."

"I didn't want or expect his help. You know that."

"He should have done his duty by you. And me," she added with a whisper.

"Dear, don't — "

"Yes, I know. Don't speak or think badly of him. He was a man, and I quote, 'zealously committed to honor.'" Charie had hoped to lighten the mood, but her mother's expression told her she'd failed miserably. "I promise to be home for dinner. I couldn't endure a scolding from *Madame* Jeaneau after listening to *Monsieur* Rubenevski. *Au revoir*," she called over her shoulder as she headed to the door.

Opening it, she stifled a cry when she realized the obese man she'd glimpsed earlier still lurked outside her mother's dressing room.

Not wanting her mother disturbed, she closed the door quickly. Ignoring him, she set off down the hall, her ballet slippers making but a wisp of sound. As she approached the stairwell, the man's heavy tread followed. He was a persistent someone. Irritated, she twirled around.

"*Madame* Marin's next performance will be tomorrow night," Charie explained impatiently in

French.

"I'm not here to see *Madame* Marin." The man replied in English, his accent bearing traces of the New Yorker.

She would know—she'd lived there with her mother for the better part of twelve years.

"I'm here to see you."

"I don't understand." She replied in English.

"Aren't you Charice Marin, *prima danseuse* of the *Ballet Eleganté*?" The man drew forth a handkerchief to wipe his damp brow. The hallway was anything but warm.

She was chilled, and the man before her added fear to her chill. Charie reined in her imagination, and though the ardent admirers and theatre crew had departed, her mother and Lizzie were not far away and could easily hear if she called out. Even so, she pulled her cape closer.

"I am. What do you want?" She made no attempt to hide her annoyance.

"Is there somewhere we could speak privately?"

Charie hesitated, distrustful and aware of the lengths some obsessive devotees could go. Crossing her arms, she rubbed her hands over her woolen cloak, hoping to restore warmth. The cloak covered her practice tutu and ragged leggings; clothing that provided little protection on a raw October afternoon. This was what she deserved for running out of rehearsal. "You can speak to me and my mother."

"This matter doesn't concern your mother. It concerns you and your father."

"My father?" Charie regarded the man incredulously, odd that she'd just mentioned her father, something she rarely did.

Now this complete stranger referred to him.

Suspicion mounted as she narrowed her eyes. "There's no reason to speak with you or anyone else about my father. I've never met the man."

"I represent an individual in New York who wishes very much to become your patron. He's asked me to present his offer, which, should you accept, would prove lucrative."

"My father isn't involved in my career or my life. You should speak to my mother."

"You are wrong." His voice raised a notch with insistence. "Your current patron, Count—"

"There you are, *Mademoiselle* Marin. I've looked all over for you. Rubenevski is beside himself with worry." Strong fingers gripped Charie's upper arm as the deep, richly accented voice penetrated her apprehension. Pulling her gaze from the irritating bald man, she raised her head.

Stormy green eyes met hers with such intensity her knees nearly buckled—the man from the theatre?

Before she could gather her wits, she was ushered down the stairs, the pudgy man sputtering and cursing as he was left behind, unable to keep up with their rapid descent. Upon reaching the lower level, she snatched her arm free—no small feat and undeniably painful, and then turned upon this new, unwelcome presence.

"Just who—" Charie's voice died in her throat as she took a good look at the man.

Nearly a foot taller than she, he exuded a physical strength that both frightened and attracted. His topcoat hung open, and the cut of his serviceable jacket conveyed the fact he was no slave to fashion. The neck cloth was haphazardly tied, and the buttons on his vest matched up one hole lower than they should have. Untamed hair hung unconventionally long; that lock still falling boyishly over his brow. But it was his face that sent her reeling. The scar she'd glimpsed earlier ran a jagged path from his left temple to his jaw, marring his sculpted features.

Gasping, she pressed her hand to her chest, "are you?"

"An angel of mercy when compared to the man with whom you were previously conversing." His English was flawless, but flavored with a hint of the Slav. There was no trace of a smile; no jesting gleam in his eyes. They remained a frigid green, and his scarred jaw twitched with vexation.

Hackles rising, Charie forgot that seconds earlier she'd been terrified.

"It's time you returned to rehearsal." He reached out as though to take hold of her already bruised arm.

She stepped back. "I was planning to do so. Without your help. I don't know who you are or why you're here, but you're not welcome." With that pronouncement, she strode past him, wondering how *Monsieur* Rubenevski's fit of temper had precipitated such strange events for her.

She was more than ready to return to the rehearsal if it would make the odious New Yorker and the iron-jawed eastern European go away. Wrapping her cloak closer, she braced for the wind and mist.

"You don't understand." The man fell into step beside her. "I'm escorting you to the theatre. Unless you want that man to rejoin you?"

Something in his tone made her pause and look behind her.

Sure enough the short, fat man was in pursuit.

11

Without thinking through her actions, Charie grabbed the man's hand and broke into a run.

****

They finally slowed when her companion diverted them down a narrow alley, not far from the theatre.

Winded, with a catch in her side, Charie gratefully leaned against the cold, stone wall of a deteriorating, windowless shop and drew a shaky breath. She glanced at the man who watched her with an unnerving intensity.

He appeared unaffected by their frantic race, his breathing steady. "You kept up with me. Rubenevski has trained you well."

"I beg your pardon?" Charie focused her rage and anger at this irritating, outrageous man. She would've been better off talking with the other stranger.

He'd not been nearly so intimidating. And he'd been close to disclosing something about her father.

"You possess surprising stamina."

"My stamina is not a topic of discussion. And given the fact my pursuer is no longer a threat, I can find my way back. Alone."

"I think not. My instructions were to locate and return the 'temperamental' ballerina post haste. That's what I'm doing."

"Who 'instructed' you?" Charie snapped.

"The count."

"Count Stanislov would never refer to me as temperamental."

"He did today." The jaw was twitching again.

"How do you know him? You will explain or I shan't move a muscle."

Rather than reply, he swept her up in his arms as though she weighed no more than a sack of potatoes and proceeded towards the entrance of the alley.

Furious, Charie kicked her legs and pummeled his solid muscled chest ineffectually. "Release me—I demand that you release me. Now." Unexpectedly she found herself sitting in a puddle looking up at her tormentor, who had the audacity to laugh. The nerve of him.

Leaping to her feet, she rushed him. Deftly stepping aside, he allowed her to sprawl face first into another puddle. Pushing herself up, she prepared to launch another attack, but the man was gone.

How could he just leave her? Was he such a coward that he would desert her now?

Charie was of a mind to search for him, but she knew she had to return, with muddy face and cloak. What had she done to deserve this irritation?

"I lost my temper." Charie made the admission aloud while shaking her head. She should never have let *Monsieur* Rubenevski upset her. Logic and reason would have served her much better than dashing angrily from the theatre. She wouldn't do that again. "So, Lord, I have learned something. Never again will I abandon a rehearsal."

Brushing what grime she could from her person, she trudged towards the theatre, properly humbled and subdued. Entering through the side entrance, she hoped to avoid notice. Her efforts failed as the members of the *corp de ballet* swarmed her.

Mirenda LaTalle—Mira—threw her arms about her. "I was so worried, *mon ami*." Her friend spoke rapidly in French. "You were so brave to defend me. The count has been beside himself since discovering you ran out. You've never done anything like that before. There's a mysterious man with Count Stanislov. A scar runs down the side of his face, but even so, he's the handsomest man I've ever laid eyes upon. Count Stanislov sent him after you." Mira paused and drew a deep breath. "Are you all right, Charie?"

Rather than answer, Charie broke from her best friend and wended her way through the chattering dancers, searching for the ballet company's Russian patron.

He found her first. "Charice, I thank our God above that you are unharmed. There is someone I'd like you to meet. Allow me to introduce a good friend and fellow lover of the ballet."

As the tall, scarred man hovered into view, his lips tilted mockingly, her fury mounted.

All the Bible lessons taught her by her mother evaporated.

The annoying thought she'd seen him before hovered on the fringes of her anger and sharpened her tone. "You—you!" The words wouldn't come. Her frustration and embarrassment demanded demonstration.

She slapped him.

2

"I'm sorry, so very sorry." The *prima danseuse's* voice conveyed contrition, and quite out of character with what Domitri Auberchon had previously observed.

Rubbing his stinging jaw, he glared, not trusting himself to speak.

"I don't know why I did that. Please forgive me. But you left me face down in the mud." Irregular grayish smudges marred her creamy cheeks and the tip of her nose.

He was momentarily consumed by the oddest sensation to produce his handkerchief and wipe away the dirt. "No less than what you asked for. I believe you told me to release you."

"I did, but I had no idea you would do so in so ungentlemanly a manner. I am truly sorry I slapped you, but you have some apologizing to do, as well."

It took everything within Domitri not to laugh at Olar's pretty powder puff.

And what else could she be considered, for certainly there was very little of substance contained inside that lovely head covered in glorious chestnut curls.

"If anything, you should thank me for rescuing you from that obnoxious man."

"I was handling him well enough on my own."

"Is that why you grabbed my hand and ran when

you realized he was following?"

"I merely wanted to hurry back. You were dawdling."

"Enough!"

The bellow caused Domitri and the American ballerina to cease their argument and look at the count.

The short *Monsieur* Rubenevski hovered at the count's side, his face red with anger.

"I do not waste my money on temperamental ballerinas. Charice, you will resume rehearsing and Domitri, you will come with me. Now."

Domitri noticed with some satisfaction that Charice Marin's eyes widened, and she shuddered at the count's bark.

Turning about, she cast off her cloak, revealing a trim and toned dancer's figure enhanced with soft curves, then rushed out upon the stage while the *corp de ballet* assembled. Charice took her position; toes pointed, arms curved, and raised her face, meeting his gaze. Something deep in her violet tinted eyes spoke to him, igniting a long dormant spark in the pit of his stomach.

Banishing the sensation, he turned to his former father-in-law.

"So she was where I sent you. I was certain she would run to Matilda. Their bond is strong."

"*Mademoiselle* Marin was there, but not alone. An overzealous admirer was pestering her. However, I am glad she is your concern and not mine. She is too spirited for her own good."

"There was a time when you admired spirit." Olar Stanislov spoke in French, although the two could have just as easily conversed in Russian or English.

Domitri's mother was a Russian native, and he'd

learned English over a two year period while living in New York City.

"Sophia's spiritedness was different." Domitri fought the wave of bitterness that threatened. "Never have two women been more unlike. There is no comparison."

"Oh, really?" Olar seemed surprised by his reply. "Do not allow Sophia's untimely death convince you she was perfect. I, her father, knew well her faults. Yet, her charm overshadowed all defects."

Sophia Stanislovna had been an ethereal dream who vanished far too quickly. If only the accident had claimed him as well, there'd be no emptiness in his heart. As it was, he was forced to endure the memories and a jagged scar that reminded him constantly of his loss. Couldn't Olar see how his words affected him?

"I'd rather not speak of her." Domitri replied with a civility he was far from feeling. "You asked me to join you today to assist you. So far all I've done is follow a tantrum-throwing, ill-mannered ballerina and been slapped for my efforts. In what way am I to assist?"

"You already have." The count's reply confused Domitri.

Pondering the man's words, his gaze was pulled to the stage where the wayward imp was performing her Act II solo to the familiar strains of Adam's *Giselle*.

He'd seen Carlotta Grisi dance the role in the premiere performance four years earlier at the Paris Opera House. But never had he witnessed a more compelling execution.

Lured from Olar's side, Domitri peered through the part in the curtains, transfixed. Movement surged within him in a way it hadn't in seven long years. He'd not so much as stepped foot on a stage since Sophia's death. At that moment, he was overwhelmed by the urge—the need—to join Charice Marin on the stage, bathed in the golden glow of the gas lamps.

Physically gripping the curtain, he drew a deep breath when her Albrecht, a *danseur* of some renown, joined her for their *pas de deux*. The music filled him, lifted him; allowed him to remember a happier time.

"You know you should be out there." Olar's whispered words drifted over his shoulder. How could Olar even suggest as much?

Domitri had only danced with Sophia—she had been his life and his world for five magical years. Until the train wreck. Blinding pain replaced the music—he was once again holding her in his arms, her body battered and crushed while fire and steam rained down and the few surviving passengers screamed and begged for mercy.

"*Non; jamais.*" His tone was brusque as he released the curtain. Quickly, he moved from his view of the stage and dropped heavily upon an overturned crate, running his hands over his face. A fierce chill enveloped him.

"I suppose I should tell you the real reason why I asked you to meet me today." Olar stood before him, hands folded upon the gold wolf's head topping his cane. A signet ring caught the light of a lantern hanging on the wall and glittered hypnotically. "Sophia would not want to see you like this. You have mourned too long. And you are wasting the magnificent talent God gave you. It is time you rejoined the living, Domitri."

The count's words caused him to lower his hands and look up at the man whom he had always respected and admired. It was unusual to find a wealthy man who could have anything he wanted, yet chose to live simply in close communion to the Lord and Savior. Olar's one and only passion was the ballet.

Sophia had once confided to Domitri that Olar had dreamed of being in the ballet but his parents had quashed any such notion. Perhaps God had given Sophia her love of the ballet so that Olar could watch her attain what he'd been denied.

"I am living."

"But you're not dancing."

"When Sophia died, the dancing died, too." Domitri was certain the twisted flesh of his scar pulled tighter. He nearly winced.

"Many families lost loved ones in that accident. You were not alone. God spared you for a reason. I believe—"

Whatever it was that Olar believed was never revealed for there was a howl of rage followed by rapid fire Russian that even Domitri had trouble following.

Coming quickly to his feet, he reached the stage before Olar and the theatre crew.

Judging by the wildly flailing arms of Rubenevski and the equally flailing arms of Charice's male partner, the two glaring at one another, Domitri reasoned they were arguing.

Antoine Valmiere, an athletic *danseur* prone to bragging and prancing, was not one to make friends, but Domitri had learned to tolerate him. Admittedly, Valmiere could give an amazing performance when he put his mind to it, but those occasions were rare.

Olar had confided on their drive to the theatre that Valmiere was not the first choice, but the desired *danseur*, Aleksei Ullavich, had a commitment to the

Imperial Ballet in St. Petersburg.

Domitri swallowed a chuckle when Valmiere marched off the stage, and then leapt theatrically into the orchestra pit.

"Break your leg and your neck," Rubenevski bellowed in Russian at Valmiere's departing back. "See if it matters to me." Turning to Charice and the others in the company, he shook his shaggy gray head, his longish beard quaking with his uncontained rage. "Too many distractions—first you, Charice, and then Valmiere. I will not tolerate this."

"Need I remind you I pay you to 'tolerate' this sort of thing?" Olar spoke in Russian as he walked up to the agitated man.

"There is nothing you can do to me to make me accept such behavior. Hire another ballet master. I can walk two blocks over and be taken on just like that." Rubenevski snapped his fingers in emphasis of his words.

"*Monsieur* Rubenevski, you are free to seek employment elsewhere. The Paris Opera will undoubtedly find a use for your abilities. So, if that is your wish, please take your leave, so that my ballet company can practice."

Domitri glanced at Charice, whose lovely face displayed bewilderment and guilt. She stepped forward, drawing all eyes. Even her walk was graceful and controlled. Who could ignore such beauty?

"I fear I am to blame."

Dimitri marveled at her flawless French, rare for an American.

"My emotions ruled my head earlier, and now everyone is upset. *Monsieur* Rubenevski, please let us practice. We all want to do well and make you and

Monsieur Phillipe and Count Stanislov proud. Please give us another chance."

"How can you practice when you have no partner?" Rubenevski demanded.

"I can dance with her," spilled from Domitri's lips before he realized what he'd said. He was now the center of attention.

Rubenevski's look was incredulous, Olar's expression one of smug delight, and Charice's one of horror. The look on her face made him want to laugh.

Unbeknownst to anyone, including Olar, he'd given lessons for the past two years, using the huge basement level in his Paris townhouse as a studio.

And when no one was around and Muzette, his housekeeper and cook, did the marketing, he danced to the music that had never left his soul. Being here today had brought it all back. Perhaps it was God's will that he dance again even though he'd vowed not to after losing Sophia. He'd found contentment as an instructor at the *Academie de Paris*, teaching Russian and English. Yet, something deep inside urged him to dance.

"That's preposterous," Charice exploded. "If this is some sort of cruel jest, you are truly in need of help. What makes you think you can dance?"

"Allow me to properly introduce my son-in-law, Domitri Auberchon."

Charice's mouth snapped shut, and Domitri saw her convulsive swallow. It appeared she had at least heard of him, although when he and Sophia had danced on the Paris stage, Charice would have been but a child.

"You were Sophia's husband," she spoke slowly and softly. "Of course—I should have known. I saw you and Sophia dance in New York on my twelfth birthday. It was a marvelous performance. Do you recall that night, Count Stanislov? That was the night we met for the first time."

"Yes, I remember that night well, my kitten," the count said, and smiled at Charice affectionately. It was obvious to Domitri that Olar was fond of Charice—but whether as a father or something more, Domitri couldn't guess.

But Charice would never replace Sophia in Olar's heart. Sophia had been the man's flesh and blood child.

"Shall we start?" Domitri's tone was intentionally impatient as he shrugged out of his overcoat and shed his jacket. He disliked all the attention his suggestion had created and sincerely wished he'd kept his mouth shut.

"But how can you do this?" *Monsieur* Phillipe demanded, his curled mustache quivering in outrage.

How fortunate he'd finally decided to join what was becoming a circus, Domitri thought ironically.

"*Mademoiselle* Marin could not possibly dance with you—you have not danced in years, and you are much too large to partner with her."

"Henri," Olar spoke up, "Domitri is only filling in. He is not taking Valmiere's place. Rubenevski wants a full rehearsal. Here is a way to have it."

"He is right," Rubenevski declared. Even though the Russian could roar worse than a bear, Domitri knew the man was exceptional. He had been the ballet master of his mother's company when she had been the *prima danseuse* of the Imperial Ballet.

That was before her marriage and his birth. Now she was content to teach ballet to little children, make her colorful quilts, and sit before the fire with his father. How different their lives were when compared to the whirlwind days of their youth.

"We will begin now."

"But…" Charice began.

She was completely ignored as Rubenevski clapped his hands and urged everyone into their places in Russian.

Domitri watched her shoulders raise and lower as she released a deep sigh, and then obediently took her place, vaguely aware that Rubenevski was reciting his steps.

Walking several paces away from where she stood, Domitri drew himself up and sucked in a deep breath to cover his nervousness. For all his outward bravado, he was suddenly scared to death. What if he messed up dreadfully or even, worse, dropped Charice? What was left of his career could be quickly destroyed over the next few minutes. *Lord, I have once more jumped into something without asking for Your direction and guidance. Please help me not to look completely ridiculous.*

The orchestra tuned up, and Domitri broke into a sweat.

Then the music began and the dancers commenced their steps.

Suddenly, Domitri was swept away into a world he'd thought lost to him forever.

****

Charie tamped down outrage just in time for her to take the first steps toward Domitri Auberchon.

The nerve of the man to think he could simply waltz in and partner her. The next time she saw Antoine she planned to tell him exactly what she thought of arrogant *danseurs*.

But when her gaze met Domitri's, she forgot her anger, plunged into emerald green pools that shook her to her soul. How could a man be so handsome and so infuriating all at once, she silently demanded, as she raised her arm and he took her hand.

His touch sent delicious shivers racing through her, and for a moment, she forgot where she was and why she was standing on a stage. Then her gaze fastened on his again, and her feet began to move of their own accord, as though unseen angels swept her along. She glided effortlessly with Domitri, who was amazingly competent for someone who'd been away from the ballet for so many years.

They flowed easily through the *pas de deux* of Act II, and after the execution of the *sissonnes*, Domitri lifted her. It was as though she weighed no more than a feather pillow.

When her toes again touched the stage, they moved in sync and in such harmony, Charie felt as though they had danced together forever. She'd never felt this with any of her partners. Tears gathered in her eyes as the notes of the music died away, her face now cupped by Domitri in his role of Albrecht.

For the first time in her life, she was caught up in the beauty of the music and the movement, unable to separate the two.

Who was this Domitri Auberchon and how had he so turned her world upside down?

His eyes were haunted and melancholy, almost as though she had turned into the *wili* that she portrayed in the ballet. Something made her want to stroke his cheek and assure him she wasn't a ghost—that she was very much alive.

A slight smile touched his lips as he placed a fingertip on Charie's mud — smudged nose.

She started to speak when startling applause erupted all about them. Pulling away, flustered and embarrassed, Charie slowly turned to see Rubenevski wiping tears from his eyes, Phillipe clapping the count on the back, and the company hopping about excitedly.

Domitri was motionless.

"*Brilliante!*" Phillipe declared. "*Magnifique!* I have not seen such magic since I witnessed the premier performance of *Giselle* with Grisi and Petipa. The *ballottés* were marvelous. Rubenevski, you will tell Valmiere not to return. Ever. Count Stanislov, we must talk. Come with me."

"There will be no talking," Domitri interjected tersely. "I was merely accommodating *Mademoiselle* Marin. There will not be a repeat performance."

Voices exploded all around as Phillipe bellowed in French and Rubenevski raged in Russian.

To her amazement, the count took hold of her arm and Domitri's and ushered them off the stage and away from the brewing ferment. He shoved them into a small dressing room, slammed the door and braced it with a chair so that no one could enter. Stanislov turned about to face them, arms folded across his chest, his look determined, his jaw steely and inflexible.

Glancing at Domitri, Charie noticed that his expression was very similar, the scar more pronounced at the moment.

Shivering, she wrapped her arms about her, though the temperature of the small, cramped space did not cause her discomfort. *Dear God in Heaven, something is about to happen, and it frightens me. Please bring me through this. I have always liked and admired the count, and he has been good to me. I can't imagine that he would want to do something that would hurt me. But this Domitri Auberchon—I don't know what to make of him. Help me, Father. Please help me.*

"Domitri, you and I both know that Valmiere is not the one to dance this role. The only way that Charice will dance to her fullest potential is if she is partnered with someone of equal skill. You could be that partner."

"But I will not be. I told you I would never dance on stage again. I cannot."

"What you mean is that you will not. You cannot simply fade away because you lost your wife. She was my daughter, and not a day passes that I do not mourn her, but she would want me to live—to move forward. And Sophia wants the same for you. This is your chance, Domitri."

"I do not appreciate your underhanded way. This is beneath you, Stanislov. I have never known you to be anything less than straightforward and candid. Why?"

"Why?" the count repeated, and then laughed sadly. "How else would I have gotten you on that stage so that you could see how much you still love the ballet?"

"Don't I have some say in this?" Charie demanded, and then realized how petulant she sounded. Even so, she continued. "In no way am I partial to Antoine Valmiere, but to consider dancing with this—" here she paused as she searched for a suitable description of the man who had become both a tormentor and rescuer over the course of a few hours. "—very tall man, I must protest."

"Did you not feel it, Charice?" the count asked

excitedly as he met her gaze. She couldn't tell him before Auberchon that she'd never felt so wonderful.

"The sheer beauty of your movements—like a picture of Heaven. I saw something within you as you danced that I have never seen before. I am asking you to trust me, Charice."

"I would like to pray about it," she insisted, though the fight whooshed from her leaving her weak-kneed.

Domitri possessed a commanding, fluid gracefulness that was manly, yet yielding.

Partnering with Valmiere was like dancing with a strutting peacock who wanted to make sure everyone saw him preen.

"I will think on this tonight."

"Good," Stanislov declared. "And you, Domitri? What say you on the matter?"

"I, too, must pray," he replied brusquely.

Charie arched a brow questioningly.

"Yes, I do pray," Domitri retorted as he fastened his angry glare upon her.

It seemed to her that the last thing he wanted to do was partner her. Why should he bother to pray?

"May we leave?" he asked.

To her surprise, the count chuckled.

"Certainly." Stepping aside, he allowed Domitri to pass.

Taking up the chair, Domitri hurled it across the room, and then threw open the door, a multitude of faces and bodies huddled just beyond. Domitri snorted in disgust, and then plowed a path.

Phillipe and Rubenevski rushed the count.

"What did he say? What did she say?"

"They have to pray about the matter." Those were

the count's final words as he moved past the curiosity seekers.

****

As Lizbet fussed with her disobedient curls before the mirror of her alabaster vanity, Charie learned that Markham Fitzhugh was dining with them that evening.

Fitz, Matilda's shortened version of her agent-manager's name, was a welcome guest in the Marins' Paris home and frequently dined with them.

But when Lizbet let slip that the second dinner guest was to be Baron Bauerhausen, annoyance brought Charie to her feet. Drawing a deep breath, she raced from her bedchamber, leaving Lizbet standing open-mouthed before her vanity.

"*Maman*, how could you?" Charie demanded as she burst into her mother's room directly across the hall.

Matilda, also seated at her vanity, quickly turned. "How could I what, dear?"

"Invite that odious, obnoxious man to our home. You know I dislike him."

"He's here to discuss a new play for me. The baron wishes to provide financial backing if I agree to perform in Frankfurt. I've always wanted to visit."

"But you don't speak the language. He's doing this to irritate me."

"I doubt he would dine with us simply to irritate you. It's been nearly a year since you refused his suit."

Charie clenched her fists at her sides, taking deep breaths to keep from shouting at her mother, who had turned back to the mirror of her vanity, lightly dabbing a bit of color on her cheeks.

"You're not the one he was 'showering' with affection. I thought I would never discourage him, and now you bring him here? Perhaps you've developed a fondness for him."

That brought Matilda back around, her brows lowered in a rare show of anger.

Charie realized she'd gone too far.

"You know very well that's untrue. I have no feelings for the baron beyond that of a possible business relationship. He is much too young for me. Charie, I ask that you be polite this evening. The baron is here on business and business only. I'm sure he regrets his silly behavior. You must be flattered that he was so smitten."

"I'm not. Had the count not intervened, the man would still be hounding me."

"Ah, yes, the count. Your knight in shining armor." Her mother's tone held a trace of rancor. "He always comes to your rescue."

"It's his sense of responsibility. Today, after I left the theatre, he sent someone after me because he was worried. And with good reason. Did I tell you that short, heavy man waiting outside your dressing room wanted to talk to me about my father?"

"Your father?" Matilda's face paled to the point Charie feared she would faint.

Should she call for Lizbet?

"I thought you said the man represented an individual from New York who is interested in becoming patron of the ballet."

"I forgot to tell you the part about my father." *It's a wonder I can think straight after everything that's happened today.* "The man insisted on speaking to me and my father. What an odd request."

"It is." Matilda quickly turned back to her mirror and attempted to rearrange a curl that coiled perfectly.

Charie sensed her mother wasn't being completely honest. Details of her father had always been inadequate, at best. "Could you contact him—my father—and see if he knows the identity of this potential patron? Does he still live in New York?"

"No." Her mother's tone was uncharacteristically sharp. "I won't be contacting him—not for any reason. He isn't in New York."

"I see."

Her mother's vehemence was unsettling.

"But dinner with the baron—" Charie hesitated.

"Will go smoothly if you keep your comments to yourself. There's nothing to fear. If I detect inappropriate behavior on the baron's part, I will ask him to leave."

Nodding, Charie left her mother's room, though she paused once she was back in the hall. Perhaps she could obtain the whereabouts of her father from someone else and write to him about her strange encounter. She had no desire to establish a relationship with the man; she just needed a few answers.

Fitz might be able to help her—she'd corner him before the evening was over.

****

Her mother proved to be right, and the baron, who had sent Charie roses daily for six months the year before, seemed to have focused his attention elsewhere.

Blond, tall, and dashing, he exuded a confidence that easily turned a female's head, but not Charie's.

When he'd decided to woo Charie after witnessing her performance in *Marionette*, nothing Charie could do or say would dissuade him from his pursuit.

Charie finally confessed her dilemma to Count Stanislov, and the baron's amorous overtures ceased. A tremendous relief, for the man was overly fond of wine and too suave to be trusted.

Now as she sipped water from her goblet, she watched him, deep in discussion with Fitz, and found herself unintentionally comparing him to Domitri Auberchon. Both men were tall and handsome; Domitri's appearance somewhat flawed by the prominent scar. But Domitri had the athletic, *danseur*'s build. There was no forgetting how effortlessly he'd lifted her when they'd danced.

Unexpected warmth slid through her as she recalled the brief minutes he'd held her while performing the *pas de deux*.

Is anything wrong, dear? her mother mouthed silently to her from her place at the head of the elegantly appointed table resplendent with crystal and gold-rimmed china.

Charie shook her head and smiled reassuringly.

It was then the baron addressed her. "I can hardly wait for your opening night, *liebchen*. I've heard wonderful things about this ballet. You are certain to outshine Grisi."

"I only hope to give my best. My desire is that my love of the ballet will show through to the audience. There's no expectation that I'll surpass Grisi's performance."

"Which you won't if Valmiere is not replaced," Fitz pointed out as he stabbed his veal with intensity.

Charie shifted her gaze to the charming, slender

Englishman.

His gift of negotiation had secured her mother many a successful contract over the course of her acting career.

Fastidious in appearance and in business, Fitz never left a detail to chance, and the graying man of indeterminate middle age took pride in his accomplishments. "Several sources say he made a spectacle of himself today."

"As did I." Charie glanced down at her plate, her meal hardly touched. She was embarrassed by her earlier behavior. Would she ever put that behind her? Had she behaved herself, Antoine would never have stormed out, and she would never have danced with Domitri. More importantly, she wouldn't be sitting here thinking about him and how strong his arms were. "This seemed to be the day for fits of temper."

"But I also heard Olar found a replacement. He actually convinced his son-in-law to dance with you during rehearsal."

Her mother gasped, her fork clattering to her plate.

All eyes turned to Matilda.

"You said nothing of this," *Maman* accused, locking gazes with Charie.

Charie squirmed.

"You danced with Domitri Auberchon?"

"He replaced Antoine. That's all—just so *Monsieur* Rubenevski would cease fuming. We managed to finish rehearsal. Do you know *Monsieur* Auberchon?"

"I know of him."

Once more, Charie sensed her mother wasn't telling all.

Matilda had lowered her eyes, pushing food about

on her plate. Mention of this man disturbed her.

"I, too, know of him," Bauerhausen said. "I have seen him dance with his late wife, your Count Stanislov's daughter, Sophia."

"I only saw her perform once, but I've never forgotten how wonderful she was," Charie said.

"Indeed," the baron agreed. "Sophia was like a forest sprite floating across the stage. They were very good together—she and Auberchon. Sophia Stanislovna was killed in a train wreck outside of London, and Auberchon was badly injured. Rumor was he swore he'd never dance on the stage again after losing Sophia. You, *liebchen*, must have convinced him otherwise."

"I convinced him of nothing. He volunteered to help out when he saw Antoine leave." Her words tumbled out much too vehemently, and her mother frowned.

"Amazing," Bauerhausen replied, his eyes conveying the fact he found the situation anything but. He always wore a smirk.

At the moment, Charie had no tolerance for his attitude. "Domitri Auberchon was merely appeasing the count, who'd wearied of Rubenevski's whining."

"Why don't we have dessert?" Matilda suggested, skillfully redirecting the conversation. "Amalie," she said, and then rang the bell by her plate. "Amalie, dessert please."

As *Madame* Jeaneau came towards the table bearing a silver tray, Charie noticed the pallor of her mother's face and the gleam of speculation in Bauerhausen's eyes.

Charie knew before the night was through she would have a private word with Fitz.

3

If Fitz thought it odd that Charie trapped him in the sitting room, while her mother escorted Bauerhausen to the door, he said nothing. Taking a seat, he crossed his leg at the knee and adjusted the crease in his trousers.

Drawing a deep breath, Charie pushed the door closed, and then leaned against it. "Fitz, I had the oddest thing happen today at *Maman*'s theatre. As I was leaving, a man stopped me, saying he represented a party in New York who wished to become my patron. I told him he needed to speak with *Maman*, but he said this concerned me and my father. What did he mean? I know you handle *Maman*'s personal affairs, so I thought you might know the whereabouts of my father."

Fitz's composure evaporated as he tugged nervously on his flawlessly tied cravat. "What was this man's name?"

"I don't know. I was so frightened, I didn't ask. Fortunately, Count Stanislov sent Domitri Auberchon to the theatre to bring me back to practice. When we left together, the man ended his pursuit."

"What exactly did he say?" Fitz looked as pale as her mother had at dinner.

"He said that he wished to speak to me and my father about the interested party's offer. I explained my father has no say in matters. Do you know where my father is? Does he live in the States?"

"I—no; I'm certain he's not in America." Beads of sweat dotted his forehead.

Charie had never seen Fitz perspire.

Why was he nervous? Perhaps her father was a criminal. Or worse.

"Would you help me contact him?"

"That's not possible. Charice, speak to Matilda. It's not my place to reveal this information."

"I've asked before with no luck. *Maman* hates my father, and with good reason."

"I can't help you, Charice." Fitz came to his feet and hurried up to her as though he couldn't get away quickly enough.

Seeing she had no choice, Charie moved aside so he could open the door.

"I must respect your mother's wishes. You'll have to ask her about your father. But if you should ever be approached by that man again, let me know immediately."

"Do you think he poses a threat?"

"Unlikely, but he has no right to give you a scare. Give him my name, and tell him to contact me. There's no need to concern yourself with complicated matters. You must focus on your dancing." Opening the door, he dashed out.

A few seconds later, she heard him speaking to her mother in the entrance hall. Then his voice dropped, as did her mother's.

She was certain they were discussing her conversation with Fitz, and heat flooded her cheeks. Charie was old enough to know the truth about her father. She had no desire to reunite with him, but as he was apparently alive, she wouldn't mind meeting him.

Just once. Did she look like him or possess any similarity in mannerisms or temperament? What harm could there be?

Aggravated with her mother and the secrecy, she made her way to the kitchen, surprising *Madame* Jeaneau and Paulette, the scullery maid, now tidying up.

"I'm going out for air." Taking her old cloak off a peg on the wall, Charie wrapped herself within its folds. After letting herself out, she slipped around the side of the townhouse and made her way to the cobblestone street. After hailing a cab, she was soon on her way to Count Stanislov's. She would talk to him.

Perhaps he knew of her father's whereabouts.

****

Jules's announcement that *Mademoiselle* Marin had arrived to see Olar unsettled Domitri. And intrigued. And presented an interesting way to spend the evening. Having just finished a late meal with his former father-in-law, he rested on a divan in the count's study, legs propped on the arm while thumbing through a journal devoted to the ballet.

Olar sat in his favorite chair, smoking his pipe and reading the Bible. At the announcement by the very proper English butler, Olar put his Bible aside and stood, while removing his pipe.

Domitri swung his legs to the side and sat up, discarding the journal. An odd excitement warmed him.

"Please show her in, Jules. And have *Madame* Orenska bring tea and those wonderful scones she baked earlier."

The butler nodded and after delivering a quick, bobbing bow, returned to the foyer.

Domitri stood. "I'll leave."

"Nonsense. I've enjoyed your company immensely. I'd nearly decided you planned to ignore me during my stay in the city while preparing lessons for your mischievous pupils." Olar's voice held gentle teasing. "But certainly you could spare a few minutes to chat with a beautiful ballerina."

Domitri shook his head. "It's bad enough you tricked me into dancing with her."

"You don't fool me, Domitri. You weren't 'tricked' into anything."

Domitri withheld comment for Charice Marin chose that moment to enter the room.

As Jules assisted Charie in the removal of her well-worn cloak and revealed her stunning beauty, Domitri fought the urge to sink back down on the divan, his knees suddenly weak. It wasn't as though he hadn't noticed her comeliness that afternoon, but her charm then had been her dishevelment; loosened curls, torn leggings, the same old cloak.

Now she stood before him as regal as a princess; dark red curls in obeisance, frock of gold and green highlighting a winsome form, and gold slippers peeking out from beneath her fashionably shorter skirts.

As soon as she noticed him, her eyes widened in panic, as though she would turn and flee. Who did she think he was? The big, bad wolf?

He nearly chuckled as he recalled dancing the part at the age of ten.

"I didn't know you were entertaining." Her shock made her breathless. "Jules should have told me."

"Charie, what a marvelous surprise." Olar's voice conveyed warmth and sincerity as he bestowed a fatherly hug upon the statue-still Charice. Taking her hand, he led her to the plum upholstered settle near the piano. "Domitri has entertained me, regaling me with the antics of your esteemed peers from the pages of the *Journal de Ballet*. Did you know that Taglioni is rumored to be enamored of her Russian cobbler?"

"No, no—I didn't." She glanced uneasily at Domitri, and then looked back at Olar, managing a small smile. "I suppose a ballerina could form an attachment to a man who holds her feet in his hands."

"Is that what it would take to win your affection, *Mademoiselle* Marin?" As soon as he uttered the words, Domitri wanted to kick himself.

To his amazement, she laughed, the sound like silver bells caressed by a gentle wind, stroking his wounded spirit. *This isn't good.* Giving in to his weak knees, Domitri sat. He was much too interested; a heat flaring beneath his breast unrelated to his proximity to the blazing hearth. His heart, left behind in the carnage and twisted metal of the train wreck which claimed Sophia's life, beat strong and rapid.

"It would take much more than that, *Monsieur* Auberchon. He would have to hold my heart in those hands, as well."

"I shall keep that in mind."

"See that you do." She was in jest, but her words ignited a spark.

Flaming coils knotted in the pit of his stomach. Averting his face, he pretended to examine the cover of the journal as Olar took a seat opposite Charice.

The count ended the tension. "Tell me what brings you out so late of an evening? You should be resting your toes."

"*Maman!*" burst from her lips, and a torrent of French followed, spoken almost as flawlessly as a native.

His father had often discussed matters with his mother in his native French because he believed his little son could only understand his mother's Russian.

But Domitri had understood words in both languages as young as two years of age. By the time he was six, he could read and speak Russian and French. He followed the conversation between Charice and Olar easily.

"She invited Ludwig Bauerhausen into our home to discuss 'business.' Can you believe it? *Maman* believes it's acceptable to entertain the lecher if he offers to back a play even though he hounded me for months. I don't understand her."

"Did he insult you?" Olar asked, his jaw twitching in vexation.

Domitri had heard of the man, though never met him—a German nobleman known for his amoral pursuits and limitless spending. He was not the sort of man to respect an innocent maiden. Anger surged.

"He was on his best behavior. I know it's wrong and not at all Christian to hold a grudge, but he was insufferable last year." She shuddered.

Domitri clenched his hands into fists to keep from reaching out to comfort her.

"But I have intruded upon your quiet evening. I shouldn't have come." She started to rise but Olar reached out a hand to halt her.

"You have brightened what would have proven to be a dull evening."

Domitri lowered his brows, unsure how to take

Olar's comment.

"Bauerhausen—he's left your home?"

"*Oui*. He left before me. I'm disturbed by something else, Count Stanislov." Now her eyes darkened, and her face paled. "Do you know where my father is?"

Silence descended, a silence broken only by the hiss and snap of the fire as it devoured the wood.

Domitri watched the emotions flit across the face of his father-in-law; grief, anger, love, regret. What in Charie's question could have caused Olar to experience a myriad of feelings simultaneously?

"Why do you ask, child?" Olar's voice was unsteady.

"Today, at *Maman*'s theatre, I was approached by a man who said he represented an individual in New York who wished to become my patron. I told him he would have to speak to *Maman*, but he insisted on speaking to my father. My father has nothing to do with me or my dancing. I've never met him."

Olar's expression was troubled, and he slowly rubbed his silvering Vandyke beard.

"This is the same man I spoke of to you earlier," Domitri said, recalling the squat, irritating man. "When I found *Mademoiselle* Marin, this man was proving himself an annoyance."

"*Monsieur* Auberchon helped me elude him. I was alarmed by the man's persistence. I'm not sure I properly thanked you, *Monsieur* Auberchon." Her words held a ring of sincerity as she met his gaze.

Domitri nodded. "I'm glad I could assist. Who do you believe sent this man to Mademoiselle Marin, Olar?"

"I'm fairly certain he was sent by Anapol

Chervenkof. Chervenkof is an ardent admirer of your mother, Charie, and is looking for an opportunity to bring her back into his circle."

"*Maman* has never mentioned him."

"That's because she doesn't return his feelings. She has gone to great lengths to avoid him. I fear this is another ploy meant to encourage Matilda to reconsider his suit. The man is unscrupulous."

"And what of Bauerhausen? She'd rather deal with a debauched noble than an unscrupulous admirer?"

"Perhaps," Olar answered Domitri. "I only know that Chervenkof can be difficult, and he doesn't like to be crossed. Rumor has it that he was once involved with Russian revolutionaries."

An evasive memory tugged at Domitri's mind while he silently repeated *Anapol…Anapol.*

"And he's closely connected to Tammany Hall in New York City," Olar added.

Though Domitri had lived in Europe all of his life, he'd read about the notorious Tammany Hall and the political influence wielded by those belonging to the organization. He also knew that funds collected by this same group were not always used appropriately.

Yet, for the most part, those incidents were deliberately and effectively hushed. Expected behavior for those brash, cocky Americans, he reasoned.

"But my father—how does he fit into all of this? Does he belong to this Tammany Hall?"

"*Non,*" Olar replied emphatically. "He has no connection whatsoever."

"So you know him—you know where he is?" Charie's excitement spread over her revealing face. She was like an artist's palette, drawn and redrawn again and again as her emotions varied.

Domitri was mesmerized and openly stared.

"Why do you want to know, Charie?" Olar asked, drawing Domitri's attention back to him. The count's voice held a deep sadness.

"Why does Anapol Chervenkof think my father has anything to do with decisions that affect my dancing? Tell me where he is. Please."

"I—cannot say. It is your mother's wish that his whereabouts remain unknown."

Charie stood, her expression angry and frustrated. "I expected such an answer from Fitz, but not from you. I knew you would be honest with me."

"Charie, I wish with all my heart that I could be, but it is best this way. Do not be angry with me."

"I am angry—with you and *Maman*. Did she make you promise not to speak of this, or are you being difficult because the two of you don't get along? Whatever your grievance with each other, you should both put it behind you. I am sorry to have bothered you." She started across the room, her head lowered as she struggled with what Domitri suspected was tears.

The urge to comfort returned with frightening strength, but he remained seated.

It was Olar who followed her, catching up to her before she left the room. "Don't leave like this, Charie. Please stay until you're composed and have some tea. I've already instructed Jules to ask Madame Orenska to make you a cup of the Russian tea you like so much. Don't return to Matilda as you are now. She will have my head on a platter if she believes I upset you."

That brought a slight smile to Charie's lips.

Olar took hold of her chin and raised her face so that her beautiful, glistening eyes met his. "I would never intentionally hurt you. What I do or say is to protect you, and though you think you don't need protection, you do. It is a joyous duty that our God above has assigned to me. And I take my duties very seriously. So, stay. Have tea and one of Rena's English scones that Jules taught her to bake. She will be very disappointed if you don't have one." Olar spoke to Charie in a soothing manner reminiscent of the way he'd always cajoled Sophia when she was in a temper.

As Domitri watched the interaction, he noted Olar's fatherly manner and Charie's daughterly response to his overtures. Were they aware of the connection that existed?

For a brief moment he was envious, wishing that Charie held him in the same regard. Not as father to daughter, but as friend to friend. Or—perhaps more?

Once the tears vanished and Charie was laughing at something silly Olar said, the count led her back to her recently vacated seat.

Domitri excused himself, but he didn't think they heard. He headed for the door, which Jules quickly opened, bidding him goodnight. An uncomfortable regret invaded as he commenced his walk through a cold, misting rain bound for his apartment and studio. Regret that he'd decided seven years ago to give up on love.

****

After receiving a stern lecture from her mother for leaving the house without telling her, Charie retired to her bedchamber. Before attempting to sleep, she took up her Bible and silently read one of her favorite passages in Psalms.

Praise ye the Lord. Praise God in His sanctuary; praise Him in the firmament of His power. Praise Him for His mighty acts; praise Him according to His excellent greatness. Praise Him with the sound of the trumpet; praise Him with the psaltery and harp. Praise Him with the timbrel and dance; praise Him with stringed instruments and organs. Praise Him upon the loud cymbals; praise Him upon the high sounding cymbals. Let every thing that hath breath praise the Lord. Praise ye the Lord.

"Oh Lord," she whispered aloud as she pressed her Bible to her chest and closed her eyes. "I'm so unsettled. So much happened today that makes no sense. Yesterday, everything in my life was in order, but now this stranger, by merely mentioning my father, has caused uncertainty.

"There are so many questions I can't answer, and no one is willing to share the truth. And I don't know what to think about Domitri Auberchon. I know he was once a great *danseur noble*, and today, he danced with me as though we'd partnered many times before. It seemed as if he could sense my movements—as though we were one.

"I know that's silly, Lord. But what if he agrees to replace Antoine? I'm not sure I can work with him. But I want to dance and do my best. What would You have me do, Heavenly Father? *Maman* always taught me to turn to You in all things, and I'm so uncertain. I know this request is foolish, Lord, but I'd like to meet my father someday. These things I ask in your Son's precious name, Amen."

Lying against her pillows, she sighed deeply. At this rate, she wouldn't get any rest. And Lizzie would be shaking her awake just after dawn. Turning on her side, she looked out a window, watching the light rain splatter the panes of glass.

Why had Domitri left so suddenly tonight? Had her presence bothered him? Or had he other business? Perhaps a lady love was awaiting him somewhere. He was handsome enough to have many female admirers.

She wondered about his marriage to the count's daughter and only child, the beautiful Sophia Stanislovna, who was still spoken of in revered whispers. It was just as Bauerhausen had said—Sophia floated on the stage, small and petite and ethereal; her face sculpted by a heavenly artist. Such a tragedy that she'd died. So sad for the count. And for Domitri.

Slowly, Charie drifted to sleep. In her dreams, she danced through an emerald green forest filled with woodland creatures. Just as she neared a brook, a dark, hulking figure emerged from the shadows and advanced, baring fangs. Turning away, she ran, but stumbled and fell.

Just when the monster was nearly upon her, strong arms swept her up and away. The hooded rescuer kept his face averted, but once out of the forest and into the sparkling sunlight, she saw his scar, running from temple to jaw—her gallant was none other than Domitri.

But leaving her frightened and unsettled was the monster that'd given chase. Who was he—the man from the theatre, the Chervenkof man from New York, or, much worse, perhaps—her own father?

****

By ten o'clock the next morning, Charie was feeling more herself, all the angst and confusion of yesterday nearly banished as she was comfortably surrounded by the sights and smells of the theatre, stage hands lighting the gas lamps which illuminated the dance floor.

Mira chattered nonstop in her lilting French, pleasantly lulling as Charie tied her slipper ribbons about her ankles in the exact manner taught to her by her ballet instructor, *Madame* Erlaine, eight years ago on her very first day of training at the Paris Opera.

It was the first of many things the dear woman had shown her through the years, and though *Madame* Erlaine was no longer living, every time Charie stepped out on the stage she sensed the woman's spirit.

Adella Erlaine had never reached the greatness of Grisi or Taglioni, but she drew from each pupil their full potential, a fact not lost upon the prestigious *le Théâtre de l'Académie Royale de Musique*.

Charie would always fondly recall those days.

"You aren't listening, Charie." Mira's accusation forced Charie to look up and focus on her friend of nearly five years.

Mira had been a frightened girl of fourteen when she'd presented herself at the Paris Opera. A runaway from a rural area in southern France where friends and family had scoffed at her love of dance, she'd been destined for marriage to a middle-aged man who owned the largest sheep farm in the province.

Charie recalled her first glimpse of Mira—what a difference from the shy, scared child she'd been. "I'm not," Charie confessed as she stood and adjusted her billowing skirts, giving Mira a smile. "I'm just so glad today is today."

"Well, of course today is today," she agreed impatiently. "I said isn't Domitri Auberchon the most mysteriously handsome man you've ever seen?"

Reality crashed, forcing Charie to recall every painful, confusing, angering moment of the day before. She prayed she'd not say something regretful. "Why ask me that?" A tiny ache commenced above her left temple. And she'd been so sure this day would be normal.

"Because he just arrived with Count Stanislov." Mira pointed to the stage where the count was shaking hands with Phillipe.

Domitri was standing next to him. And he was dressed to dance.

Charie quickly looked away, her face aflame with indignation and anger. What should she do? She'd thought after her long talk with Count Stanislov, he understood her feelings.

How could he do this? Why would the count, whom she'd considered her dearest friend, place her in this awkward position?

Now she would have to tell him, in front of everyone, that she would not dance with Domitri Auberchon. Not now, not ever.

Forgetting Mira, Charie hurried out on the stage before she lost her nerve. A little voice whispered inside her head, *You've told Me you don't want to dance with him, but you haven't given him a chance. Don't forget, he's suffered. This could be his last chance. He has a gift—a gift I gave him. Let him use it.*

Charie halted, raising her eyes heavenward but seeing only the beams and rafters of the stage ceiling. "Lord, don't make me do this," she whispered aloud. "I don't like him—I mean, he's tall and, and, really tall and—handsome." A tiny sob escaped as she dropped her face in her hands. "I'd rather dance with someone I don't like."

"Then we should do well together." The deep, stirring voice caressed her ears in charmingly accented English.

She immediately dropped her hands, looking up to see Domitri standing directly before her. Alternating chills and heat shook her. *Surely this can't be Your will, Lord.*

"Are you all right?" There was a note of concern in his voice.

"I'm—quite—well."

He has a gift—let him use it.

How would she feel if someone tried to keep her from dancing? How would she feel if she'd endured a tragedy similar to that of Domitri Auberchon? "I take it you've decided to accept the role of Albrecht."

"That would be correct." He gave her an irresistible grin, fueling her irritation. "I heard that *Monsieur*s Phillipe and Rubenevski convinced Valmiere last evening over a large bottle of wine that he'd be better suited for the lead male role in a new Perrot project. It's rumored that Perrot is creating a ballet for Fanny Elssler."

"I don't believe there's a bottle of wine large enough to make Antoine Valmiere relinquish a paying job for a 'maybe' job. How much did the count pay him?" Charie folded her arms disapprovingly as she awaited Domitri's answer.

He chuckled. "And to think I was misguided enough to believe there was little happening here," he tapped the top of her neatly coiled braids, courtesy of Lizzie.

Charie bristled.

"You know Olar far too well."

"For your information, I am not an ignorant

American. Nor am I a vapid ballerina who only thinks of herself. As for Count Stanislov, his actions are prompted by concern for me. He is the closest thing I've ever had to a father." She paused to draw a deep, shuddering breath.

"Forgive me for misjudging. I fear you hold a very low opinion of me."

"I don't have any opinion of you." *That was an untruth if ever I've uttered one.* "It doesn't matter to me who I dance with."

He arched a brow.

I've uttered another lie. "Let's just practice," she sputtered in frustration, marching forward.

Domitri caught her arm, and she looked up. His emerald eyes ensnared, sending her heart into dizzying *pirouettes*. "Did you pray about this, about us?"

Charie was powerless to force a flippant remark through her lips. She had no choice but honesty. "Yes," she whispered.

"So did I." His voice was low. And warming.

"What did He say?" she asked.

"He said that you have a gift, and you should use it."

Charie drew a sharp breath. His words duplicated those she'd imagined hearing just moments earlier.

When Domitri's gaze fastened on her parted lips, his head lowered.

What was happening?

"It is good to see that the two of you have worked through your professional differences." *Monsieur* Rubenevski barked close to where they stood, and they jumped apart. "Now, if the two of you would be so kind as to join us for rehearsal."

Stunned by the unexpected exchange, Charie drew

herself up and proceeded towards her spot on the stage. She dared a glance at Domitri, his expression unreadable from his position several feet away.

Looking out over the empty seats, she saw Count Stanislov seated in the front row, wearing an expression that reminded her of the cat that had just sampled the cream.

4

Charie was lost in a daydream, her fifth for the day to be exact. It was something she inexplicably slipped into each time she was not required to dance, and could simply watch Domitri working with the choreographer, Henri Phillipe.

It was a fascinating process, the way *Monsieur* Phillipe asked Domitri's opinion, and then actually gave it consideration.

Any time she made suggestions, she was told to perform the steps as she'd been instructed and not to delay practice. That rubbed her already frayed nerves, so rather than dwell on the slight, she daydreamed.

She was a fairy princess held captive in a crumbling tower and her beloved knight was coming to her rescue. The music in her head made her sway and dip with abandon in what she believed was an unobservable part of the stage. Suddenly she realized stage activity had quieted. Prickles spiraled down the back of her neck, a sure sign that someone was watching. She stilled.

Rubenevski barked. Again. "Come out on the stage, *gospoja* Marin." It wasn't a request, it was an order. "Phillipe wishes to confer with you."

Aware all eyes were upon her, Charie did as she was told, stopping before *Monsieur* Phillipe and Domitri.

"Those steps—do them again," Phillipe

demanded. Didn't any of these men know how to ask nicely?

"I wasn't doing anything in particular. I was just— moving."

"That was the beauty." Domitri was clearly excited. "At the precise time you become a *wili*—the ghost, dance as you just did—as though the music comes from your soul. It will be more effective than the choreographed steps."

Charie looked at Phillipe, and then at Rubenevski, awaiting an outburst in either Russian or French. She'd made a similar suggestion two weeks ago and earned an ear-singeing lecture.

Now, both men remained silent.

"You really want me to dance my own steps?"

"Yes, please," Domitri urged.

Without waiting for the orchestra to play so much as the first note, Charie went easily into a flowing series of *pointe* turns, *chassés*, a *gargouillade*, weaving *piques*, bends and sways. Dancing from her heart and her soul, the freedom allowed her love of ballet to guide her feet rather than the stern instructions of *Monsieur* Rubenevski. Charie was again the pupil and *Madame* Erlaine was encouraging her to dance for the love of it.

So she danced the dance of a broken-hearted young girl, deceived by her love; robbed of life and any chance at happiness. And when she executed her last *pirouette* and came slowly to a stop, her feet again earth bound, hands crossed at her throat, head bowed, she breathed a silent thank you to the Lord for allowing her to do what she loved.

If no one enjoyed her dancing and if there were those who disapproved, no one could take away this marvelous joy. From her earliest years, all she'd ever dreamed of was moving to the beautiful music, whirling and leaping; drifting and soaring.

Embarrassingly aware of the deep silence in the theatre, she dared to look up, bracing herself for the chastisement surely to come.

It was Domitri who broke the nearly unbearable silence as he began a slow clapping that was quickly emulated by the other observers.

Within seconds, the applause was thunderous and looking out into the theatre, she saw Count Stanislov on his feet as he, too, clapped.

Fortunately, Mira chose that moment to run up to her, throwing her arms about her. "I've never seen you dance more wonderfully. It was amazing—you are amazing."

The other dancers surrounded Charie, lavishing her with praise.

Rubenevski shouted, and everyone hurried back to their places.

Domitri joined her and took her hand.

Shyly, she raised her gaze.

"It is an honor to dance with you, and I am glad that you are willing to accept me."

"We were meant to dance together."

Emerald brilliants flared in his eyes at her words. Whatever had prompted her to say that?

Phillipe interrupted, ending the moment. "Enough. I humored you, *Monsieur* Auberchon, by permitting *Mademoiselle* Marin to perform her own choreography. Now, could we please rehearse the real steps?"

"They will be changed," Domitri said, still in possession of her hand.

She wanted to be grievously offended, but failed to summon so much as pique.

"You are not the choreographer." Phillipe stomped to where they stood, his hands fisted on hips. "I make that decision." There was a moment of silence as all awaited his next words. His bluster ebbed. "I suppose we could work in some of the steps."

"I suggested that some time ago," Charie said, torn between surprise at Domitri's response to her dancing and anger at the fact that Phillipe was willing to make changes based upon Domitri's opinion rather than hers. "You told me there would be no changes."

"Charie, if *Monsieur* Phillipe is willing to bend now, let him," the count suggested from his front-row seat. "It doesn't mean your idea was unworthy. Domitri has simply reinforced the need to highlight your talent with new choreography."

Charie struggled with pride and acceptance. If she meekly agreed, these men would continue to think her opinions of little worth—if she threw another tantrum, they would label her "difficult." What would God have her do?

"Make peace," she whispered to herself. Why was doing the right thing so difficult? "Very well." Charie failed to restrain the lift of her chin as she directed a cool glance at Domitri.

To her dismay, he grinned. Far too charmingly.

"Shall we practice?"

She was certain she heard the count's relieved sigh even though quite some distance separated them. *I must be driving the count near to madness.* That wasn't at all her intention, but the advent of Domitri had turned her into someone she didn't know. She prayed she hadn't made a mistake in agreeing to dance with the unnervingly handsome *danseur*.

****

"The headmaster at the academy was far from pleased when I told him I would be spending the next month performing your ballet," Domitri said, breaking the silence that had slipped between Olar and he as they rode together in Olar's carriage.

After a week of rehearsing the part of Albrecht with Charie, Domitri teetered in that precarious realm of clutching memories while enticed into the present. That realization angered and saddened. With every passing day, Sophia slipped further away, just like the fairy creature she had portrayed in their last performance together in London at Her Majesty's Theatre, just mere hours before the wreck.

But now the pain and agony had inexplicably lessened. "*Monsieur* Garnier assured me that if I didn't get this 'dancing' out of my system and present myself at the start of the term in January, I should consider myself released from employment."

"You won't need to return. There's a ballet I want you and Charie to work on for Christmas, and then a spring performance that will be most appropriate for the Lenten season."

"Olar, we're ten days away from the opening of *Giselle*. Charie told me she begins rehearsals for *Long Ago in Bethlehem* the latter part of November. And now you're talking of another ballet the first of the year. You never pushed Sophia so hard."

"I am not pushing Charie. If she wishes to pass on *The Pearls of Esther*, that is ultimately her decision. But having heard the music and read the libretto, I believe it would be good for her. And for you."

"Did you not hear me, Olar? I have to return to the classroom in January. I am only dancing the part of Albrecht as a favor to you."

"So you have no desire whatsoever to dance with the most magical and engaging creature God ever made?"

"Olar, I cannot forget Sophia." Irritation laced his voice. Irritation at Olar or at himself?

"Nor can I. But can you say to me that Sophia was the dancer that Charie is? I cannot forget what I saw that first day you practiced together and told Charie to dance as she was moved to dance. There is a beauty within her that spills forth with every step and turn she takes. You cannot deny it."

Domitri gritted his teeth, wrestling with anger. "I return to my teaching position in January." He spoke louder than required in the close confines of a carriage.

"We will discuss this later, Domitri," the count announced with that air of authority that was ingrained in those of noble birth. Olar rarely invoked such a tone unless displeased. "Ah, we have arrived."

Domitri looked out the carriage window to see a myriad of lights spilling from the numerous windows of the home of François Robert, the director of the *Ballet Eleganté*.

Part of an elite and wealthy Parisian group, which also included the director of the famed Paris Opera, Robert was renowned for his lavish entertaining. The evening's event—his daughter's eighteenth birthday—had inspired the man to compose a guest list of notables primarily from the dancing stratum of society.

Domitri had made Robert's acquaintance when he and Sophia had performed *Romeo and Juliet* in Paris. He was as tolerable as one could hope of a man engaged in his profession, and Domitri had never known him to be dishonest.

Within minutes, Domitri and Olar were ushered into the grand salon, where the guest of honor—a giggling, gangly eighteen year old—greeted them. The young girl blushed beet red when Domitri kissed the back of her hand, and then immediately dissolved into more giggles.

It was a relief when other newcomers forced him to move on.

A tray bearing flutes of champagne was thrust into his face and after waving the servant on, he clasped his hands behind his back and slowly meandered among the guests.

Marie Taglioni was seated in a high-backed chair reminiscent of a throne, Robert and his pleasantly plump wife in attendance, as well as several other members of the Parisian dance community, including Rubenevski and Phillipe.

Moving further into the gilt festooned, crystal burdened space, he spied Fanny Cerito and her husband, dancer and choreographer, Arthur Saint-Léon. They, too, were surrounded by admirers.

Véron, the most famous director of the Paris Opera and now retired, was notably absent. To this day, Domitri believed Véron had contributed much to the ill will that existed between Taglioni and Elssler. So it was no surprise that Fanny Elssler was nowhere to be seen.

Further on, Olar was conversing with Matilda Marin.

Domitri had seen Charie's mother on the London stage eight years earlier in her widely acclaimed portrayal of Joan of Arc. Her performance was riveting, and Domitri remembered how Sophia cried when St. Joan had been tied to the stake.

Stage life hadn't hardened or aged Matilda, surely attributable to her Christian faith, which, Olar assured him, was unshakable. It was hard to believe this lovely, sophisticated woman had grown up on a farm in the rural South of the United States and had reached such heights in her career without compromising her faith or herself. And to have raised such a beautiful, unaffected daughter—

Violet rimmed eyes met his across the room, luminescent and brilliant, reflecting the myriad candle flames dancing about the ballroom.

Shaking himself of his momentary surprise, he swept Charie head to toe, taking in the discreet, but flattering décolletage of the elegant ball gown of blue and silver. She looked every bit the fairy princess; Domitri pulled to her without realizing his feet moved.

Just as he neared, another man slipped between them, tall and muscular with perfectly combed blond hair. Within seconds, this man led Charie to the dance floor, even though she cast him a pleading look over her shoulder.

Domitri started to follow until a hand rested on his shoulder. Turning, he saw Olar.

"That is Bauerhausen. No need to start anything."

"Charice doesn't want to dance with him."

"Perhaps, but she's in no danger. It's better she dance with him than that one."

Reluctantly dragging his gaze from Charie and the baron, Domitri looked in the direction Olar indicated, focusing on the back of a man of average height, garbed immaculately, and currently fawning over Marie Taglioni, who'd at last arose from her throne.

"We have greater problems than the baron. That is Anapol Chervenkof."

As though the man heard Olar speak his name, he looked around, his gaze fastening on Domitri.

Shock gave way to foreboding. "Nap Rheyev?" Domitri breathed aloud.

****

When Charie realized Domitri had no intention of rescuing her, she resigned herself to dancing with the baron. Not that he was a poor dancer—if anything, he was exceptional. She simply did not want to encourage him.

"That long sigh tells me you are less than pleased that I whisked you away from that washed up *danseur*."

"You know that isn't so, for you've seen him dance."

"That's true, but he's been retired for years. If he is still as good as you say, why would he have given up?"

"He was in mourning. Obviously, you've never been in love."

"I could be," he teased.

Charie almost smiled, and then caught herself. She mustn't encourage him in any way.

"*Mein liebchen*, will you be angry with me forever? Now that I will be working with your mother, cannot we at least be friends?"

"I'm not convinced my mother is doing the right thing, but she has managed her own affairs long enough to know if she's made the right choice. As for being friends, I am more than willing to put the past behind us. But I have no intention of becoming one of your admirers."

"You say that with such conviction, Charice. What if I set out to change your mind?"

A tart reply had been on the tip of Charie's tongue until she noticed Domitri and the count, heads together in conversation.

Count Stanislov's expression could only be termed as grim, and she feared he and her mother had argued again.

"No reply?" Bauerhausen asked, drawing her thoughts back to her current dilemma.

"I'm sorry. I really can't finish this dance. If you'll excuse me." Charie slipped away quickly, weaving a path through the other dancers. Seeing that her mother chatted with the newly wedded Fanny Cerrito, she decided to join them.

She'd taken but a step in their direction when the face of a man came into view. Horrified, she froze.

"You remember me?" His voice was more irritating than it'd been upon their first meeting at her mother's theatre. Why was he here?

"I do. If you'll excuse me."

His pudgy hand fastened on her arm, and her heart skipped a beat. How could he think she'd so much as consider speaking with him given his abominable behavior?

"Release me."

"Ernest Altby of New York," he unnecessarily announced while his grip tightened. "You'd do well to come with me if you have any care as to your mother's welfare."

Knee weakening alarm raced through Charie, and she looked about desperately, luckless in sighting anyone she knew.

This heinous man dared threaten her mother?

Looking wildly around once more, she noticed a dark-haired, dark-eyed man approaching, his features pleasant and his temples liberally touched with silver, giving him a look of distinction.

Perhaps she could yet escape this Ernest Altby.

"There you are," she cried out with forced gaiety, wrenching free of Altby and taking hold of the stranger's arm. "I believe I promised you this dance."

The man chuckled. Was he willing to play along?

"I can see, Altby, that once again you've failed to charm Miss Marin." The voice held a trace of an accent but he spoke perfect English. "This time I will talk some sense into her."

Too terrified to protest, she allowed the man to sweep her back among the dancers. His face and manner were outwardly pleasing, but his words sliced her with shards of fear.

"Never send a minion to handle an important matter. Now that I've met you, Miss Marin, allow me to introduce myself. I am Anapol Chervenkof, and I plan to become very important to you; just as important as I once was to your mother. But first, let's talk about your father."

"*Mademoiselle* Marin, I believe this is the dance you promised." Relief flooded Charie as Domitri expertly maneuvered her away from Anapol Chervenkof. Anger spread over the smooth features of Altby's employer.

Charie only cared that Domitri was guiding her very far away. "Where have you been?" She'd meant to express her gratitude, but terror clouded her thinking.

"It's nice to see you again, too," he replied, a tiny

twitch in his jaw and a forced smile telling her he was displeased.

And with good reason, she admitted. "I'm sorry. That wasn't kind of me. I've been nearly out of my mind with fear. First that odious man from the theatre, and then this Chervenkof—what is going on?"

"No one is going to hurt you." He spoke softly, the warmth in his voice chasing away the icy fear.

Lowering her gaze, Charie hoped he wouldn't realize his effect. She was in a state, and she didn't like it. What had become of the normal Charice Marin? How could that one fit of temper from a week ago lead to so many complications?

"We are going to dance together for a bit, and then discreetly slip away to meet the count and your mother. I'm sorry that the evening will be cut short."

"I'd rather be anywhere than here. Anapol Chervenkof has frightened me more than Ernest Altby—that's the man from the theatre," she explained when he gave her a puzzled look. "He works for Chervenkof."

Domitri nodded in understanding, but his expression was grim as he guided her around the other dancers. When they neared a door on the far side of the ballroom, Domitri paused and opened it. Taking her hand, he pulled her through, shutting and locking it behind them. After glancing quickly about the dimly lit hall, he chose a direction.

Charie was all too glad to follow. Her relief was tempered by a chill and chattering teeth.

Traveling countless corridors, they finally arrived at what looked like a servant's entrance.

Domitri went through the door and they found themselves in the laundry room.

Occupied by one woman seated behind a long table, her head rested atop a stack of folded linens as she napped. Hearing them, she jumped from her stool and scurried away, shrieking in French.

Charie ran as Domitri increased his strides, rushing through the stone-floored space.

This time he found a door that opened up to what appeared to be the kitchen garden.

The cold air enveloped Charie with frigid intensity, a gasp forced from her lips.

Recognizing her discomfort, Domitri paused and removed his coat, settling it about her shoulders. Before she could thank him, he resumed their flight, gripping her hand tightly. They reached the circular drive, and Domitri guided her towards the carriage that Charie recognized as the count's.

As the driver, Petrov, helped her in, she realized neither her mother nor the count awaited them.

But her evening cloak was lying on the seat as though someone had prepared for this sudden departure.

Domitri settled beside her and rapped for the driver to leave. The carriage set off quickly and in no time reached a brisk pace, leaving the Robert mansion behind.

"You said we would meet Count Stanislov and my mother." Charie handed him his coat, and then lifted her own fur-lined cloak.

Domitri took it and settled it about her shoulders, their gazes momentarily meeting. Charie warmed immediately.

"They are awaiting us at my atelier not far from the *Champs Élysées*. We thought it best not to return to your home or the count's."

Should she be frightened or angered? Could she trust Domitri Auberchon? Why was it so hard to summon outrage at this man's audacity? Had the baron done this, she would be audibly furious. Instead, she sat meek and accepting.

"Do you think Chervenkof would present himself at either residence?"

"It's hard to say." Domitri's firm lips pressed together in displeasure.

"*Monsieur* Fitzhugh, *Maman*'s agent, should tell him to leave us alone. This Chervenkof acts as though he knows something he could use against *Maman* and me." Charie shuddered.

"I believe Matilda could better answer that. Anapol Chervenkof is not a man with whom you'd want to associate."

"How would you know?" Even though little light filtered into the carriage, the street lamps illuminated enough of Domitri's face to allow Charie a glimpse of his tension.

His jaw flexed. "He once tried to kill me."

5

"What?" Charie pressed her hand to her throat. Shock speared.

Domitri sighed, transferring his gaze to the window. "I knew him as Nap Rheyev. That's why I failed to connect him to the name Chervenkof. Nap— Anapol—lived with his unmarried mother in a room over the baker's shop a few blocks down the street from my boyhood home in St. Petersburg. He was a few years older, and all the young boys looked up to him.

"When he was about a score and two, he joined a group of revolutionaries and quickly moved up through the ranks. He enticed many a young boy into leaving school and joining the 'cause.' He even approached me." Domitri shook his head and chuckled bitterly. "Nap wouldn't take no for an answer—no one refused Nap. We fought—with fists—and though I was younger, I came out with sore knuckles. He had a broken nose. After that, he left me alone. The last I heard of him, he'd managed to turn his revolutionary activities into a healthy source of income."

"How?"

"Through the extortion of innocent citizens. They are frightened into giving their hard earned *rubles* to support Russian freedom. It's been going on for years. My mother's country is filled with those who think violence is the only way to achieve reform and change.

Not that there isn't a need, but there are better ways to approach the situation. Apparently, Chervenkof has decided to direct his attacks on citizens of another country using his trademark blackmail and intimidation."

"This Chervenkof should be in prison. Why don't you go to the Paris authorities and tell them what you know?"

"Tell them what? I believe that my former tormentor is possibly a Russian revolutionary posing as an American entrepreneur and is up to no good? They might want me to be more specific and provide proof." There was no missing the sarcasm in Domitri's voice, so Charie fell silent. He made perfect sense.

"I don't see what he stands to gain if he becomes patron of the *Ballet Eleganté*."

"Nor do I. But my mind doesn't work like his."

The carriage slowed and looking out her window, Charie noticed they were passing the *Arc de Triomphe*, completed ten years ago as a symbol of Napoleon I's military victories.

It seemed ironic to her that the city would complete a monument for a man who ended up in exile. Monuments in the United States were built to honor heroes and Founding Fathers of the country.

"We're here." The carriage halted before a four-storied, unimposing brick structure that looked as though it may have once served as a warehouse.

Domitri helped her alight, and then grasped her hand as he led her towards the door.

There wasn't so much as a speck of light shining through any of the windows. It was clear that her mother and Count Stanislov were not within.

"I shouldn't go in. Not until my mother and the

count arrive." She intentionally pulled back, unwilling to pass through the door he'd just unlocked and opened.

"Muzette is upstairs, though most likely asleep. She will be our chaperone."

Was Muzette Domitri's mistress? If so, the woman would not be a suitable chaperone. What should she do?

"Muzette is my housekeeper and cook and just turned three score and two."

Now he was reading her mind, Charie thought, feeling sheepish and silly.

As if Domitri Auberchon had any designs upon her person. He'd once been in love with the incomparable Sophia Stanislovna.

Charie could never compete with her.

Somewhat reassured, she passed through the door, and then allowed him to guide her up a narrow flight of stairs.

"My living apartments are upstairs, and I use the lower level as my dance studio. I'd like you to see it sometime. I instruct some of the young men I teach at the *Academie* in the evenings and on Saturdays. Even though I retired from the stage, the love of the dance is still in here." He tapped his heart.

"But now you're out of retirement," she reminded. "You'll be performing again before hundreds of people. It will help you move on."

"It won't help me forget Sophia." His words were uttered harshly as he paused on the steps.

She couldn't see his face, but she knew he was angry. "I didn't mean that you would forget her. I simply meant that it would give you a chance to share your talent."

"You've never lost someone you loved more than life itself. There isn't any way you could understand my grief."

"Perhaps not." Why did her voice quiver and the liquid pool in her eyes? She was grateful for the darkness. "But I know that God wants you to go on living. And I do mourn for someone—for a father who is as lost to me as though he was dead. My mother made the choice that I was never to know him without ever asking me how I felt. So, I do understand how you feel, to some extent. I didn't mean to offend."

"You didn't offend me," he said, and then sighed. "This week I've thought less about Sophia and more about my dancing. I feel disloyal because I pledged to never dance on the stage again. Now, I am breaking that promise."

"Which is my fault." Tears filled Charie's eyes. "I never meant for you to do something you didn't want to."

"That's not the problem. I'm doing exactly what I want to do, and I'm partnering a beautiful, talented young woman possessed of a remarkable gift. And I'm beginning to enjoy her company." He paused, reaching out to tuck back a straying curl. "Far too much."

A gasp died on her lips as Domitri cupped the back of her head. Could he mean to kiss her?

She might be a score and one, but her mother's sheltering and the count's protectiveness had insulated her from men and their amorous pursuits. Not even Bauerhausen had managed a kiss; not for lack of trying.

A pleasant heat crept through her as her heart raced, and she tentatively rested her hands on his chest, aware of his thudding heart.

Unexpectedly, Domitri pushed her back as though she was loathsome to his touch.

Before she could manage a coherent word, light flooded the narrow stairwell and a head peeked out the door, gray braids swinging free from beneath a lacey mobcap. "Is that you, *Monsieur* Domitri?" came the elderly woman's high-pitched voice, her words spoken in French. "Hurry up. I will prepare the hot tea that you like so much."

That finished whatever had magically flowed, and then abruptly ended seconds earlier.

Domitri, now cold and aloof, took great pains to avoid contact as he motioned for her to climb the remaining steps ahead of him.

Something strange twisted about Charie's heart as she brushed at irritating tears, and she wondered if it was hate—or something else?

****

It was a relief that Olar and Matilda arrived at his apartment not long after the disaster on the stairs because Domitri could finally focus on something besides Charice Marin's shattering effect.

Muzette, now in her role of housekeeper, presented cups of the strongly brewed tea he preferred, the water boiled in the samovar his mother had insisted he take when he left home. The woman also brought in a tray of tiny sandwiches and cakes.

So while his guests ate, Domitri stood by the large window overlooking the broad expanse of the *Champs Élysées* pondering his foolish behavior.

I can't have feelings for her, Lord. I simply can't. What of Sophia? I was about to kiss Charie. What does she think of me? I should tell Olar that I can't perform with her. What if these feelings grow stronger?

And what if they do? came the inaudible response.

Slowly, Domitri turned away from the window and gazed upon Charie, who accepted a steaming cup of tea from Muzette, chattering away in her non-stop French.

Charie glanced at him, and then quickly looked away, understandably angry.

There was no denying her beauty, her features nearly identical to her mother's and her hair bearing traces of her mother's vibrant red. But her chin was firmer and more pronounced, as were her nose and cheekbones. Though she lacked her mother's brilliant blue eyes, hers were dark pools of ambergine, glistening at the moment as they reflected the low lamplight. The shadows that danced about her were strangely similar to those that highlighted Olar's classically sculpted face.

A twinge of unease curled through Domitri, but he dismissed the sensation. His emotions and senses were unnaturally heightened.

"Join us, Domitri," Olar said. "We may as well explore the issue and see where we stand."

"This isn't necessary," Matilda protested. "Charie has had a fright, and the best thing for her right now is to go home. Olar, you are making far too much of this. You're turning it into something akin to cloak and dagger."

"Am I?" he asked tersely as he faced Charie's mother, his jaw noticeably tensing.

Domitri joined them, taking a seat on an old, threadbare couch Muzette had long wanted her upholsterer brother to re-cover. Domitri simply saw no reason to do so. "I think it's time you told Charie about your involvement with Chervenkof."

"Involvement?" Charie asked as she set down her cup, fear robbing her lovely face of all color. "*Maman*, I thought he was nothing more than an overzealous admirer."

Her mother released a deep sigh, bringing her gloved hand up as she rested her chin on the back of it, her elbow propped on the arm of her chair. It was a theatrical pose, but Domitri surmised it came naturally to Matilda Marin.

"Two years ago, Charie, when I spent the summer in London during the Shakespeare revival and you were with the ballet company in Italy, I met Anapol Chervenkof. He claimed to be an American of Russian descent, a New York businessman on holiday in London. Chervenkof was kind, considerate, and generous. We spent a lot of time together, and he asked me to marry him." Here she paused and flicked a nervous glance at Olar, whose jaw still twitched. "I believed God was gifting me with another chance at love so I seriously considered his proposal.

"Then Fitz discovered that Anapol was a Russian national obtaining arms and weapons in America illegally, and then sending them to Russian revolutionaries. I realized it was I, not our Lord, who was encouraging the relationship so I explained to Anapol that I could no longer see him. He was enraged, but I truly believed that once he calmed, he would be gentlemanly enough to honor my request.

"I never said anything to you, Charie, because I didn't want you to worry. I thought the matter resolved until last year when Anapol presented himself at my dressing room after my first performance of

Helen of Troy. He asked me again to marry him, and I declined his proposal. He flew into a rage, frightening Lizzie so badly she went for help."

"And you didn't tell me?" Charie asked, unshed tears pooling in her eyes.

Domitri fought the urge to comfort her.

"I didn't want you dragged into something so unpleasant. After all, it was of my own making. When he threatened me, I was angry. When he made threats against you, I was frightened. I finally confided in Olar."

"What sort of threats?" Domitri asked, the old animosity resurfacing with a jarring force.

So Nap had graduated from harassing the corner baker to intimidating a woman who rejected his advances. It sounded as though Rheyev's—Chervenkof's—few remaining principles had vanished. While his greed intensified.

"He said he'd see that I never acted in another play, and that he would make sure Charie never danced again." Matilda shuddered.

The blood pumping through Domitri's veins boiled—the mere thought of anything happening to Charie filled him with fury. He clenched his hands into fists.

"I can't believe he's here in Paris." Matilda sobbed. There was nothing pretend in her anxious, tear-filled eyes.

"I can," Domitri said. "We lived in the same neighborhood in St. Petersburg, but our lives took very different turns. Chervenkof joined a group of malcontents bent upon overthrowing the Russian monarchy while terrorizing local shop owners. He went by the name Nap Rheyev, then."

"What about my father?" Charie asked.

Matilda and Olar exchanged uncertain looks.

"Where is he, and what is his connection to Chervenkof? Ernest Altby, the man who accosted me at *Maman*'s theatre, said that his employer—Chervenkof—wanted to speak to me and my father about the ballet company. My father needs to know this criminal is making things difficult for us. My father hurt you, *Maman*, but surely if he knows we're in trouble, he'll help."

"I'll worry about that, *chaton*," Olar spoke gently, using the French endearment for kitten. "Do not trouble yourself."

"But I want to speak with him. Surely no harm can come from that."

"The hour is late, and everyone needs their rest," Olar insisted as he stood. "And don't forget that practice begins at seven o'clock in the morning, Charie. We can talk more about this later."

"No." Charie came to her feet, facing Olar and her mother. "I'm tired of the secrecy. Why don't we report Chervenkof to the Parisian authorities?"

"Charice, it is not so simple, and it will take time to work things out," Olar said. "In the meantime, you must avoid Chervenkof. I will make sure you and Matilda have a companion at all times. I don't want you to be alarmed."

"How can I not be alarmed? Why did we scurry away from the soiree so quickly if there was nothing to worry about? Why did Altby tell me I should speak to Chervenkof if I cared about my mother's welfare? You're not telling me everything."

Another worried look passed between Matilda and Olar, who almost imperceptibly nodded his head.

But for now, the count was right. It was time for Charie and her mother to return home.

Domitri almost chuckled in despair. He would be the least likely of them all to get any sleep as he replayed in his mind those moments with Charie on the darkened stairway.

"We should do as Olar asks," Domitri said, and the count looked at him thankfully. "We can't accomplish anything tonight, nor can we resolve the Rheyev-Chervenkof problem. The important thing to remember is to not go anywhere alone—either of you." He looked pointedly at Charie, whose face reddened at his obvious referral to her flight from rehearsal a week ago.

There was no need to minimize the severity of the situation. Chervenkof couldn't be trusted. And though Domitri knew of Nap's criminal tendencies, the frequent and frightened looks Matilda directed at Olar indicated there was more than a thwarted courtship fueling Chervenkof's ire. If he was to help Olar, Domitri needed to know the entire story. And he would learn the truth.

"I agree." Matilda stood, drawing her cloak around her. "Thank you for your hospitality, *Monsieur* Auberchon. Please compliment your housekeeper on the cakes. They were delicious." She walked to the door, Olar behind her.

Charie didn't follow. Silence slipped over the room, and then Charie, huffing in frustration, snatched up her cloak and proceeded to the door.

Domitri took advantage of her departure, coming to his feet and hurrying to her side to assist her with her garment.

She glared up at him as she reluctantly accepted

his help.

"I'm sorry," Domitri whispered.

"You should be," she retorted under her breath, but loudly enough for him to hear.

By then, Olar and Matilda were waiting, and there was no time for further conversation, not that such would have helped.

He'd ruined their tenuous friendship. Opening the door for his guests, he watched them descend the narrow stairs, Charie behind her mother and Olar.

She paused a moment and looked back at him. Tears glistened on her lashes.

****

"Charie, are you asleep?" Matilda's voice intruded into Charie's restlessness, and she lay perfectly still upon her bed, torn between feigning sleep so that her mother would go away or responding and inviting her mother in.

She opted for the latter and sitting up, called out. "No, *Maman*. I'm awake."

The door swung open and her mother entered, clad in a simple ivory dressing gown. She made her way across the room lit by a single lamp, and then took a seat on the edge of Charie's huge bed, much as she had during Charie's childhood when she would read her a bedtime story.

"Perhaps I was wrong to keep you in the dark in regards to your father."

"It seems I've been left in the dark about many things." Cherie regretted her tone, but it couldn't be helped. She was hurt. And angry. "Why didn't you tell me about Anapol Chervenkof?"

"I've been so careful to avoid entanglements," Matilda said sadly. "After my relationship with your father failed, I found solace in you and my acting. That worked well until you grew your wings and flew away. Now, we're often apart—I'm here and you're there. And it's lonely. That summer in London was the first time we'd been separated. I knew those times would occur more frequently.

"Then I met Anapol after one of my performances. He was much younger than I, but I was flattered by his attention. He was charming and congenial, and," here she paused as though gathering her thoughts, "attractive. When Fitz uncovered Anapol's illegal activities, I was ashamed and embarrassed. It wasn't something I wanted you to know."

"You always worry about me. Why can't I do the same for you? That's what people do for those they love."

"And you must know how very much I love you."

Charie smiled at her mother and reached out to take her hand.

Matilda folded hers over Charie's.

"I want you to know how much I appreciate what you've done for me. You took me with you, no matter where you went. You raised me and educated me and showed me a world I would have never seen had I been one of those little girls sent away to boarding school. You encouraged my love of ballet and supported me. You've always been there for me. I will always be here for you."

"I have been very foolish, Charie. I've brought this disaster upon us."

"The count will aright matters."

"Ah, yes. Olar to the rescue." Her mother uttered a

sad laugh. "As badly as I hate to admit it, he does have a way of stepping in just when he's needed."

"That's a good thing." Charie hesitated, and then drew a fortifying breath. "*Maman*—did you love my father?"

A ghost of a smile touched her mother's lips as her eyes looked beyond Charie into the past. "What was there not to love about him? Handsome and courtly, just like a prince from a fairytale. I fell in love hard and fast, and when he asked me to marry him I couldn't say 'yes' quickly enough."

"What happened?" Charie was absolutely amazed that her mother poured out her heart in a way she never had before.

"His family 'happened.' There were certain expectations of him and specific responsibilities he was required to fulfill. Marrying me was not in keeping with those expectations and responsibilities. He chose to follow his family's wishes."

"He didn't try to save your marriage?"

"He did. He asked me to give up acting and live at the family estate. There was a young child by his first wife. That wife died in childbirth. It was understandable he'd want to be with the child. But I didn't want to give up the stage."

"By then you were—" here Charie paused as she sought a delicate way to say her mother had been pregnant. "—in the family way."

"I was. And I was overjoyed. But even so, I didn't want to abandon the stage and move far away to another country. I know now that I was selfish. I should have been more willing to compromise. I erroneously believed he should give up everything for me. But that's all in the past. This is the here and now, and we must be happy with what we have." She shook Charie's hand in emphasis to her words.

"But this Chervenkof—?"

"Olar and I will work it out."

"If you're willing to let him help, have you put aside your hate?"

"I've never hated him—we just see things differently. Under the circumstances, we can work together. Now, get some sleep."

"I don't think I can. Something else happened tonight that is most disturbing. Domitri was very attentive and protective towards me when he helped me escape Chervenkof. He completely changed when we reached his apartment; cold and unfriendly. What do you know about him?"

"He is a superb dancer, and Olar considers him the son he never had."

"He was married to his daughter so that's understandable."

"It has more to do with his strength of character. It was difficult for Domitri to accept Sophia's death, and Olar said Domitri entered a period where he blamed God for taking her from him. I cannot say where he stands at this time, but as he's dancing again, I believe he is moving past the tragedy. I fear, however, if he found himself attracted to another woman, he would struggle with guilt."

"Could he be attracted to me?" Charie knew she shouldn't care, but there was no denying she was both hopeful and frightened by the possibility.

"I'd say he's interested. But you should pray about this. The last thing I want is for you to be hurt or make the mistakes I've made."

"Isn't that part of life, *Maman*? You can't protect

me forever. I am of an age to make my own choices and decisions. But I will pray. I always feel better sharing my burdens with the Lord."

"You know what we should do?" Matilda asked, and Charie shook her head. "We should take a holiday in the spring and visit Virginia. Your grandparents and aunts and uncles and cousins haven't seen you in five years. What do you think about that?"

"I'd love to. But *Maman*, what I'd really like is to meet my father. Would you mind that so terribly?"

"No, dear. You have a right. Just be patient with me and give me some time. There are things I need to work out first. Your father's life is complicated, as is our relationship. May I ask patience of you?"

"Of course." Charie squeezed her mother's hand. "Thank you for allowing me to dance. I can't imagine doing anything other than what I'm doing right now."

"I know how important it is to be able to follow your dream, but don't rule out love and marriage, and perhaps, children."

"I haven't, *Maman*. This probably sounds silly, but I want to be truly, deeply in love with a man and he with me. That would be the only way I'd give up the ballet."

"It's not silly. It's what every woman hopes and prays for. You've a good head on your shoulders, Charie."

"I get that from you."

"And your father. He's a good, decent man, dear. You must not harbor the man any ill will. One day I hope to make you understand why things happened as they did."

"But until then, I'll be patient," Charie promised.

Then, just as she had many a night during her

childhood, Matilda leaned over and kissed the top of her head, erasing Charie's fears and uncertainty.

It was a good feeling.

6

Charie wasn't sure what to expect from Domitri the following day when she arrived at the theatre minutes after the sun peeked above the horizon.

He was already there, warming up, clad in leggings that were more ragged than hers.

She paused at the door, not ready for him to see her so that she could watch.

A perfectly fluid combination of sinew and bone, Domitri's thighs and shoulders reflected honed muscles that responded to jumps, leaps, and *allegros* effortlessly. Watching him spiral and turn left her breathless. When he raced across the stage in pure abandon and reckless spontaneity, she wanted to mirror his movements.

At any moment, she expected him to tumble, but he soared without mishap or misstep. Entranced by his performance, she moved closer, his presence magnetic. When she reached the stage, he noticed her, stopping suddenly, the light from the gas lamps highlighting the moisture that beaded his brow and neck.

"Don't stop."

"Join me," he suggested as he squatted at the edge of the stage. "Why don't we practice before the others arrive?"

"I—well, why not?" Charie removed her outer garments, and then quickly slipped on her ballet shoes. After tying the ribbons, she hurried around to the side of the stage, and Domitri met her at the edge.

Grasping her wrists, he effortlessly pulled her up, and then immediately swept her out upon the stage performing a series of weaving *tours*. He called out the steps, and she easily followed.

Her breathlessness returned; in no way connected to the pace, but a result of his proximity and her efforts to mesh her movements perfectly with his.

With her back to him, Domitri lifted her, pivoted slowly, and then released her. As her feet touched the floor he turned her about to face him.

"I apologize for last night." His voice was low and husky, unbidden warmth heating her flesh. His green gaze was intense and hypnotic. "I never meant to offend you."

"I know." Her voice was hardly above a whisper.

"I wanted to kiss you."

"You were angry."

"I was angry with myself. It had nothing to do with you. Actually," he shook his head, "it has everything to do with you."

"I'm confused."

"We've spent too much time talking." Certain he would kiss her, she rose up on her toes.

The staccato tap of a cane ended the moment, and both of them looked out into the theatre. It was Count Stanislov, looking as dapper as ever, walking towards them.

"The two of you are practicing early." Count Stanislov closed the gap between them, his progression halted by the orchestra pit.

Charie blushed as the count looked at them with narrowed gaze. The two of them practicing alone could initiate damaging rumors, the last thing she needed or wanted.

"You know I've always practiced early. It's easier to rehearse if I'm warmed up." Domitri's reply held no trace of alarm, so Charie relaxed.

"I don't recall you arriving so early before." Count Stanislov leveled his gaze at Charie.

She reddened more even as she replied. "I didn't sleep well last night. Rather than toss and turn another minute, I got up. I didn't awaken *Maman*, Lizzie, or *Madame* Jeaneau, but I left them a note. I ate a cold croissant and came straight here."

"Alone?" The count thundered, and his face grew redder than hers.

"I took a cab. I was quite safe."

"Charie." Domitri's tone was much softer than the count's. "You cannot forget our warning. You must not go anywhere alone."

"I know you're concerned, but I won't be wrapped in a cocoon, no matter how good your intentions. Now, if you'll excuse me." Quickly, she left the stage, the earlier joy of dancing with Domitri banished. Tears rolled down her cheeks as soon as she deemed herself out of sight, but the arrival of several members of the company forced her to hastily wipe her eyes.

Mira who was, as always, full of chatter, asked Charie about *Monsieur* Robert's birthday celebration for his daughter.

It wasn't long before *Monsieur*s Phillipe and Rubenevski arrived, both men issuing orders and instructions with military precision, making everything seem normal. The rehearsal day had officially begun.

****

"You dance like wooden sticks," Rubenevski raged in Russian.

Domitri glanced at Charie, her hands folded before her as she stoically bore the man's wrath.

For those who couldn't understand one word spewing from his mouth, the man's gestures and facial expression were an universal indication of displeasure.

Unfortunately, Rubenevski was right; he and Charie were dancing as though those brief minutes together that morning had never happened, when they had danced as one, executing their steps in anticipation of one another's movements.

Oddly, he'd felt more as one with Charie than he ever had with Sophia. Sophia's dancing reflected her desire to be the center of attention. And she'd never lost an opportunity to capture that.

Charie danced for the pure love of it.

"We will break. Be back here at a quarter of the hour."

A member of the group translated the man's words into French and the dancers moved apart.

Charie scurried away with the ballerina whom he'd come to realize was Charie's best friend, Mira.

The flaxen-haired girl whispered something to Charie as they left the stage.

Sighing, Domitri headed towards the opposite side of the stage only to find Olar waiting.

"I wish to speak to you about Charice." The count's expression told Domitri the man was troubled. "I do not want you to take advantage of her. I suspect she is enamored of you."

Domitri snorted. "You saw how we danced out there. That's not how an 'enamored' young woman dances with the object of her affection. She doesn't care for me."

"Nevertheless, I see something in her eyes and her manner when she is around you."

"You were the one who wanted me to take the role of Albrecht. If you've changed your mind—"

Olar's raised hand halted his flow of heated words. "I haven't changed my mind. Leave Charie alone if you cannot give your heart to her. You told me you could never love another as you did Sophia."

"And was it not you who told me I could easily develop feelings for your protégé? Make up your mind, Olar. Besides, you know me well enough to know I would not engage in a dalliance—not with Charie, or any woman. You've carried your responsibility to the point that you sound like a worried father."

Olar's face noticeably paled, briefly. Then the angry red returned. "There would be no greater irresponsibility on my part should I ignore my duty to Charice and her mother. Though Matilda and I sometimes disagree, I consider her under my protection. Markham Fitzhugh is too pompous to be bothered with anything other than what earns him a salary."

"Do I detect a hint of jealousy?" Now was a good time to find out what actually existed between the count and the American actress.

"There is no reason to be jealous of Fitzhugh. I have no care as to whom Matilda keeps company."

"That's reassuring. So the frequent squabbles are genuine?"

"They are genuine differences of opinion. Domitri, don't change the subject. Do not hurt Charice. Now, we must discover what Chervenkof hopes to gain by threatening Matilda and Charice."

"Perhaps he pines for *Madame* Marin." Domitri said as he walked over to a stool and picked up a towel lying upon it. He wiped his wet brow and neck.

"Though his monumental ego suffers from her rejection, I doubt that alone would cause him to retaliate."

"I don't know," Domitri said, almost to himself. "I, too, have a feeling he's after something more based on our previous acquaintance—something that would benefit him either financially, or politically."

"All the more reason to closely watch Charice and Matilda. A man pursuing money and power is dangerous."

"I am curious about the looks that passed between you and Matilda last night. There's something you're not sharing."

Olar raised a brow. "Concern yourself with the ballet, and I'll deal with other matters."

"But you've asked me to keep watch over Charie and her mother. I have a right to know everything."

"Not now, Domitri. Things are—complicated. Ah, there is Rubenevski. Try dancing with more enthusiasm, Domitri. You're not being paid to be a handsome statue."

Domitri had no opportunity to reply for Rubenevski was snapping orders again, and his presence was loudly demanded, front and center.

In the back of his mind, however, niggled the suspicion that Olar possessed a large piece of the puzzle. And that piece might prove crucial.

****

Charie loved Saturday mornings. She and her mother would walk to their favorite bakery on the *Champs Élysées* and enjoy hot chocolate and beignets.

People passed by the wide window strolling down the boulevard.

This Saturday was no different except Olar sent his carriage and driver, Petrov, and Mira joined them.

The day before at rehearsal, Mira had whispered to her in strictest confidence that she'd made the acquaintance of an artist who wanted to paint her. She'd encountered him in the park as he painted a group of children, and they'd struck up a conversation.

Charie was skeptical of the man, certain that Mira should not pose for a total stranger. However, she agreed to accompany Mira to the man's atelier.

The problem was how to elude her mother after they breakfasted. Especially when she and her mother had been warned not to go anywhere alone.

But Charie would be in the company of Mira, and, therefore, not alone.

It was Matilda who presented the opportunity Charie secretly sought.

"Would you girls mind terribly returning in the carriage without me? Fitz is to meet me here, and then accompany me to Baron Bauerhausen's residence. We plan to finalize the contract today for my next play."

"*Maman*, are you sure this is wise?" Charie couldn't help but worry that her mother was making a poor decision. She didn't trust the baron.

"Charie, you know that good plays don't just happen—they require lots of money. The baron is willing to assume that financial obligation. This in no way involves you, and no one is expecting you to act any differently towards the baron. I most heartily support your choice to reject his romantic overtures. But he is a shrewd man of business and seems to make a success of whatever he undertakes."

"But you'll be in Frankfurt. What about my performance in *The Pearls of Esther*?"

"Dear, Frankfurt isn't that far away. I'll be able to attend some of your performances. And Olar will be at every one. Now, can I count on the two of you to go straight home?"

Charie opened her mouth to protest further until she looked over at Mira.

Her friend intentionally widened her already large brown eyes, a clear indication that she was soundlessly urging Charie to agree. Recalling her promise to Mira, she bit back the words on her tongue. "We will return home." *Eventually.* Not exactly a lie, but far from the truth.

"Thank you." Her mother seemed relieved. "I can always count on the two of you."

The bell over the bakery door jingled and looking at the entrance, Fitz came in. Immaculate in a charcoal gray suit and maroon cravat, he gave them a courtly bow when he reached the table. "What a charming picture the three of you make this *bon matin*. Have I arrived too early?"

"Right on time," Matilda announced. "I'm ready if you are."

Fitz took her gloved hand and assisted her from her seat.

"Now remember what I said. Straight home. Or Olar will have my head." Matilda leaned over and kissed first Charie, and then Mira, then allowed Fitz to lead her from the establishment.

Mira looked over at Charie, excitement dancing in

her eyes. "Oh, Charie, just for a short while. I promise we won't stay long. He offered to show me his paintings, and he's so very talented."

"Mira, when I say it's time to go, we must leave. I don't want *Maman* or the count to discover our deception. But I did promise to help. You have the address?"

"Oh, yes, Charie, thank you," she cried happily. "You are going to see why I want to pose for him. He is so handsome."

"And probably looking for an easy conquest."

Mira's lips drooped at her words.

"You must be very careful, Mira. You know what I've gone through with the baron."

"But you are a star of the ballet, Charie. Many men have vied for your affections. What I can't understand is why you haven't fallen in love with one of them."

"Because I am waiting for the man with whom God would want me to fall in love. No man as yet has professed love for both God and I."

"I would think loving you would be enough," Mira said, clearly confused.

"It's not, Mira. That's what I've been trying to tell you. If a man loves you, he will respect you and want what's best for you. And above all, he will honor and serve the Lord."

"Suppose you never find anyone like that?"

"Then I'll continue to dance and thank God for the opportunity He has given me. Now, do I have your pledge that this will be a short visit?"

"*Oui.* I should not want you to be in trouble with your *maman* or the count."

"We should hurry." Rising, Charie smoothed the wrinkles in her skirt of cream and rust velvet, the walking suit a recent gift from the count. She felt very sophisticated in the ensemble; a jaunty hat covered in the same velvet perched on her curls, a pheasant's feather fastened to the brim.

Mira looked very pretty in a frock of copper silk.

Slipping her arm through Mira's, Charie smiled. "So we're off on an adventure that must be our little secret."

Mira giggled and the two walked towards the door of the bakery.

****

Mira's "adventure" took them into the heart of bohemian Paris.

Not surprising, Charie silently admitted, as the carriage stopped before a building that looked as though it hadn't seen repair or upkeep in over a hundred years.

One side of the four storied structure sagged and bricks were crumbling on the other side.

Charie turned to Mira, no longer sure she wanted to keep her promise.

"Mira, this," she gestured at the apartment, "doesn't look like somewhere we should be. Are you sure he lives here?"

"Positive," Mira confirmed. "He told me I would find his abode quite disreputable, but it's all he can afford until he makes a name for himself. Can't we just see if he's in?"

"The building looks as though it could fall down any second. We should go home."

"I understand if you don't want to come in with me. But I'm going to see him."

Before Charie could stop her, her friend pushed open the door of the carriage and leaped down.

Charie had no choice but to follow, calling out to Petrov to wait for them as she gave chase.

Mira flew through the door-less entrance and started up the rickety stairs.

Charie was close behind, self-conscious when heads poked through partially open doors. The building, which had seen better days, was apparently home to several people, none of whom looked especially dangerous.

When Mira reached the highest level, she knocked on the scarred door.

A tall, lanky young man opened it, his hair brown and closely cropped and his beard neatly trimmed.

He looked exactly as Charie had imagined a starving artist would look.

He embraced Mira and kissed her upon the lips. Apparently, this relationship had progressed further than Mira had revealed.

"You came, my pet," he greeted in French. "I so feared you would not."

"I can't stay long."

Before the man could drag Mira within his questionable atelier, Charie made her presence known.

"I am Mira's friend." When Charie spoke, both of them turned to look at her.

Mira smiled in relief. "Pierre, this is my best friend, Charice Marin."

"Ah, Mira has told me so much about you." Releasing Mira, the man took Charie's hand. "You are the *prima danseuse* of the *Ballet Eleganté*, are you not?"

"And you are?" she inquired rather than answer.

If Mira was willing to plunge into an ill-advised

relationship, it was up to Charie to protect her.

"Pierre Gouneau. Welcome to my humble home." Backing away, he extended his arm and indicated that Mira and Charie enter.

Charie followed her friend, taking in what obviously was Pierre's home and studio, amazed at what he'd done with such a mess. Things were orderly—even the space devoted to his painting was organized and neatly arranged.

What struck Charie forcibly was the man's talent—portraits and landscapes littering the floor and walls, and each work more amazing than the one she glimpsed before. Pierre Gouneau was gifted. Charie was especially intrigued by scenes of children in park settings.

"Mira, come see the finished painting of the *les petits* in the park," Pierre urged, and Mira joined him at his easel.

Charie did the same, fearing she'd misjudged this man.

"Charie, this is the one he was working on when we first met," Mira explained excitedly. "It's a painting of a group of nannies with their little charges in their perambulators. Isn't it amazing?"

"It's lovely." Charie glanced at Pierre and found him gazing with adoration at Mira. *He's smitten*, Charie realized, regretting her assumption that Pierre's interest in Mira was improper. "Truly lovely."

"Has Mira told you I wish to paint her? There is nothing lovelier than a woman who floats on air. Rather like an angel, *non*?"

"I agree." Charie laughed. "But ballerinas are far from angels. Sometimes we fall more than float."

Laughter filled the space, and Pierre asked them if

they cared for tea.

After accepting, Mira and Charie walked about the atelier, remarking on the spectacular north light that filtered through the high windows.

That produced another laugh from the young man who seemed to be filled with *joie de vive*. "Yes, but when it rains, water leaks through the windows and I am flooded. And there is very little the fire in my hearth can do to chase away the cold. That is why I sleep and live in this very tiny corner of the room." He swept his arm to indicate a bed, old couch, a few chairs and a table missing a leg positioned directly before the fireplace. "I am always happiest when spring arrives."

Over tea, they learned that Pierre was from a province in eastern France, born in a village near the Swiss border.

His father owned sheep—here Mira and Charie exchanged glances and both nearly giggled—and his mother spent her days watching over his eight younger brothers and sisters.

He, the eldest, had been expected to work with his father. But from his earliest recollection, he'd loved to draw and paint. So, much to his parents' disappointment, he'd journeyed to Paris.

He'd been in the city for three years, but had only sold a dozen or so of his paintings. It was nearly impossible to break into the elite society that ruled the Parisian art scene.

"I wonder if Count Stanislov could help?" Charie asked aloud, while pondering Pierre's problem. "He travels in wealthy circles and knows influential people. I'll ask him if he could put in a word for you. Of course, he'll want to see your work."

"I'll gladly show him. I've heard of this count—he

is Russian, *non*?"

"Yes," Mira answered. "And he's brought in the most fascinating man to dance the role of Albrecht with Charie's *Giselle*. You should see Charie when she dances with him."

"Perhaps, after I am done with the portrait of Mira, you and your partner would pose for me?" Pierre asked hopefully.

"I don't think so," Charie demurred. "We aren't good friends. Domitri—I mean *Monsieur* Auberchon—is only dancing the part as a favor to the count."

"But he likes you, Charie. I can see it in his eyes. The two of you are perfect for each other."

"Not according to *Monsieur* Rubenevski. You heard what he said yesterday."

"He was in a bad mood."

Wasn't he always, Charie thought and almost laughed.

"Yes, Pierre," Mira continued, "you must paint Charie and Domitri."

"Only after I paint you. When can we begin?"

"I can't come alone. Charie, when can you come with me?"

"Mira, I—it's difficult—oh, I don't know. It will be hard to escape *Maman* and the count. And performances will begin soon. We'll be so busy."

"Charie, please," Mira begged. "This means so much."

"Tomorrow," she suggested, not sure how she'd work it out. "After church."

"Wonderful!" Pierre enthused. "I cannot wait. I will see both of you tomorrow."

Goodbyes were exchanged, and then Pierre walked them down to where the carriage and Petrov waited. But when they reached the street, there was no sign of the count's conveyance. Pierre's gaze reflected worry.

"What do you think happened? Shall I walk you home?"

"It's much too far, Pierre," Charie said. "We'll find a cab to take us back. Petrov must've misunderstood my instructions."

"I feel badly about this. It is because you visited me. I hope no one will be in trouble."

"No more so than usual." Charie smiled ruefully. "Mira and I must go if we're to be home before dark."

After assuring Pierre once again they would be fine, they set out on foot, uneasily aware they were somewhere they shouldn't be. To make matters worse, fog curled in spectral wisps.

"I'm so sorry, Charie." Mira broke the silence.

"It's not your fault, Mira. I can't believe the man drove away and left us. That's not like Petrov."

"Perhaps he had an emergency. Maybe we should return to Pierre's. Petrov might be there now."

"But if he isn't, we'll be found out, and there'll be all manner of drama."

"What does that mean?"

"It means I'll never hear the end of this. Let's hurry."

Locking arms, they rushed away from the bleak, fog shrouded buildings and scurried past pedestrians who paused to give the two nicely dressed women a closer look.

Charie finally spotted a waiting cabby, dozing high up in his seat, and releasing Mira's arm, ran to it before someone else could grab it. She had almost reached it when someone took hold of her arm.

Thinking it was Mira, she stopped and turned. To her horror, it was Anapol Chervenkof.

"Imagine running into you here, of all places, Charice. You're far from home and the watchful eye of your *maman*."

"I am on my way home," she said, wrenching her arm free, her heart hammering far too loudly. Out of the corner of her eye she saw Mira approaching. She hoped the girl realized something was amiss and wouldn't join her.

"Then you'll allow me to escort you home. My carriage is close by."

"I think not. Good day."

"I insist." Again he grasped her arm and this time he pushed her forward. She tried to lock her legs, but he put his arm about her waist. Lifting her off her feet, he moved forward.

"Put me down! I'm not going anywhere with you."

"You have no choice, Charice. Besides, it's time we became better acquainted. After all, I may soon be your new papa."

"That won't happen." By now they had reached Chervenkof's carriage, and his driver held the door.

Charie had to act quickly or would soon be Chervenkof's prisoner. The baron, at his most amorous, never frightened her as badly as Chervenkof did just now, his eyes cold and unfeeling.

"I will not go anywhere with you."

"You don't have a choice." With that he hoisted her up.

Charie refused to capitulate. *Lord, help me. I know I brought this on myself, but please help me.* Grasping the doorframe, she held on, kicking at Chervenkof's legs.

Managing to strike his shin, he released her, shrieks of pain rending the air.

Racing from the carriage, Charie's hat flopped and flipped, eventually dislodging so that it dangled from the side of her head.

Gloved hands took hold of her arm, and fearing it was Chervenkof, she started to pull away.

"It's me, Charie," Mira cried. "Who is that man?"

"Mira, listen to me. Take a cab and go to the count's home. His residence is on the Rue de la Mer. Tell him that Chervenkof is following me."

"Where are you going?" Fear widened Mira's eyes, and she spoke breathlessly.

"I'm not sure, but I have to get away from here. Go Mira. Hurry!" Glancing behind her, she saw that Chervenkof had spotted her, coming towards them with a limp. "Go, Mira!" Lifting her skirts, Charie dashed towards a group of people, pushing her way through. Frantic and desperate, she lifted her eyes towards Heaven, taking note of the *Arc de Triomphe*, barely visible through the fog.

Domitri's studio was near the *Champs Élysées*. If he was at home, surely he'd help. Not daring to question her decision, she ran towards the familiar landmark, praying she could elude Chervenkof.

7

"What you must remember, gentlemen," Domitri said as he walked down the evenly spaced boys positioned at the barre, ranging in age from twelve to fifteen, "is that a man can exhibit both gracefulness and power at the same time. But the power must be developed, and it is developed by repeating these boring, and I quote *Monsieur* Devone…"

One of the older boys turned beet red in embarrassment.

Domitri had overheard him complaining to two others that *barre* work was unnecessary and boring. "…*Barre* exercises. So before we can *cabriole* and *entrechat* and partner a beautiful ballerina, we develop power. Are you—"

The door to the studio slammed open, a disheveled and mussed Charie staggering through.

He almost laughed until he noticed the moisture rimming her violet-gray eyes, her paleness, and her expression of absolute terror.

"You will practice your *ronds de jambes* until I return." Quickly crossing the floor, he reached Charie.

Her eyelids fluttered closed, and he feared she would faint.

Without hesitation, Domitri lifted her in his arms and hurried from the studio, aware of his staring, motionless students. Taking the steps up to his apartment two at the time, Domitri bellowed for

Muzette.

The housekeeper had the door open by the time he reached the upper level, and he rushed through the room, entering his bedchamber. Lying Charie upon his bed, he quickly loosened the buttons of her fitted jacket and those around the high neck of her blouse.

Muzette waved smelling salts beneath her nose causing Charie to stir.

Coughing and gagging, she managed to open her eyes. Confusion darkened her expression until her gaze rested upon Domitri. Sitting up, fear shadowed her face as she grasped the front of his sweat-dampened tunic.

"Mira—is alone," she choked out. "Chervenkof—" She coughed again and Muzette quickly thrust a glass of water at her. Cherie took it and drank gratefully. "Chervenkof followed me. I believe Mira got away."

"Charie, what are you saying?" Domitri's heart plummeted at the thought of Chervenkof pursuing either woman. "You're not making sense. Take a deep breath. Start again." He sat on the side of the bed.

"Mira and I visited a friend of hers, and when we left, the count's carriage and Petrov had disappeared. We decided to take a cab home, but while we searched, Chervenkof appeared. He tried to force me into his carriage, but I slipped away." Charie paused to draw a deep breath. "I told Mira to take a cab and go straight to the count's residence. Then I traveled here by foot, hoping you'd be in. Thank God you were." She threw her arms about his neck and sobbed against his shoulder.

His arms went around her, tightening instinctively and protectively. Something happened—his heart pounded as though he'd leapt circles around a stage a dozen times, and his hands shook. Holding her awakened his every nerve; heightened his every sense. Softness and warmth enfolded him, the hint of lilacs teased his nose, and her loosened chestnut curls covered his chest. Without thinking, he pressed his lips to the top of her head.

"You're all right now, Charie. You're safe." Slowly, he pushed her away so that he could look into her teary eyes. "Why were you and Mira without an escort? You know what Olar said." If he thought speaking to her sternly would alleviate the earlier sensations, he was sadly mistaken. He battled the urge to pull her close again.

"I know. But Mira wanted me to meet an artist who has asked her to pose for him, and *Maman* left with Fitz to sign contracts with Bauerhausen. We were supposed to go straight home in the count's carriage, but I didn't want to disappoint Mira. When we were ready to leave, the carriage was gone, even though I told Petrov to wait. I can't imagine what happened to him."

"I can," Domitri said grimly as he stood. Walking over to the windows, he began to pace.

Muzette took his place on the bed and sponged Charie's face while she reassured her in French that all would be well.

"What do you think happened?"

Looking to his side he saw that Charie had left the bed and joined him.

When he glanced at Muzette, she shrugged and shook her head.

No one could keep Charie confined if she chose not to be. It was an infuriatingly attractive characteristic; one that could easily land her in danger.

It was his job to point that out.

"It's possible that Olar's driver was lured away." He didn't add that the man might have come to harm. "You sent Mira to Olar?"

Charie nodded, the movement loosening the last tenuous hold her fashionable hat had on her hair, and the elegant chapeau dropped to the floor. She didn't bother to retrieve it. "I was certain Chervenkof would follow me, not her. And I knew that the count would help. Oh, Domitri, I never meant for this to happen. *Maman* will lecture me, and the count will be so angry."

"I am angry with you." His stinging words brought fresh tears to her eyes. Grasping her shoulders, he shook her slightly to emphasize his words. "What were you thinking to disobey? Was it that important that Mira visit this artist?"

"She's in love with him, and he with her. I'm glad we visited." Charie's quavering voice held defiance. "I am sorry I've caused trouble and interrupted your class. But I'm not a child, Domitri."

"Then stop acting like one. What would I have done if something had happened to you?"

"What?" Her eyes reflected confusion; the tears no longer spilling over her smooth cheeks. "Why should you care what happens to me? We don't even like each other."

"How foolish of me." Domitri fisted one hand, wrestling with the need to shake sense into her and kiss her trembling lips. "You're absolutely right. A spoiled, petulant ballerina is the last person on which I would waste my time."

"And I don't need an arrogant, unfeeling *danseur* trying to control my life."

"Apparently, you need someone in control. You're doing a poor job. It's a miracle you can tie your laces without help."

"Don't insult me. But then, I suppose having been married to Sophia Stanislovna, all other ballerinas pale in comparison." Her words wounded.

It was as though a blade had been thrust into his aching heart and twisted.

Domitri's instinct was to lash out. "No one can compare to her."

Charie's eyes darkened with hurt and bewilderment, and she staggered back, breaking his hold.

The urgency to set matters aright made him reach for her.

She backed further away.

"Charie, I didn't—"

"Domitri, Domitri!" Olar's bellow preceded him before he burst into the apartment.

Grasping Charie's hand, Domitri rushed to the parlor to find an enraged Olar and a wild-eyed Mira.

"Domitri, thank God you're here. Charie…Charie, you're here?"

"I'm so sorry," Charie sobbed, pulled her hand from Domitri's, and rushed to Olar.

He quickly folded her in a fatherly embrace.

"I know I did wrong. Don't tell *Maman*. Please."

"I'm only glad you are unharmed. When Mira arrived at my home shortly after Petrov, who was bleeding and beaten, I nearly lost my mind. Tell me what happened."

"Why don't the three of you sit here and sort things out," Domitri suggested dryly. "I still have a class downstairs that I need to dismiss."

The three did as he'd recommended, huddling together on the old couch.

Shaking his head, Domitri left them, feeling very much the outsider.

****

"You're quiet tonight," Matilda observed as she and Charie dined informally in the sitting room, a linen clad table and two comfortable chairs positioned before the fire.

Olar had delivered Charie to her frantic mother about an hour earlier, explaining that she and Mira had visited with him rather than return home. Another half-truth that was also a half-lie.

Charie struggled with her conscience as she pushed the food about her plate. "Didn't you have a nice time visiting Olar? He does have a lovely home. I just wish you'd have shared your plans this morning."

"We didn't plan the visit; we somehow ended up there."

"That's an odd way of putting it. I want to forewarn you that the baron will be dropping by later. After spending time with him today, I really believe he's changed."

"In what way?" Charie was surprised by her mother's words.

"I believe he's sorry he frightened you. He's not used to a young woman who is neither swept off her feet by his title, nor impressed by his romantic overtures. He truly seems fond of you."

"What are you saying, *Maman*?" Anger raged through Charie as her fork clattered to her plate.

"I'm saying I believe he wants to make amends."

"Is he a Christian?"

"The right influences could push him towards the path of faith. I believe he simply needs a friend."

"You can be his friend, *Maman*, but I will not. You've struck your deal with him; now you'll have to live with the consequences."

"That's an unkind thing to say," Matilda said sadly. "Are any of us fit to judge another?"

"All I know is that I can't be his friend. He's insufferable."

"Don't allow your infatuation with Domitri Auberchon preclude a relationship with another man. Ludwig Bauerhausen is wealthy and powerful. Domitri Auberchon is a penurious *danseur* who survives on an income provided by a teaching position."

"*Maman*, it's not like you to measure one's worth by their bank account. What happened to love?"

"Love sometimes comes later, Charie, if you open your heart and your mind. I only want to make sure you are well cared for and cherished. Domitri is still entrenched in the past. I would not want you to constantly wonder how you measure up to Sophia Stanislovna, both as a dancer and a wife."

"*Maman*, you are worried about something that will never happen. Domitri makes no secret of the love he still harbors for his late wife."

Domitri's earlier remarks had wounded. Deeply.

Charie would have little trouble quelling any and all romantic notions. "He considers me a child, much like some other people."

The look her mother gave her assured her she'd made her point. "I know you're not a child, but until this matter with Chervenkof is resolved, we have to be careful. Charie, I'll never interfere in your personal life. But I can share my fears and concerns."

"I accept that. But I'm in no danger of falling in love."

"I told myself the same thing after I met your father. And look what happened."

"But you did fall in love with him. We all make mistakes."

"And isn't it wonderful that we have a loving Savior who is willing to forgive us for all of those mistakes?"

"I hope you'll understand if I stay in my room while the baron is here."

"Certainly." Matilda smiled and reached over to pat her hand. "Is there something else you'd like to share?"

Suddenly, the dam burst, and tears spilled over her cheeks. The words tumbled from her lips as Charie recounted the story of how Chervenkof had followed her and Mira, had the count's driver beaten, and then tried to force her to go with him.

Her mother's face paled, but she said nothing until Charie finished.

Now Matilda's dinner remained untouched. Rising from her seat, Matilda went to Charie, kneeling beside her chair as she hugged her. "My darling daughter, I never meant for you to be drawn into this. I'm so sorry. And so grateful to God for seeing you safely to Domitri's. Why didn't you tell me this sooner?"

"For the same reason you didn't tell me about Chervenkof. I didn't want to worry you. I'm unharmed and so is Mira, and I've learned a lesson. But I made a promise to Mira. Do you think you could accompany us after church to her beau's atelier? He wants to begin a painting of her."

"Of course. And I can bring the script along and look through my lines for the new play. What a pleasant way to pass the afternoon."

"Well, it might be a little chilly, because Pierre is extremely poor. And there are lots of cracks in the walls and around the windows."

"Good heavens. Where does the boy live?"

"In an apartment building that looks close to falling into rubble. Pierre barely gets by. But he's extremely talented. And charming."

Matilda smiled. "Then we must see what we can do to help this young man, if he is as talented and likeable as you claim. Go upstairs and tell Lizzie to help you with a hot bath. Now that I think on it, your ensemble was a mess when you arrived. I should have known you didn't pass a quiet, uneventful day with Olar. By the way, you weren't wearing your hat."

Laughter suddenly bubbled out upon Charie's lips. "I believe the poor thing is roosting somewhere in Domitri's apartment."

They both laughed.

Charie's tears miraculously dried.

****

Matilda kept her promise.

After the service at the small, but lovely, protestant church that Charie and her mother attended since taking up residence in Paris, they took a hansom cab to the flat that Mira shared with three other ballerinas from the company.

Mira was waiting for them on the stoop, clearly

surprised to see Matilda with Charie. But the eagerness to visit Pierre overrode her uncertainty, and when she joined them, she was full of her usual chatter.

Upon arriving at Pierre's derelict residence, Matilda gazed at it in horror.

"Your Pierre lives here?" she gasped.

"On the very top floor," Mira announced happily. "He's not the only one who resides in the building. There are others living on the lower floors."

Her mother's expression was so incredulous, Charie had to stifle a giggle as the driver came around to help them out.

Matilda remained silent on the climb to Pierre's apartment, but she was obviously dismayed by the abysmal living conditions.

Pierre greeted them at Mira's first knock, and within minutes Pierre had captivated Matilda. So much so, she promised to find him a more hospitable abode and even went so far as to suggest that Count Stanislov might want to see his paintings.

Mira changed into the costume for her role in Giselle behind a large screen in a corner of the chilly apartment, and Pierre spent the next four hours painting until the position of the autumn sun could no longer provide the light he needed.

Charie was fascinated by the man's sure strokes and how, with just a few, he was able to capture Mira's form, already bringing a hint of life to the undefined face.

By the time they made their farewells, Matilda had invited him to dine with them Wednesday night, insinuating that there might be the possibility of a commission.

When Pierre humbly declined the invitation,

stating that his Bible group met on Wednesday evenings, Matilda promptly changed the invitation to Friday.

Once the times were established, Mira included in the dinner arrangements, the three women left with the understanding that Mira would return with her chaperones the following Sunday for another sitting.

Charie noticed that Mira and Pierre exchanged a quick kiss while her mother was exiting the splintered door, and there was no denying the devoted look that passed between them.

Matilda immediately assumed the role of mothering mentor on the return trip, commenting aloud that Olar would certainly take Pierre under his wing and assist in finding the young man a better place to live.

By the time they delivered Mira to her apartment, the girl was beside herself with excitement, certain that Pierre's talent would soon be discovered, earning him well-deserved recognition.

Charie and her mother enjoyed a quiet ride to their townhouse, welcoming light pouring from the myriad windows.

Lizzie met them at the door, and the expression on her face told them something was very wrong. The woman was so upset she rambled in Swedish until Matilda calmed her enough so that she repeated herself in English.

"Forgive me, Madam Matilda, I am so shaken I cannot tink," the woman said breathlessly, her hand pressed to her chest. "Come vith me and I vill show you vat vas delivered vile you vere out today."

Charie and her mother followed Lizzie into the sitting room.

A portrait of her mother rested against a table. Red paint had been dashed against it, rivulets of the now dried liquid running down her mother's lovely face. A card was attached.

Matilda removed it, her hand shaking as Lizzie talked on. "The man vho delivered it seemed nice enough, and the painting, it vas vrapped. Ven I pulled away the paper, this is how it looked. I am so sorry, Madam Matilda. I vould have sent the man avay vith this terrible picture."

By now Matilda had opened the envelope and pulled out a single, folded sheet. She read aloud. "'I warned you.'"

Three words that filled Charie with unspeakable dread.

The note slipped from her mother's hand as she collapsed upon a chair.

Charie picked up the note. It was signed, "AC."

There was no doubt as to the identity of the sender. And there was no doubt he intended Matilda Marin serious harm.

"*Maman*, we must contact my father. Perhaps he can help. He needs to know about this."

"He already does," she replied wearily, lifting a face to Charie that had aged ten years in a matter of minutes. "Olar is your father."

****

Though the day had been pleasant for autumn, Domitri spent his Sunday restless and dissatisfied. He'd devoted the morning to Bible study and prayer. But no amount of prayer or scripture reading could erase what was inside him. He could no longer deny his attraction to Charice Marin. He could no longer deny Sophia was a fading memory. He was a man torn, angry, and confused.

When he'd told Charie she could never compare to Sophia, he'd hoped to hurt her as badly as she'd hurt him. What he'd really been thinking was that Sophia could never compare to Charie.

There—he'd admitted it. But no relief accompanied the confession. For Charie believed him to be egotistical, domineering, and emotionless.

"Lord," he spoke aloud, "what do I do?"

There was no answer. Sunday was the day Muzette spent with relatives, and she'd not return until the morning. He felt the isolation; the loneliness. Leaving his seat by the parlor window, he walked to the door of his bedchamber.

He clearly recalled the vision of Charie as she'd lain upon the counterpane, her dark hair with its vibrant red highlights spread over the white linen, her face displaying an ethereal innocence.

It was impossible to deny the pull, the yearning that pounded in his ears and rushed through his blood, reminding him of the connection between man and woman.

Turning abruptly, Domitri fled the apartment and ran down the stairs as though pursued by ravenous wolves. Entering his studio, he shed his shirt and began to dance. His movements reflected the fury and angst that warred within him. Pushing hard, his heart felt close to bursting and his lungs burned. Faster and faster he spiraled until there was no control. Then he slipped. He landed on his bottom.

Domitri groaned, welcoming the pain for it cleared his head. He couldn't care for Charie. Not now; not ever. Even setting aside the memory of Sophia, Charie presented other problems.

She was determined, stubborn, disobedient, willful...talented, beautiful, graceful. Angelic.

Running his hands over his face, he expelled a deep sigh. From somewhere came the words of a familiar and beloved passage from Psalms 30. *O, Lord, thou hast brought up my soul from the grave: thou hast kept me alive, that I should not go down to the pit...weeping may endure for a night, but joy cometh in the morning...Thou hast turned for me my mourning into dancing: thou hast put off my sackcloth and girded me with gladness...*

"Was there a reason I survived the wreck? Guilt consumes me, Lord. For so long I've believed I should have died, and Sophia should have lived. I never planned to care for another woman—not as I cared for Sophia. Charie is in danger, and I'm not sure I can protect her. What if something happens to her? I can't involve myself. Involvement requires commitment. Commitment leads to a place I don't want to be."

Weary and spent, he leaned his head against the rough wall, draping his arms over his knees. His eyes grew irritatingly moist and he wiped his hand over them, disgusted by his weakness.

And I was with you in weakness, and in fear, and in much trembling.

The verse from First Corinthians eased his mind, steadied his pulse, and slowed his heart. He had to face this situation, without fear, without trepidation. He would clean up, dress, and pay a visit to the Marin home. He would apologize to Charie for his harsh comments and set matters aright.

She might choose to have nothing to do with him beyond a forced professional relationship. But at least he'd be right in his soul.

Rising with just a smidgeon of discomfort concentrated in the vicinity of his backside, he left the studio and made his way up the stairs, much more slowly than he'd gone down them minutes earlier.

8

Charie had no idea what time it was—she only knew that it was late as she sat in the elegant salon of her mother's townhouse facing a woman she'd always considered her best friend and confidante; trusted and loved.

To think that for Charie's entire life, her mother had withheld the identity of her father; allowed her to meet, form an attachment to, and come to trust the very man who was her father without telling her the truth. The foundation upon which her life had been built lay in shattered pieces.

She knew that her mother and the count were speaking earnestly to her, but heated anger thrummed in her ears and garbled their voices.

"I allowed my father to convince me that my duty was to the Stanislovs."

"I didn't want to give up the stage."

"I never meant to hurt you."

"I only hoped to save you greater pain."

Upon hearing the word "pain," Charie finally roused herself from her shock and glared at the two people she now considered supremely selfish.

And they considered themselves Christians.

How ironic, Charie thought bitterly.

"The one thing I am sure of is that the two of you have lied to me. I believed that my father was a dishonorable man who vanished because he didn't want the responsibility of a family. The truth of the matter is that my father feared losing his title and my mother was afraid she'd no longer be the most sought after actress in America and Europe."

"But we gave you all of our love," Matilda insisted. "Olar found a way to be with you—he has tried to be a father to you."

"Why couldn't you have told me the truth from the beginning? Even though you divorced—"just saying the word caused her to shudder, "—you didn't have to leave me in the dark. Why did you do this?"

Matilda looked at Olar, tears rolling down her cheeks.

Out in the hall, the tall case clock chimed the hour of ten.

Charie was scheduled to be up by half past five and at rehearsal by seven. She wasn't sleepy, too filled with fury to be anything other than wide-awake.

Olar took her mother's hand and squeezed it reassuringly.

The display of tenderness irked her, knowing the two hadn't loved each other enough to remain married.

"Charie, when I met your mother in Venice, it was as though Heaven had opened and dropped an angel into my life. From the first moment she stepped out on the stage in her role as Beatrice in *Much Ado About Nothing*, I knew that I loved her. I had been widowed for several years and though my marriage had been a good one, it was an arranged match, and sadly, I never fell in love with Asenka, although I did come to care deeply for her.

"I had a beautiful little girl who was already training in the ballet and away from home much of the time. So I was alone, and I felt that God had given me another chance to love. There was a whirlwind courtship, and I convinced your mother to marry me within two months of our first meeting.

"We were still honeymooning in Venice when my father arrived. He had recently learned from his physician that he had an illness that would most likely claim his life within the year. While he was still strong enough, he wanted to see me and convince me to return to the family estate, for my eldest brother had decided to take monastic vows. I told him I wanted to make my home with my new wife. It was Matilda who made me rethink my choice."

Charie looked at her mother, not sure she'd heard correctly. "What does he mean?"

A fresh pool of tears formed in Matilda's eyes. "I realized I shouldn't come between Olar and his father, given the fact the man was dying. In my heart, I knew he should honor his father's request, but I also knew I wasn't ready to leave the stage and become chatelaine of a Russian castle.

"Everyone told me I was foolish to give up what would have been a fairytale existence. But I was very young, and I couldn't see beyond the here and now. I told Olar that I had mistaken infatuation for love, and that we should arrange a discreet separation and divorce.

"By the time the ink dried on those documents, I was four months along with you. I didn't share my news with Olar, and returned home to Virginia to await your birth. Fortunately, my parents allowed me to stay with them until you were born, then kept you until I could hire a nanny willing to travel. You were about ten months old by that time."

"Had I known of your existence, Charice," Olar continued, picking up the threads of the story, "I would never have allowed your mother's so called 'mistaken infatuation' keep me from doing my duty as a father. As it was, I assumed my role within my family and devoted myself to Sophia."

"So that first time we met in New York," Charie looked at the count, "I was watching my very own sister dance. Sophia Stanislovna was my sister," Charie repeated in a whisper, shaking her head in bewilderment. "And Domitri is my brother-in-law."

"Was, Charice," Olar gently corrected.

"After I learned of Sophia's unfortunate death, I knew that Olar had a right to be told the truth—that he hadn't lost everyone he loved. That was when I told him you were his daughter." Matilda gave her a teary smile. "Up until then, I allowed him to think you were the result of a liaison with a former beau in my home town."

"You let him believe that you were—that I was a...a—" Charie couldn't bring herself to say the word. It was too horrible to utter.

"I didn't see another choice. I couldn't allow Olar to suspect you were his child. For a long time, I feared that if he knew, he might try to take you from me."

"You are the one who always told me we have no reason to be ashamed," Charie cried. "That we should hold our heads up proudly and not be bothered by idle talk and hurtful gossip."

"Charie, I was very wrong."

"Charice, by the time Matilda told me you were my child, I already loved you as a daughter." Olar's eyes were clouded with tears. "I watched you grow from a shy, uncertain child into a confident and talented ballerina. When I discovered you were my daughter, I was beside myself with joy."

"If I wasn't the one at the center of this melodrama, I might feel some bit of sympathy for the two of you. But I am, and I'm angry and hurt. How could you do this? You were only thinking of yourselves."

"There were so many times I wanted to tell you," Matilda said, her voice catching on a sob. "I love you, Charice, and I only want you to be happy."

"And why did you," Charie pointed at Olar, "force your son-in-law to dance with me knowing all along of my relationship to Sophia? Does Domitri know the truth?"

"No. I think it would be best if he was to remain unaware of the relationship."

"So you've lied to him, too." Charie shook her head, and then laughed bitterly. "It all makes sense now — how you," she again pointed at Olar, her finger shaking, "magically cleared the debts of the ballet company. How I was amazingly and suddenly elevated to *prima danseuse* status."

"I had nothing to do with that," Olar said. "Rubenevski recognized your talent. The company has enjoyed phenomenal success in Europe and America ever since. God has bestowed upon you a marvelous gift."

"I'm a fraud and a sham. I'm not at all who I thought I was. I can never forgive you. Never." Fury brought her to her feet, hands clenched at her sides. "I've heard about as much as I can tolerate without saying something dreadful or hurtful. Forgive me for not complacently accepting the truth." Her words were sarcastic and biting.

Matilda winced.

A forceful knock sounded on the door.

Fear darted into her mother's eyes, and Olar came to his feet.

Charie's breathing grew shallow as she contemplated who might be on the other side of the door.

Chervenkof?

Another spurt of pounding galvanized Olar, and rising, he hurried into the hallway and made his way to the door just as a mob capped *Madame* Jeaneau appeared, clad in a voluminous dressing gown. Olar waved the woman back.

"Yes?"

"Olar." It was Domitri.

Why was he here? Could this night hold any more surprises?

****

"It's Domitri. Let me in."

Olar immediately complied.

Charie now stood a few feet behind the count.

Domitri entered, brushing past Olar, his gaze fixed on her. The cold clung to him, his face reddened from contact with the biting wind.

Taking her hands, he looked down at her, his expression unreadable, his breathing labored as though he'd been running. His touch chilled and warmed.

His gaze bored into hers, and it was as though she was lost in a sea of emerald green. A lock of his black hair fell boyishly over his forehead, and without thinking, she freed a hand and brushed it back.

Domitri's eyes darkened as he grabbed her hand

and brought it to his lips.

The contact shook Charie into remembrance. With remembrance came betrayal and disappointment. And the knowledge she could never be anything more to this man than *Giselle*. The lie she'd lived for more than two score years sealed her fate. "Why—why are you here, Domitri?"

He released her hand, and then looked around.

Olar still stood by the door, *Madame* Jeaneau stared open mouthed, and her mother's pleading gaze seared her, though she was several feet away at the entrance of the salon.

"I wish to speak to you in private. Please?"

"I—" Charie looked at her mother then at Olar. "I'm not well. I was about to retire."

"You're unwell? Your fright from the other day—"

"Has nothing to do with how I feel. If you'll excuse me." She backed away, severing his hold. Turning, she forced her legs to carry her to the stairs, but Domitri followed, catching her arm before she placed her foot on a carpeted tread.

"I'm certain this has something to do with me. I said things—"

"This has nothing to do with you." Her words struck her ears, cold and lifeless.

"You deserve the truth."

"No, I don't." *Because I can't tell you the truth. Because my parents have deceived me all of my life. Because you were once married to my sister.* "Goodnight, Domitri." She wondered if her abrupt dismissal was worthy of an acting accolade. An hysterical laugh rose up within her, but never passed her lips.

Mounting the stairs, a weight settled in her chest making it difficult to climb. She wanted to cry and rail and blame everyone but herself for her troubles. But that was not the way of the Lord. That was not the way to live her life.

"Charie!" The urgency in Domitri's voice halted her.

Looking over her shoulder she peered down at him.

"I—I care for you."

His words pierced, carving a jagged wound she feared would never heal. It was time to end things. To end what had never been anything more than a foolish fascination and ridiculous attraction. "I'm sorry I cannot say the same."

Her heart in shreds, she raced up the few remaining stairs as though pursued by rabid dogs. Once within her room, she fell to her knees by her bed, the tears rushing torrentially over her cheeks and splashing the coverlet. "Oh, dear Lord," she sobbed aloud. "What has happened? Why has this happened?"

****

"Domitri, Charie is overwrought," Matilda Marin offered, her eyes bright with unshed tears as she hurried up to him. "Just before you arrived, she—Olar—we were not in agreement over an important matter. Don't take her words to heart."

"What important matter?"

"There's something I want you to see, Domitri." Olar motioned for him to follow.

Domitri glanced up the stairs once more, but presenting himself at Charie's bedchamber was not an option. Reluctantly, he moved away and joined Olar.

The count led him through the dining room,

beyond the kitchen, and into a space used for storage. Lighting a lantern, he motioned towards a painting covered with a cloth and propped against the wall. Olar pulled the fabric away.

Domitri wasn't certain what he saw. The face was Matilda's, but it had been marred by red paint, slashed across the canvas and reminiscent of blood.

"This came with the delivery."

As though in a dream, Domitri accepted the note Olar extended. Opening it, he read. "'I warned you. AC.'" Domitri met Olar's troubled gaze. "Chervenkof?"

"Undoubtedly."

"Olar, the authorities have to be notified. When was this portrait painted?"

"Chervenkof commissioned it when he and Matilda," Olar swallowed hard, and then continued, "were romantically involved. I don't believe the artist had anything to do with the defacement."

"Chervenkof couldn't possibly hope to regain Matilda's affection. His intention is to frighten her. But for what purpose?"

"I have no idea. I fear for Matilda. And I fear for Charice. Chervenkof must know Matilda would do anything to keep Charice from harm. As would I."

"This," Domitri gestured at the painting, "is why Charie is so upset?"

Olar hesitated.

"She is also upset over a decision Matilda and I made. "

"Something you don't wish to discuss?"

"Not tonight."

Domitri shook his head, dissatisfied with Olar's answer. Out of respect, he held his tongue. "What can I do?"

"Go home, Domitri. We'll talk more tomorrow. I will spend the night here—in the guest room—just to assure myself the night passes without incident. As for Charice's behavior, as Matilda said, she is not herself. Do not take her words to heart."

"I only wish to help."

"I know, Domitri. Nothing can be accomplished tonight."

"Then I'll take my leave." Moving out of the small room, he retraced his steps.

Matilda awaited him in the hall. "I'm afraid I haven't been very hospitable this evening. Things are—unsettled."

"I understand, *Madame* Marin. I hope matters will soon be resolved. I'm sorry that Chervenkof has targeted you."

Matilda was sad. "I have brought this on myself. I erred in judgment, and now I am reaping the consequences. I just don't want Charie hurt." Her voice broke on a sob.

Domitri took hold of her hand. "I will do everything I can to make sure no harm comes to her. I care deeply for her."

"Thank you, Domitri."

Domitri continued on to the door and let himself out, met by chilly gusts and a misting rain.

****

Domitri arrived at the theatre early the next morning, but Charice was already there.

Sitting on the stage, she'd drawn her legs up to her chest and encircled them with her arms, her head resting on them.

He wasn't sure, but he thought he detected soft crying. Noiselessly he approached, carrying the elegant chapeau she'd left at his flat. Then a board squeaked beneath his slipper-shod foot and she jerked, lifting her head, and then coming to her feet.

She brushed at her eyes and smoothed the layers of tulle that cascaded from her waist.

"I didn't mean to startle you," he offered apologetically as he quickly joined her. "I believe this is yours."

Charie took it from him. "How kind of you to bring it to me. Thank you." Turning away, she walked towards the wing.

He followed, and just as she passed into the shadows, he gently grasped her arm.

She looked up, her eyes dark, luminous pools that tugged at him.

"Charie, I must be honest with you." His voice hoarsened with emotion. Had Sophia made him feel this way? Charie's presence rattled his senses and left him reeling from an overpowering need to hold her and protect her. With Sophia, he'd sensed an invisible hand holding him at a distance, as though her noble blood inspired a certain aloofness. He'd never felt that with Charice—but she was American, and Americans didn't give much thought to titles and privileged birth.

"Honest?" Her voice trembled, and she seemed close to shedding more tears. "Have you lied to me, too?"

"What?" Her question confused him. "No, I mean, I haven't told you how I truly feel. I tried to tell you last night and made a terrible mess. I told you I cared for you, but I know it doesn't seem that way. In fact, you probably believe I've pushed you away. I didn't mean what I said to you about Sophia. I was angry."

A sob tore from her throat, and she buried her face in her hands. Was she crying from joy or horror?

Domitri had no way of knowing, so he gathered her in his arms.

"You can't mean that," she cried, looking up at him. "It wouldn't be fair to Sophia."

"Sophia has been dead seven years, Charie. I know that I have to put that part of my life behind me. You're so different from Sophia—so open and honest, so beautiful, and gifted with an incredible talent. I'm not sure what I'm feeling or why I'm feeling this way. Will you give me a chance?"

"But I'm not so different from Sophia. If you only knew. This can't be—you mustn't care for me. It would be wrong. You would be hurt." Charie attempted to free herself, but he tightened his hold.

"Charie, listen to me. I saw the painting. I know you and your mother are in trouble. I want to help. I want to protect you. I know Chervenkof—how his mind works. Have you no feelings for me at all?"

"I can't." The words seemed torn from her soul. Wrenching free, she rushed away.

Domitri determined to follow until Rubenevski made his ill-timed arrival, insisting the two of them needed to discuss the details of one scene.

By the time he managed to slip away from the ballet master, the other dancers had arrived.

He'd lost his opportunity.

****

Several days of frustration followed, Charie never

permitting herself to be alone with him. Practice was grueling as opening night drew ever nearer, and though Charie endured the regimen, tireless and committed as ever, she lacked the élan that was so much a part of her performance.

Two days before the ballet's opening, rehearsal having just ended and twilight settling over Paris, Domitri was about to leave the theatre when he noticed Charie, her friend Mira, and three other girls gathered on the street near the Stanislov carriage. Curious, he walked closer with every intention of eavesdropping.

But he was prevented from doing so for Petrov, now recovered from the attack, hurried around to open the door for them and Olar's valet, Yuri, hopped out to assist the women.

Domitri wasn't sure when he made the decision to follow, but within seconds he'd hailed a hackney cab and issued instructions to follow the gold embellished carriage.

He was surprised when Petrov halted the carriage before an old building, displaying the name *hôpital des soeurs de l'espoir*—Hospital of the Sisters of Hope. And beneath that, carved in the marble, was an angel cradling a child in its arms.

Instructing the man to stop, he paid the fare and let himself out.

****

"Why must I play the man again?" Vionette Verdun wailed in French as she theatrically pressed the back of her hand to her forehead.

Charie laughed as she tied her well-worn practice slippers in preparation of the impromptu performance she, Mira, and three other female members of the ballet would perform for the children at the infants' hospital.

Charie first learned of the hospital a few months earlier when a younger sibling of a member of the corp was admitted to the facility. The child was devastated that she would miss her older sister's performance.

Charie decided she and a few of her friends could bring the ballet to the child. And, having danced that one time, Charie's heart had gone out to the children, some so ill and near death that it broke her heart.

The little girl recovered and was now home with her family, but there were so many others who hadn't been so fortunate. Now, Charie, Mira, and the three girls Mira roomed with visited the hospital whenever time permitted, hoping to bring some joy into the children's lives.

With *Giselle* to begin its run in two days, there would be little opportunity to visit over the next month. Hopefully, the time spent dancing at the hospital would take her mind off her troubles—minor when compared with those the children faced.

"You are the tallest," Charie reminded Vionette in the girl's native language. "You've played the prince before without complaint."

"And you are the, ah, smallest in the chest," Heidi Thorsten pointed out practically.

Charie feared the girl's comment did nothing to soothe Vionette's pride.

Vionette huffed. "So you are saying I am good for nothing other than playing the role of a man? Why, *Monsieur* Rubenevski says I am an elegant swan with a long neck."

"*Monsieur* Rubenevski is a Russian, and to him a bear vould be graceful," Heidi's twin, Helga, said.

Heated discussion commenced and Charie wondered if they'd be dancing at all.

"I will not play this Beast," Vionette gestured at the fierce lion-like head borrowed from the costume room of the ballet. "You shall perform without me. Mira, you can play the beast."

"But I'm to play the housekeeper," Mira protested as she adjusted a pinafore over her billowing ankle length tutu. "And I'm already dressed. I don't want to change now."

"*Beauty and the Beast* has to have a beast," Charie said. "Besides, you'll be able to discard the head for the last scene."

"The last scene," she repeated petulantly. "In the meantime, I'm stuck with this huge thing on my head."

"You should be used to that," Heidi said. "You've carried a huge ego for years."

"Girls," Charie interrupted, aware that tempers and pride were out of hand; fearful their raised voices would be heard by the sisters. Coming to her feet, she planted her hands on her hips. "I will play the beast and Mira will play Beauty. Vionette, you can be the housekeeper. But we must hurry and make the costume changes for the sisters have asked us to be ready to perform as soon as the evening meal is over. So let us switch costumes—"

"That won't be necessary."

9

The male voice came clearly through the closed door.

Charie immediately recognized it, whirling with a gasp. "Domitri? Why are you here?" A lump lodged in her throat.

"If I'm not mistaken, you were instructed to have an escort at all times."

Charie clenched her fists in aggravation. "Yuri is with us."

"You have to admit he is not the most physically intimidating. I've never seen Yuri do anything more violent than slam a door. And have you forgotten poor Petrov was beaten senseless?"

Her companions' eyes widened, clearly frightened by Domitri's words.

"You're not needed," Charie stated firmly.

"Oh, yes you are," Mira cried, rushing to the door and throwing it open.

Fortunately, all present were decently attired.

Domitri poked his head within, his green eyes meeting Charie's defiantly.

She elevated her chin in challenge.

"You can play the beast," Mira said. "Vionette will be so happy."

"It is my wish to make Vionette,"—he smiled at the girl and she blushed— "And all of you happy."

Charie rolled her eyes.

Domitri shifted his gaze to Charie.

Squirming inwardly, she debated the wisdom of dancing with him. How could she allow him to touch her knowing her relationship to Sophia? It would be a betrayal; an insult to her half-sister's memory. Why must Domitri appoint himself her protector? No one would bother her and her friends here at the hospital.

There was no ignoring Vionette's relieved look.

Sighing, Charie knew she had no choice but accept Domitri's offer. "Then dance the role of Beast if you are so determined," she responded uncharitably, fully aware that God was not pleased with her sharp words. But didn't He understand what a terrible predicament she was in?

Nothing I can't help you with, she practically heard Him say.

"We haven't anything for you to wear."

"I have my practice clothing with me. Allow me to change and be your Beast." He swept her an exaggerated bow.

With a huff, she stomped past, her arms folded disapprovingly, aware that the others trailed behind. She feared this would prove to be a long evening.

****

The performance moved flawlessly, Domitri no stranger to this ballet though it was rarely performed.

Monsieur Phillipe choreographed it early in his career, never receiving the acclaim of those choreographed by him the past ten years or so.

The resident nuns hovered over their rapt charges, many children in wheelchairs and others in possession of crutches, all eyes focused in unrestrained joy.

A quartet of sisters sat in a corner, providing the music, their cornettes flapping like huge white bat wings as they swayed with the rhythm, violins tucked beneath their chins with a piano accompanist—a young priest—beside them.

When the last act came to a close and Domitri, now freed of his beast head, pressed the rose into her hand, Charie almost forgot she was performing for an audience, so lost in the magic of the moment—a woman who had brought happiness and love into the life of one believed to be unlovable.

Domitri's head dipped as though he might kiss her, and she drew back. There was no mistaking the hurt in his eyes.

After changing, they visited the excited, chattering children.

Charie was captivated by a wheelchair bound child who explained in detail how his scheduled leg surgery would correct his problem and allow him to dance like the "Beast."

On the boy's other side was an extremely ill child in a small cot, her face white as the sheet covering her, her dark eyes huge and shadowed.

Domitri sat with this child, holding her hand.

Charie's new friend began to chat with Heidi, who was teasing him, so Charie focused her attention on Domitri's conversation with the little girl.

"You made a good beast," the child praised in her tiny, angelic voice.

Charie feared the frail child didn't have much longer upon earth.

Domitri chuckled softly as he tucked a blanket about her thin shoulders. "Did I make a good prince, once I learned how to love and be loved?"

"Oh, yes, a most handsome one. And Beauty, she is so very lovely."

"Yes, she is. But you know, beauty is more than having pretty eyes or soft hair. It has more to do with what's in here." He lightly tapped her chest.

"*Le docteur* says that my heart is very weak, and there isn't anything to make it stronger."

"If you love, your heart is strong. Never forgot that," Domitri said softly.

"*Monsieur* Domitri, I wish that I could dance like her." The child turned her thin face and gestured at Charie.

Domitri's gaze met Charie's, and she knew that her eyes were glazed with unshed tears. She managed a smile and reached out to take the child's other hand.

"You can dance like me. Imagine the music in your head, and you can dance in your mind."

"Maybe when I get to Heaven, I will dance with the angels," the child offered hopefully.

Unable to answer, Charie came to her feet. Leaning over, she kissed the child's unnaturally cool forehead. "You must believe you will dance one day."

The little girl seemed happy with that, and with strength sapped, allowed her lids to close.

Fearful that she would burst into uncontrollable sobs, Charie slipped away and rapidly crossed the large open room, stepping into the drafty hall. Just as she thought her emotions were under control, Domitri appeared.

"Are you unwell?" The need to be in his arms caused an ache in her chest, but the thought was improper and impossible. Moving a few steps away, she hastily brushed at her eyes.

"No, no, I'm fine. It's just that child—"

"Suzette," he provided the name. "One of the sisters said that she has little time left. I pray that her passing will be gentle."

"Why doesn't God heal her?" Charie demanded, suddenly angry as she turned upon Domitri. "She is a sweet, innocent child who brings such joy even though she is so very ill."

"Charie, we know that God doesn't promise ease and comfort in this life. His promises lie beyond what we know here and now. We must take that on faith."

"I know," she whimpered brokenly. Without fully understanding how she came to be there, she found herself in Domitri's arms, one of his hands pressed to the back of her head as she rested her cheek against his chest, savoring his warmth and assurance. Clinging to him, she cried; cried for Suzette and the other children who might never be able to return to their families. Their next home might be that prepared for them by God.

When her tears ceased, Domitri cupped her face in his hands and raised her face. "Charie, what did you mean when you said you couldn't care for me."

"I," she began and faltered. What could she say — how could she explain? "I can't say."

Domitri's eyes conveyed his confusion. "Be honest with me, Charie. Please," he urged in a whisper, his lips far too close to hers. She had to get away.

"Charie, Raoul is asking for you." It was Heidi calling.

Domitri released her, and she hurried towards the girl, thankful for the timely summons.

"The boy says you promised to read him a story before you leave. Have I interrupted something?" Heidi looked from Charie, and then across the floor to where Domitri stood in the hall.

Charie feared her expression was incriminating, and she quickly gave the girl a tremulous smile even though she recognized Domitri's approaching tread. "Not at all. I will read Raoul his story." She turned to face him. "Domitri, you needn't wait until we leave."

"I'll wait." Judging by the set of his lips, there would be no dissuading him.

"Very well," she replied abruptly and hurried away, afraid her emotions would unravel any moment.

****

Mira and the other three very talkative young ladies had been delivered to their shared residence.

Domitri was alone in the carriage with Charie and a dozing Yuri.

She hadn't spoken a word since their conversation in the hall, and it didn't appear she planned to speak now that they had some degree of privacy. She looked out the window, but he wondered what she really saw.

"It's good of you to spend time with those children." Domitri hoped his comment would encourage her to talk.

"I enjoy it. It's far too little to do, but I love to see their smiles."

"Don't underestimate your efforts. I enjoyed it, and I wouldn't mind being part of it in the future."

"I'm sure you're too busy."

"I'm not. Charice," he said more forcefully than he'd intended, "don't push me away. It won't work."

"You don't understand."

"Then help me to understand."

The sleeping Yuri emitted a snore, and then

shifted his position, both of them anticipating his waking. But he slept on.

"Nothing good will come by pursuing answers."

Angry and frustrated, Domitri knew he was about to say things he'd regret. Rapping loudly on the roof, his action roused Yuri, who quickly sat up and tried to act as though he hadn't been asleep for a good thirty minutes.

Petrov halted the carriage and Domitri let himself out.

After he slammed the door, Charie leaned out the window. "Domitri, you're far from home, and it's so very cold."

"I need the walk," he retorted gruffly, and then turned about, striding off in a direction that would take him even farther from his residence. He needed time to think.

****

When Charie arrived at the townhouse, *Madame* Jeaneau informed her that her mother was in her chamber with Lizbet examining costume choices for her next play.

She hurried upstairs and entered her mother's room without the courtesy of a knock.

Both women turned, expressions startled.

Seeing Charie's distress, Matilda asked Lizzie to leave them.

As soon as Lizzie shut the door, Charie faced her mother, suddenly unable to say any of the things she'd planned to say. She'd wanted to tell the woman she was angry over the deception; that all the lies had caused her to lose a chance at happiness; and that now she was afraid to be alone with Domitri.

Instead, she dropped into a chair and buried her face in her hands. She heard the rustle of her mother's silk skirts as Matilda knelt beside her.

"What has you so troubled, Charie?" Her voice was soft and comforting. "Did something happen at the children's hospital?"

Charie lifted her head and met her mother's concerned gaze.

"No *Maman*, not really. I mean," she drew a deep breath to steady her voice, "there was a little girl who is so very ill. She told me she would soon be dancing with the angels in Heaven. Her words nearly broke my heart."

"But something more troubles you." Her mother knew her far too well.

"Domitri."

Matilda sighed.

"I will never be able to look at him again without thinking of Sophia. Why, why couldn't you and the count have told me the truth years ago? I could have handled the truth. Now, I'm torn and confused."

"You wouldn't be if you'd turn this over to our Lord," Matilda reminded her. "You can't know what God's plan is in the midst of what you perceive to be a disaster unless you seek His will. Both Olar and I have told you how sorry we are. We know we were wrong, but at the time it seemed that withholding the facts would be best for you."

"You let Olar walk away from you—from us. Did you ever stop to think how it would affect my life to never know my father? Wasn't that selfish?"

"Yes, it was." Matilda stood and walked across the tastefully furnished and appointed room, pausing by one of the room's multitude of mullioned windows. "I've made mistakes, Charie, and I prayed for forgiveness for years. But at some point, I had to let go of the past because although God had forgiven me, I'd not yet forgiven myself. Now I have, and I'm at peace. I can never change my choices or my actions of twenty years ago. All I can do is go forward. I hope you will come to understand."

"But Domitri—I fear I am growing fond of him. Knowing that Sophia is my half-sister, she rises like one of Giselle's *wilis* and comes between us."

"If God's plan is for the two of you to find happiness, nothing can come between you."

"*Maman*, tell me about Sophia. You must have met her."

"I did. Several times, actually, although Olar never explained our relationship to her. She was a marvel on stage. Not an exceptional beauty, but there was something about her when she was dancing that captured an audience. And when she danced with Domitri..." Matilda left the comment incomplete as she glanced apologetically at Charie. "They were spectacular together because his athleticism made up for what Sophia lacked in technical skill."

"What I'm really asking is what kind of person was she?" Charie needed to understand why Domitri had fallen in love with Sophia. Did she in some way remind him of his first wife? Could that be the source of his attraction?

"Sophia was pampered and indulged by numerous governesses who sought to protect their employment by keeping their wealthy and titled employer's daughter happy. Olar never failed to show Sophia his love, but she early on displayed a rebellious streak, which worsened as she grew older and garnered acclaim as a *soliste*. I fear that her willfulness contributed to her untimely death."

"Am I like her?" Charie asked, half fearful her mother would say yes—half fearful she would say no.

"You love the ballet just as she did—she had Olar's nose as do you. She, like you, commanded everyone's attention by merely entering a room, although you've never realized that about yourself. It is not your nature to take notice of your charm, whereas Sophia was always very much aware of hers. Does that answer your question?"

"In some ways."

"But it doesn't solve your problem," Matilda correctly assessed as she walked back to where Charie still sat. "There's only One who can do that, my dear." Matilda reached out and took Charie's hand. "Pray on the matter, child. And I will be praying that you find the answers you seek."

"Thank you, *Maman*," Charie whispered, and then stood and hugged her mother.

****

Domitri decided during that chilly walk home that he would say nothing more to Charie, nor press her for explanations. But during practice the next day, a deep sadness clung to her, which was, as far as he could determine, most unnatural. Was her present state of mind directly attributable to him or could it have anything to do with the frightening portrait sent to Matilda by Chervenkof?

But Chervenkof hadn't been seen or heard from.

Domitri fervently prayed that would remain so as

he stood in the silent wings two hours before the curtain was to rise on the opening night performance of *Giselle*.

Lost in thought, Domitri saw nothing of the stage, now filled with props and painted backdrops, as he wondered how to approach Charie. Perhaps there was no need to try—perhaps that was God's will. But her sadness only made him more determined to bring a smile to her lips.

Hearing light footsteps, he turned, pleasantly surprised to see Charie walking towards him, clad in a simple gown of moss green velvet. She gave him a small smile as she joined him.

"I was hoping to find you here, before the chaos begins," she said. "I owe you an explanation."

"I had no right to demand answers. You hardly know me. I overstepped the bounds of our professional friendship."

"In a way, you have." An odd statement to be certain, but before he could question her meaning, she quickly continued. "Thank you for all you've done— for taking Antoine's place and for your encouragement and help. I hope we can remain friends."

"Friends." Domitri had difficulty repeating the cold, detached word.

Charie nodded stiffly while dread encased his heart. "Perhaps I should have told you that some time ago the Baron Bauerhausen asked me to marry him. *Maman* says he is not nearly as brash as he once was."

"You are going to accept his proposal?" Domitri managed to keep his voice devoid of all feeling though sudden pain pierced him. Charie's words knifed as though she'd plunged a dagger into his chest. *Where are you, God? This can't be happening. I care for Charie—I more than care.*

"He does have a title and wealth." Charie's voice was controlled, but her eyes exposed her uncertainty.

Title? Wealth?

He'd believed her to be unimpressed with either. He'd been mistaken. "That matters to you?"

She lowered her eyes. "I suppose it should."

"No, it shouldn't."

Charie looked up, clearly stunned. But the stunned look gave way to resignation. Sad resignation. Rising on her toes, she kissed his cheek. Her caress ignited emotions he'd believed lost to him forever, and without reasoning his actions, he captured her face with his hands. Those violet gray eyes widened and her lips parted.

Domitri wavered, and then pressed his mouth to hers, aware that he was dancing too close to the flames of suppressed desire.

Charie stiffened but as he deepened the kiss, the tension eased and she slipped her arms around his waist. He was certain his heart would pound from his chest when she kissed him back, fearful he was imagining her response. Lifting his head, he saw that Charie's eyes were closed.

Her breathing was rapid, almost as if she had run for miles. When her lashes lifted, those mesmerizing eyes expressed exhilaration and pain. It was a bittersweet thought that perhaps his kiss had convinced her that the baron was not so good a choice, after all.

Not daring to remain with her a moment longer, he moved out of the circle of her arms and walked away, glad that the frantic ballet master and choreographer were headed towards him.

****

Just when Charie thought she'd found a way to navigate the emotional morass created by her parents, Domitri ruined everything.

His kiss convinced her she was lost. Not that she was surprised. Lost in his eyes—captivated by his touch, he'd awakened something within her that would not be denied. But how could she, in all good conscience, encourage the affections of her deceased sister's husband? Especially when he had no idea.

Her mother and Olar had unintentionally created an unimaginably painful situation.

Charie had a solution—she would never marry and devote her life to the ballet. When she was too old to dance, she'd teach, like her beloved *Madame* Erlaine. But the wonder of what could have been would always haunt her. If only he hadn't kissed her.

But he had and the curtain was scheduled to rise on her first performance of *Giselle* in less than fifteen minutes. As tiny tears slipped down her cheeks, she was oblivious to the melee enveloping the entire company, the shouting and calls that reached a crescendo as dancers scurried about.

Lost in her thoughts, Charie jumped when someone tapped her on the shoulder. Quickly turning, she was surprised to see Baron Bauerhausen.

"I apologize for startling you. But I had to wish you good luck. I know that you will give a fantastic and flawless performance just as you always do." He leaned over and kissed her on the forehead.

From the corner of her eye, Charie saw Domitri approaching, but when the baron kissed her on the forehead, he stopped.

"I was hoping you would allow me to escort you to a late supper after the ballet."

"I don't think—" she met Domitri's dark gaze from over the baron's shoulder, "that would be lovely." Charie gave the man a half-hearted smile.

Domitri turned abruptly and walked off in the opposite direction. Her heart splintered, and she felt sick to her stomach. *Oh, Lord, forgive me.*

"I shall look forward to it." Ludwig lowered his brows questioningly as though he suspected she was being less than truthful. But he said nothing more, nodded, bowed, and walked away.

"Charie," Mira called excitedly as she took hold of her arm. "Come take your place. It's almost time. Hurry, you daydreamer. Your head must be in the clouds." Mira pulled her forward.

Charie's heart was so heavy she feared she wouldn't be able to lift up on her toes. As the bright light of the gas lamps filtered beneath the as yet unopened curtains, she realized she would soon find out.

10

The ballet progressed well. Domitri was relieved and grateful that he and Charie had performed flawlessly.

But Charie's dancing reminded him of an expressionless marionette, going through the movements without any emotion or feeling.

How could he fault her, for he felt like a dancing puppet, each manipulation of the emotional strings jerking painfully. Standing in the wings, he watched Charie perform her solo, the steps of which had been changed to reflect her personal style and unquestionably the pinnacle of her performance.

Charie's execution of *pas de bourrée* and *piqué* turns took her around the entire stage, bringing her to the edge and close to the gas lamps that encircled the outer perimeter. She paused for a second, reminding him of an angel poised for heavenly flight.

A slight swaying of the outer curtain caught his eye.

But as Charie moved forward, Domitri's attention focused on her. Her grace and beauty captured something sweet and vital deep within him, and for just a moment, he imagined himself flying by her side.

The gaslight reflected off the sheer fabric of her voluminous skirt and scattered glittering prisms on the floor making little rainbow puddles...

"Charice!" he roared, leaping from the wings like a

madman. He was too late.

As Charie rose on her toes, one foot slipped in the water and she stumbled towards the lamps. Regaining her balance, she prepared to resume her turns amid the encouraging applause of the audience, but the applause was quickly drowned by shrieks and screams when the open flame of a gas light ignited the edge of her skirt.

Rushing forward, Domitri caught her about the waist and ripped the skirt away just as someone had the sense to lower the curtain to cloak the unfolding nightmare. With Charie freed of the flaming skirt, Domitri hurled the fabric across the stage where he heard the sound of sluicing water as buckets were dumped on the flames.

Gently lowering Charie, he caught her close, tenderly rocking her as she sobbed. He was afraid to look at her legs, afraid of what the fire might have done to them. But, if she was seriously injured, there was no time to waste.

By now a small crowd had gathered around them—he recognized Rubenevski, Phillipe, and Mira.

"Oh, Charie," Mira cried. "Were you burned?"

Domitri forced himself to examine her legs, noticing one small burn on her left shin.

"Not badly," Charie said, a slight catch in her voice. "Domitri was so fast. He saved my life." She looked up at him, her eyes filled with tears and gratitude. "How can I ever thank you—God must have known I would need you. Thank you," she whispered again and pressed her mouth to his scarred jaw.

Before he could adequately respond, someone grabbed his arm and pulled him from Charie.

It was a terror stricken Olar who dropped to his

knees beside Charie, her mother also on her knees and hugging her from the other side.

Domitri stood.

"Oh, my darling, my precious little one," Olar choked brokenly. "I was so fearful that I would lose you. I thank God that He kept you in His care."

"He did indeed, but He used Domitri." Charie's voice was stronger. "Domitri saw what happened."

All gazes turned to him.

"I realized there was water on the stage just as Charie stepped in it. I was close enough to get to her immediately. Someone put that water there just before she danced to that spot. I saw movement in the curtain, but I didn't see anyone."

"Thank you, Domitri. God bless you," Matilda Marin cried as she tightened her hold on Charie.

"Domitri, there is nothing I can say or do to thank you for saving Charie's life. It would've killed me had I lost another daughter."

Domitri stared at Olar, who was openly crying, but he stared not because of the tears; because of his words.

"What do you mean, Olar? I know that you think of Charie as a daughter. But she's not your child."

"She is my daughter," the count uttered hoarsely. "Matilda and I were married for a short time many years ago. Charice is our child."

Domitri's mind crashed as though he'd slipped in the water, fallen and hit his head. Charice—of course. It explained so many things.

Olar's devotion to the girl, his determination that she have the best roles and partners, her resemblance to him. Pieces slipped neatly into place. For Charie, Olar, and Matilda.

But not for him. Olar had allowed him to fall in love with his wife's sister. Guilt reared powerfully and irrevocably, forcing him to step back.

"Domitri, are you all right?" Domitri heard Charie's question, but his glare fixed on Olar.

"Why didn't you tell me? You forgot to mention the fact that Charie is Sophia's half-sister? I had a right to know."

"Domitri," Charie cried as she scrambled to her feet, "I didn't know, either. Not until a few days ago."

"Why didn't you tell me?" Domitri demanded, shifting his focus to Charie. She cringed, and he knew he presented a terrifying image.

Turning away, he nearly ran into Bauerhausen. "Charie is fine and doesn't need any assistance from you," Domitri snapped. "Did you know she was Olar's daughter, too?"

His guilty look confirmed that he did know—how, Domitri had no idea. Rather than risk a confrontation, he shoved past the man.

But Bauerhausen wasn't to be ignored. "That was uncalled for and rude, though expected from one like you." The baron's superior manner and his mangled French further antagonized Domitri.

"I'm sorry if I'm not acting the perfect gentleman tonight. That's why Charice prefers your company to mine. I am lacking in all the social graces."

"Then apologize."

"I don't believe I will right now. Perhaps another time," Domitri retorted sarcastically. He started to walk away again, but Bauerhausen grabbed his arm.

"You're nothing but a common Russian peasant. At least have the decency to show respect to *Mademoiselle* Marin and her mother."

"Stop it—please," Charie pleaded. "There are people out there waiting for us to continue the ballet. Let me change, and we can finish. I'm not hurt, and I'd rather dance than think about what almost happened."

Domitri clenched his jaw, but seeing Charie so distraught lessened his rage.

"Very well. Let's finish this night. But you'll need to find yourself another Albrecht. This is my first and last performance with you."

An uproar ensued.

Domitri shut it out. He was wounded, betrayed, hurt. And filled with gnawing guilt. How could he have fallen in love with Sophia's sister? Even worse, he was more in love with Charie, than he'd ever been with Sophia.

What sort of man was he to so easily forget the love he'd believed to be perfect? A liar, he answered his own question. Because his marriage had been far from perfect. And after seven years, there was no longer any need to deny the truth.

****

Her mother and Olar—how could she ever think of him as her father—had forbidden her to leave the house, insisting she needed to rest before leaving for the theatre. But having lain awake all night, rest was a luxury denied until she'd spoken to Domitri.

Realizing she would not be deterred, Olar had allowed her use of his carriage and Yuri before traveling on to the theatre.

Yuri and Petrov now watched her from the bottom of the stairs as she pounded on Domitri's door.

"Domitri! Domitri! I need to talk to you. Let me in.

Please...please." Allowing the tears to fall, she dropped to her knees. *I love him. I tried not to—I was so sure I wouldn't. But I did. Lord, help me. I don't know how to fix things.*

The door opened, and brushing away her tears, Charie looked up.

Domitri stood there, unshaven; the musky scent of sweat mingling with that of sandalwood, his clothing rumpled and in need of changing. "Why are you here?"

Charie started to rise, but he grasped her arm and hauled her up. He dragged her within his apartment, but left the door open.

Charie looked about frantically, but there was no sign of Muzette.

"Don't worry. Your virtue is safe. You'd be the last woman I'd let into my life."

"I know you're angry," Charie began breathlessly. "You have every right to be. I should have told you as soon as I discovered the truth. But Olar and *Maman*—they thought it best not to—I agreed to keep the secret. That was wrong."

"Why are you here?" he repeated. Domitri's bristled jaw twitched with vexation, and his reddened eyes conveyed contempt.

"Come back to the ballet, Domitri. I don't want anyone to take your place. We've come this far. Please dance the role of Albrecht."

"Why doesn't Bauerhausen find a replacement for me? He has connections."

Swallowing a sob, she struggled for a reply—a truthful reply. "He has no say in what I do."

"Shouldn't he? After all, you're going to accept his marriage proposal."

"I only said that— " her voice and courage failed her. Had there ever been a more terrible moment in her life?

"It's time for you to go. There's nothing to discuss." Yet, he continued to hold her.

She looked at his hand fastened on her upper arm. "I'm upset, too. They lied to me. My life has been a lie. I'm angry and hurt. But I never meant to hurt you."

Something softened in his eyes, and his fierce grip eased.

"If you would just finish—" Resting her gloved hand over his, her touch iced his eyes, and she quickly removed it.

"No. No more dancing for me. I was a fool to agree to Olar's suggestion. He manipulated me. I want nothing more to do with the ballet or *Giselle*. I want to be left alone with my memories."

There was no stopping the tears as she viewed his bleeding heart and soul through his eyes.

"I'm so sorry you lost Sophia. But maybe those memories aren't good for you."

"How would you know?" The heated anger returned. "You have no idea what I've been through. You live in a perfect world where everything is taken care of for you and you spin and whirl about the stage in a beautiful gown and have roses thrown at your feet. What do you know of loss and tragedy other than what you act out on the stage? Have you ever loved someone so deeply that when they were no longer there, you felt as though your heart had been ripped from you? Of course you haven't." Domitri shook his head. "I'm not fit to be around. I didn't sleep last night—"

"Neither did I," Charie whispered.

Domitri met her gaze. To her shock, he reached out and brushed back a lock of her loosened hair. She hadn't bothered to braid it, and the snarled mass fell about her shoulders.

The urge to press her lips to his hand made her tremble and her breath catch. "I'm sorry I intruded. You're right. I should leave."

He released her arm and she turned around, staring at the open door, Yuri and Petrov looking up at her. "I hope you find happiness, Domitri."

Passing through the door, she lifted her skirts and hurried down the steps. When she reached the two men, she gestured for them to leave. She dared to look up, just as the latch of the door above softly clicked.

****

Why am I here, Lord? The answer was simple, Domitri admitted as he allowed the rear stage door slam behind him. Four hours earlier, he had experienced a loss more devastating than that caused by Sophia's death. He had watched the beauty of hope and joy extinguished from eyes so lovely they spoke to his soul. And he was the cause. He was here in this detested place to help Charie. During those torturous minutes, sharing her despair and pain, his love for her nearly escaped his lips. She must never know how he felt. It wouldn't be right. Or fair.

"Domitri?" Turning, he saw Olar walking his way.

Dropping his bag, he remained motionless until his father-in-law joined him.

"I'm surprised to see you."

"You know why I'm here. I hope you weren't behind Charie's visit."

"Absolutely not. It was her idea. Matilda and I advised against it. But you're here."

"Only until you find a suitable replacement. And don't consider delaying your search. You have one week."

"It will be disruptive to bring in a replacement."

"It will be more disruptive if there is no male lead." Domitri wasn't backing down.

Olar was responsible for this—this what? Disaster, betrayal, angst, humiliation, love?

For in the midst of all the bad, the seed of love had bloomed in his heart. A seed which must be left unwatered to wither and die.

Olar shook his head.

Lifting his bag, he walked on.

Olar spoke again. "Thank you, Domitri."

Domitri kept his back to the man he'd once considered his best friend.

"But have a care. Memories can sometimes swallow one until there's no life to be lived."

Drawing a deep breath, Domitri moved forward. Things were what they were. There was no erasing the past. There was no erasing the fact he'd killed Sophia.

****

Paris
Mid—December

The curtain had just fallen upon the final performance of *Long Ago In Bethlehem*, and relief flooded Charie. Not that she hadn't enjoyed her role as Mary, but after the disaster of *Giselle,* she needed a respite from ballet, temperamental men, and well-meaning parents who had unintentionally ruined her life.

After all, Christmas was right around the corner, and she should be enjoying the preparations and festivities leading up to the celebration of the Christ child's birth. But for now, her heart wasn't in it, and it was because of Domitri.

"More flowers from the baron?" Mira asked as she slipped into Charie's dressing room unannounced and took a seat on a blue velvet upholstered divan.

Charie glanced over at the glorious array of white and red roses sitting on a low table, sprigs of holly artfully inserted among the flowers to add a seasonal touch.

"They are." Charie sighed and removed the pins from her painfully tight chignon that Lizzie had fashioned earlier.

"You know he wants to marry you."

Charie shook her head. "He knows that isn't a possibility." Guilt flared at the memory of how she'd led Domitri to believe she was seriously considering the baron's proposal. She'd hoped by doing so, she would successfully destroy any feelings Domitri harbored for her. Sadly, it appeared her plan had worked for she'd not seen or heard from him since Olar had announced the name of the new Albrecht. She squeezed her eyes hoping to banish the memory.

"Men don't like taking no for an answer. Have you seen *Monsieur* Auberchon?" Mira asked, almost as though she could read Charie's mind.

Charie's breathing accelerated, but it was momentary. She quickly recovered. "I've neither seen nor heard from him." It was a miracle she managed to reply, for her throat was tight and there was the uncomfortable sting of tears behind her eyes.

"What a mess. Who would have guessed that Count Stanislov was really your father? How tragically romantic that your mother fell in love with him, and then allowed him to fulfill his family obligations. And all the while she was carrying you."

"It was neither tragic nor romantic." Mira's words reignited Charie's anger. "It was selfish and arrogant of them to think their individual needs and desires outweighed what would have been best for me."

"I was only trying to make you feel better," Mira offered meekly and tears welled in her eyes.

Appalled at her behavior, Charie quickly rose from her seat before the vanity and joined Mira on the divan, putting her arms about the girl. "I'm sorry. I have no right to take out my frustration on you. It's just that all of a sudden everything I knew and believed in has changed. Those I've trusted all my life lied to me. I've prayed that I would be able to forgive them, and everything could be like it was. But I know it never will be." A sob slipped from Charie and Mira patted her reassuringly on her shoulder.

"Don't spend tonight thinking on the matter. Come with me to church. Pierre is going to meet me there, and after the service we are going for chocolate and beignets."

"Thank you for asking, Mira, but I'd be poor company. *Maman* tried to convince me to go to dinner with her and the count—I mean, my father. They'll be discussing our plans to travel to the Stanislov estate for Christmas, but I don't feel like listening. I suppose that's selfish of me, but I'd rather be alone."

"I wish you'd reconsider," Mira urged, clearly worried.

But Charie just wanted to go home and have *Madame* Jeaneau prepare her a cup of chocolate so she could curl up before the fire and read. "*Non.* I am decided." Charie came to her feet. "And I do not want to delay your departure if Pierre is waiting."

Mira rose, too, and grasped Charie's hand. "It will come out all right. You will see." She turned to leave and Charie watched her good friend depart.

Christmas was a time for being with those one loved—perhaps she should join her parents. Or perhaps—

"I know exactly what will lift my spirits," she said aloud and hurrying back to her vanity, she brushed out her dark red curls, her mind awhirl with plans.

****

Restless and at a loss as to what to do with himself after dinner, Domitri paced the length of his dimly lit sitting room.

Muzette hummed a Christmas carol in the kitchen while perfecting her cookies.

The scent of baking gingerbread would normally have forced Domitri to have a taste, but tonight his thoughts were unfocused and there was a sense of loneliness he couldn't shake. Which had everything to do with Charie.

Domitri returned to his classroom two days after his replacement had been found, spending days and weeks avoiding all journals and papers that might have carried reviews of Charie's performance in *Giselle*. He didn't know who'd taken his place, though he'd been sorely tempted to discover. His resolve crumbled beneath the onslaught of his need to see Charie, a need which overrode his pride and stubbornness. Securing a ticket, he caught that evening's final performance of *Long Ago In Bethlehem.*

As he'd watched Charie's graceful movements and her unequaled technique, he'd offered up another silent thank you to God that she'd been spared serious harm when her skirt caught fire. Seeing Charie dance made him wish he was the one dancing with her. Wishing he could tell her what was in his heart. But he couldn't.

"*Monsieur* Domitri?" Startled, he turned and found Muzette standing there, wiping her hands on her overlarge apron with its cavernous pockets. "I asked if the snow had begun."

"I haven't noticed," he replied, feeling foolish as he looked out the window and noticed that crystal white flakes were falling heavily. How long they'd been doing so, he had no idea.

"I am very glad that I was not asking you if the house was burning down, for if you paid as little notice to the flames as you did the snow, we would both be as browned as the little gingerbread man I dropped into the hearth." Her reprimand brought a slight smile to his lips.

"I am very sorry, Muzette, but my mind is on other things."

"Most likely on that ballerina who has stolen your heart. It is no sin to love again, *Monsieur* Domitri. It is God's will that your heart has opened to another. Why do you not accept His gift?"

Such a practical question that should have been easy to answer. How could he make Muzette understand that the guilt at having fallen in love with Charie was nearly unbearable?

"I don't deserve such a gift from Him. When I was married to Sophia, I failed to bring her happiness."

"What more could you have done?" Muzette demanded. "You loved her, you were a good husband, and you indulged her every whim. Perhaps that is where you made your mistake."

"If so, I did so out of love. Muzette, how many dozens of cookies have you baked?"

"Enough for you to take some to the little ones at the hospital. I know they have been on your mind since you told me of your visit."

"It is almost Christmas and many of them have no family."

"I will pack them up right now, and if you hurry, they may still be a little warm when you arrive. I think visiting the children will be good for you."

"There was one little girl there—her name is Suzette. She was very ill, and I fear she may not have very long to live."

"I'll pack the cookies."

****

Charie wasn't sure how she arranged so much in a short time, but there was a verse in the fourth chapter of Philippians that always gave her the energy she needed to get something done—*I can do all things through Christ which strengtheneth me.* And each item she located for the children at the hospital renewed her spirit and lent quickness to her steps.

A stop at a toy store, keeping later hours to facilitate Christmas purchases, provided a variety of playthings that could be enjoyed by both boys and girls.

Charie bought a special doll for Suzette, and while she paid for it, she prayed the child would be alive to receive it, and then quickly admonished herself for having so little faith.

Her next stop was the confectioner's shop, and though the establishment was already closed, her incessant knocking bought the proprietor down from his upstairs quarters. He professionally, though not quite cordially, bagged up the treats she requested. However, his cordiality returned when she gave him extra coin for his trouble.

Her final stop was at her own home. Rushing in, she quickly explained to *Madame* Jeaneau what she was planning.

She retrieved her Bible, planning to read to the children the story of Jesus' birth from the gospel of St. Luke. As a child, she'd always looked forward to her mother's reading it on Christmas Eve, and she'd heard it so many times she could nearly recite it by heart. Charie wanted to share that joy with the children.

Everything in readiness, she instructed Petrov to take her to the Hospital of the Sisters of Hope, to which he delivered her in record time despite the swirling snow.

Charie was glad to see that the lights were on and with the man's help, carried in her gifts. The sisters were delighted by her unexpected arrival and while one sister ushered the coachman to the kitchen for something warm to drink, several others led her into the large room which served as both a dining and entertaining hall, the very room where she, Mira, and the others gave their impromptu performances.

Just as she was relieved of her armload, a face hovered into view. Fortunately, her arms were empty for she would have dropped everything. *How can this be?*

Domitri walked toward her, and her heart commenced a series of *pirouettes* in her chest.

11

"This is a surprise," Domitri said calmly, as though discussing the weather or inquiring into one's health. Actually, his heart thudded, and uncomfortable warmth tempted him to tug on his collar though the room was drafty and poorly heated.

Charie was a vision in her stylish fur cape, Christmas red bonnet, and matching gown. Her eyes reflected the glow of the candles, the flames producing amethyst highlights. She stared at him until she realized several of the nuns watched them curiously.

"Yes, it is. What brings you here tonight?" She twisted her hands nervously.

"Muzette's gingerbread cookies. She made enough to feed me and the wife and dozen children I don't have."

Charie quickly lowered her eyelids, and Domitri noticed the blush in her cheeks. Had she ever considered him as a possible husband? Or was she currently enamored of Bauerhausen?

Domitri had imagined Charie as his wife more times than he cared to admit. That brought heat to his face, and he quickly turned away, struggling for control. When he looked back at her, he was relieved to see a slight smile touch her lips.

"Then this was the perfect place to bring them. Perhaps you could help me pass out a few gifts to the children. It must be terrible to be away from home and family at this time of year—or worse, to have no family. I hoped to bring a bit of happiness to the children. Have you seen Suzette?"

Domitri nodded, and now it was his turn to smile. "Suzette is already in her bed, but Sister Honoré tells me the child has improved since our previous visit, and that, though the doctor is cautiously optimistic, she may be allowed to return home the first of the year."

"Oh, thank God. I was so afraid—well, God has the final say in such matters. I picked up something for her." Charie spoke those last words in a whisper. "But let's give out the other things I've brought, and then perhaps we can visit Suzette."

Domitri agreed and with the help of the sisters, each child was given a toy and candy treat.

While the children marveled at their gifts, Charie picked up a box that had been tucked in a corner and whispered something to Sister Honoré.

The woman nodded and motioned for Charie to follow.

Charie caught Domitri's eye indicating that he should come. After traveling a series of long halls, their footsteps echoing loudly, and climbing a flight of stairs, they were led to a room, filled with eight beds only one of which was occupied.

Suzette was awake and turning the pages of a picture book. Upon hearing their entry, she looked up and gave them the smile of an angel. "I can't believe you are here. The beautiful ballerina and her prince."

Charie laughed at Suzette's words and hurried over, perching on the edge of her bed. "You are much too kind, Suzette," Charie said, "but yes we are here to wish you a *Joyeux Noel*."

"I'm so glad you came. You look just like a fairy princess," Suzette whispered, running her hand along the edge of Charie's cape. Then, as though suddenly remembering Domitri, she gave him a shy smile. "And you're still very handsome."

"But not nearly as elegant as *Mademoiselle* Marin," he added as he pulled up a chair and took a seat. "We are very glad to hear of your progress."

"I keep praying that I will see *Maman* and *Grandpère* soon, and my two brothers, and my kitty. She was a kitten when I was brought here, but by now she is probably all grown. I wish that I could grow up just as quickly."

"You should enjoy being a little girl," Charie said. "Here is a present for you. I hope you like it." Charie placed the box on Suzette's knees and watched the child open it.

Once the top had been removed, Suzette's cry of delight resounded in the empty room.

Peering within, Domitri saw that it was a doll with lovely blonde ringlets, dressed in a frothy, flowered tutu and tiny, pink ballet slippers. The doll was exquisite.

"Do you like it?" Charie asked almost fearfully.

"Oh, yes, *Mademoiselle* Marin. She is so very beautiful. And she is a ballerina. Just like you. I will love this doll forever. I will call her Beauty to always remind me of that wonderful ballet. Thank you." Suzette flung her arms around Charie.

Domitri saw the tears in Charie's eyes, but said nothing.

"You are most welcome. Now, you must settle down and go to sleep. Sister Honoré says that you are to have plenty of rest. I should like to visit you after

Christmas, but I won't be disappointed if you've already gone home."

Suzette giggled. She even sounded stronger, Domitri thought.

Charie was healing medicine to the child. And Charie had the same effect on him. Why was he such a fool?

"*Mademoiselle* Marin," a breathless voice called from the doorway, and they turned to see Sister Honoré standing there. "Your driver said to tell you the roads are worsening and that you must leave now if you're to return home this evening. You must come—now."

****

There was no mistaking Charie's disappointment. "But I haven't read the children their story," she said, dismay clouding her lovely features as she came to her feet.

"I know how much you were looking forward to that, but this is a matter of your safety. Perhaps you can do so another time."

"Domitri, what do you think?" Charie asked, and then chewed her lower lip.

He wanted to reach out and tuck back the stray curl that peeked out from her bonnet, but he kept his hands at his side. "Petrov knows what he's talking about. I'm sure there'll be another time to read to the children."

"Very well." Charie agreed, but Domitri could tell by the look on her face she was upset. "Thank you for permitting us to visit Suzette."

"She talks about the two of you all the time," Sister

Honoré said. "Now, if you'll follow me."

Charie whispered another goodbye to Suzette, and then kissed her on the forehead.

Domitri turned to the child as Charie hurried from the room with the sister.

"Are the two of you married?" Suzette asked as she tucked her doll into bed beside her.

"No, why do you ask?"

"You should be. Thank you for coming to see me."

"You are most welcome. You do as the sisters tell you, and grow strong again."

"I will. And I'll ask God to make *Mademoiselle* Marin marry you so you'll be happy."

"I wish you would." Domitri gave her a grin. "Sleep well," he added and squeezed the child's hand, overjoyed to feel the warmth in the little fingers. The last time he'd held her hand, the fingers had been cold and nearly lifeless. What a miracle from God.

Leaving Suzette, he hurried down the corridor, pausing to look out a long window. It was as the sister had said—everything was obscured by snow. Hurrying along, he reached the lower floor just as the front doors were opened to permit Charie and Petrov's departure. The wind and the snow drove them back inside.

Domitri pushed past them and stepped out on the portico. Although he knew Olar's man was a competent driver, he doubted Petrov could deliver Charie home without mishap given the poor visibility and deep snow. Domitri wasn't sure he could make it home, either.

Shutting the doors and joining the others, he pulled Petrov aside and spoke rapidly in Russian. He knew that Petrov's knowledge of French was limited, and he needed to make sure the man understood.

"I do not question your skill, but I fear that the horses' footing will be less than secure should you attempt to take *Mademoiselle* Marin home."

"It is as you say, but the count is so concerned for her safety. He would be terribly upset if I was not to return her home this evening. He also expects me to pick him and *Madame* Marin up after their dinner."

"Hopefully the count will be sensible and realize you could not possibly come after them in this." Domitri gestured at the door. "They have most likely found another way home. If the sisters will permit it, I believe we must stay here for the night. It is the only safe thing to do. I will face the count's wrath."

"If you feel that would be better." Petrov shrugged his shoulders. "I am willing to remain."

Domitri turned to Sister Honoré and quickly explained their dilemma, asking if they might be permitted to spend the night.

Sister Honoré wholeheartedly agreed and hurried off to make preparations for their overnight stay.

Domitri explained to Charie.

"I can't stay the night. *Maman* will be beside herself. And you're here."

"I'm afraid so, though I know that distresses you."

Her expression of dismay wiped away all his earlier feelings of peace and joy.

"Surely Petrov can get me home. He's driven through worse than this in Russia."

"Do you want him to jeopardize his life and that of the horses simply to take you home? If you'd give this some thought, you'd realize your life could be in danger, as well."

"It's just that—I can't—I mean—" Words failed

her, and she looked about her in desperation, wringing her hands.

Sister Honoré chose that time to return. "We are setting up cots for the gentlemen to sleep on near the fire in the kitchen. And you, *Mademoiselle* Marin, can use one of the empty beds in the west wing. Since you are staying, now you may read to the children."

Before Charie could say anything more, Sister Honoré was leading her back into the dining hall.

Petrov followed them inquiring of one sister in his halting French where he might shelter the count's horses.

Domitri found himself alone. God had much work if He planned to answer Suzette's prayer. Apparently, Charie would rather brave a blizzard than spend a night beneath the same roof with him.

****

Charie wasn't sure what awakened her. She was alone in a ward that had recently undergone painting and refurbishing, Sister Honoré had explained.

They wouldn't be moving any children in there until the first of the New Year.

So, Charie was alone and hungry and cold and miserable. She wondered if she could find her way to the kitchen and locate something to eat—perhaps just a bit of bread and cheese, for she was becoming uncomfortably aware of the fact she'd not bothered to eat dinner. She knew that Domitri and Petrov were sleeping in the kitchen, but she was certain she could complete her search without disturbing them.

She would tell the sisters in the morning that she'd helped herself from their larder and pay them for what she'd eaten.

Thus decided, she tossed off the blankets that were doing little to warm her and taking up the nearly gutted candle, made her way from the room and down the hall. She found the stairs and descended them easily enough, crossed the dining hall, slipped through a narrow passage and found herself in the kitchen gloriously warm and still smelling pleasantly of the stew the children had been served for dinner.

She didn't bother to look for the cots, hurrying towards a pantry that looked like a good place to store something edible.

Just as she took hold of the latch on the door, a large hand grasped her wrist and hauled her around.

She uttered a low cry, dropping her candle, but the flame immediately extinguished leaving her in the dark with an unknown presence.

Was it the cook—a maid—one of the sisters? Somehow, she doubted any of them would loom over her, as did this individual, nor possess such strength. Then, recognition dawned.

"Domitri, release me," she snapped in a whisper as she attempted to wrest free.

He did as she asked and stepped back. "I thought someone was up to no good, and I was planning to present a food thief to the sisters. Might I ask what you are about?"

"I'm hungry, you oaf," she replied irritably. "I had no dinner."

"I see." His tone was noticeably softer. "I believe there is some cheese in that cabinet, and I believe I saw a loaf of bread on the table. There's milk in the covered bucket just outside the door."

"It's dark in here. I don't see a door."

"Come here by the fire and have a seat before you do yourself or someone else harm."

She resented his tone—the nerve of him speaking to her as though she was a child. But she obeyed and took the seat he indicated near the fire, now able to see the sleeping back of Petrov, who snored.

Domitri left and a few minutes later returned with a mug of icy cold milk, a hunk of bread, and a thick slice of cheese.

Charie took what he offered eagerly and quickly consumed what she'd been given.

Domitri turned a chair around backwards and straddled it watching her.

Self-conscious, she sat the mug down and turning her head, brushed the crumbs from her lips. The experience was humiliating. "Thank you for your assistance. I should return to my room."

"What—and freeze to death? When I touched you earlier, your flesh was colder than the milk. Have you no fire in your chamber?"

"The fire couldn't be lit because the chimney is undergoing some sort of repair. I was given several blankets. But I'm still freezing," she admitted.

"Then sit here by the fire and talk with me."

"I can't do that—my presence might be misconstrued."

"We have loyal Petrov here to act as chaperone."

"There's nothing to talk about." Panic swept her for he was much too close.

The fire defined the chiseled lines of his face, obscuring the ragged scar in shadow.

"Our parting several weeks ago seemed final. I believe you told me you were through with me and the ballet."

"I don't want to speak of that," he replied tersely.

Even though she did, she thought angrily. He'd acted selfishly, inconsiderate of her and all involved in the ballet. She should return immediately to that cold, lonely chamber and suffer through the night rather than stay here with Domitri where it was warm and welcoming. "Then, as I said before, I have nothing to say." Charie stood, as did Domitri.

Once more, he caught her wrist with his hand, his fingers not bruising, but conveying physical determination. Slowly, he eased his hold, but she remained motionless. To her amazement, he raised her hand to his lips and placed a kiss on the back. "You don't have to be cold. Stay here where it's warm. I'll make a bed on one of the dining tables. I've slept in less comfortable places."

"I can't take your cot."

"Yes, you can. Goodnight." His clipped tone conveyed the finality of his words. He walked from the kitchen.

Had she been wrong to snap at him as she had? He'd had his reasons for quitting the ballet. And hadn't she, too, been furious with her mother and the count when she'd learned they'd lied to her?

Looking over her shoulder, she noticed Domitri's now empty cot and with reluctance, walked over to it. Dropping wearily, she only intended to sit. But at some point, she convinced herself it wouldn't hurt to lie down and after drawing the blanket up beneath her chin, she fell asleep.

****

The clanging of pots and the low rumble of sleepy

voices discussing the morning's breakfast preparations awakened Charie. Hastily sitting up and greeting the surprised cook and her help, she explained the reason for her presence, and then quickly rose and shook Petrov awake.

The man was not nearly so easy to rouse, but after the promise of coffee, he managed to sit up.

Hurrying into the dining hall, she expected to find Domitri, but there was no one there other than two of the younger sisters arranging the chairs for the soon to be served meal. Charie inquired as to Domitri's whereabouts and learned that he had left nearly a half an hour earlier.

Looking out one of the long windows, Charie saw that it was no longer snowing and that light was breaking through the clouds to the east. So he was already gone, without so much as a goodbye. Fine, she assured herself. Just as she'd told him last night, she had nothing to say to him.

"That's not so, Lord," she whispered aloud to herself. "I have everything to say to him and I don't know how to say it."

****

"Petrov, stop by *Monsieur* Auberchon's residence before you take me home," Charie requested as the man helped her into the count's carriage.

The sun shined brilliantly; ice and snow glistened beneath its rays, but not strong enough to melt.

She'd just bid the sisters goodbye, received hugs from several of the children, and promised to return with her friends to stage another ballet around Valentine's Day.

But Domitri's early departure bothered her. Perhaps she did have something to say to him, after all.

When she arrived at Domitri's apartment, she found the door unlocked so she slipped inside, heading to the stairs. Sounds emanating from the lower level studio caused her to pause. Pushing the door open with only the tiniest creak, she saw Domitri, dancing. Alone.

He danced as one angered, power and force reflected in his *grand jetés* as he circled the space, his intense expression telling her his thoughts were not pleasant. Even so, his movements both filled and created a void within her that had never before existed. Tears filled her eyes as she contemplated the source of his rage. Was he angry with her? Angry at having lost the love of his life? Anger over the lies her father and mother had perpetuated?

Whatever the cause, there was no mistaking he was a man gripped by emotions both frightening and overwhelming. Then he saw her.

Gasping, she backed away, and then quickly turned, planning to depart.

"Charice."

She knew she should leave as soon as he spoke her name. But she couldn't. Why had she come? To tell him something—that she was angry. That he'd hurt her. That he shouldn't stop living because Sophia died. That he should dance…that he was magnificent and amazing; that she…loved him?

"Charice." His whisper was close to her ear.

"I shouldn't have come. You left without—without saying goodbye. I was angry. You don't have to be rude. You're not the only one who was hurt. You don't understand—" He'd brought her around while she struggled with her words. Her lips fell silent as she gazed up at him, his hair damp and tangled, and partially obscuring one emerald green eye. His shirt, opened at the neck and exposing a glimpse of furred chest, clung to him.

Cupping the side of her face, he drew her closer. Charie could feel his heat through her winter clothing.

"Dance with me." His words were low, his voice husky.

"I can't—not dressed like this. I can't stay. I just wanted to—" Charie fell silent. She wasn't sure what it was she'd wanted to do.

"You wanted to what?" Domitri's tone was demanding, an edge to his words.

"I wanted to know why you left the orphanage and didn't tell me."

"I had no idea my presence or absence mattered."

"It does."

"It shouldn't. Aren't you promised to the baron?" There was no mistaking the derision in his tone.

"I'm not. And I don't plan to be."

"Why?" He placed his other hand on the opposite side of her face.

Her breathing shortened; her heart raced. It was time to leave.

His mouth was terrifyingly, wonderfully close. "Why, Charie?" he repeated softly.

"I—I don't care for him in that way."

His lips brushed the tip of her nose, her forehead, the corner of her mouth. Hovering there, his proximity was intoxicating, threatening to rob her of her last bit of control.

"I know," he whispered, and then kissed her, lingeringly, maddeningly. Thoroughly. When he straightened, Charie feared she would fall. Miraculously, she remained upright. Only because she clutched his wet shirt.

"You…shouldn't have done that."

Domitri laughed bitterly. "For once, I'm in complete agreement with you. It is a painful reminder of how Stanislov women wreak havoc in my life. Go home, Charie. It's time we moved beyond this— attraction, fascination, curious compulsion; whatever you want to call it—we've literally danced around for two months avoiding the truth."

"If that's how you feel, why did you kiss me?"

"Because," he paused as he shook his head, "I'm an idiot."

"An idiot—to care for me? Am I that unpleasant?"

"You're anything but. Please leave now, before I hurt you. Just as I hurt Sophia. She never knew true happiness with me. Nor will you. Go, before I kill your spirit and your joy. Just as I killed Sophia's."

"You're not making sense," Charie persisted, confused by his words. "Sophia was killed in a train accident."

"I was the reason she was on that train. Sophia was running away. From me."

Charie sucked in a breath.

Domitri released her, and then presented his back, walking across the room to the *barre*. Grasping it, he hung his head, his broad shoulders drooping.

As badly as she wanted to go to him to comfort, she couldn't make her legs move forward. Instead, she pressed her gloved hand to her lips to stifle a sob and fled.

****

Charie's tears dried by the time Petrov halted the carriage before the townhouse. On the ride home, she'd considered Domitri's shocking comment from various angles. What had he done to upset Sophia so badly she'd wanted to leave him? How had he robbed her of joy and happiness? How did he crush Sophia's spirit? Why had he said he would do the same to her?

She might have sat there for several more minutes until the opening of the carriage door brought her back to the present.

Expecting to see Petrov, she choked on a shriek when Ernest Altby poked his head within, and then climbed into the carriage. Fear finally loosened her tongue. "Petrov! Petrov!"

"Don't bother calling him." The man was as irritating and annoying as ever. "He has a pistol aimed at him. He won't answer."

"What do you want?" Fright was transforming to anger. How dare this man accost her in front of her home. In daylight.

"At the moment, nothing. I am here to warn you."

"Warn me? About?" Clenching her hands into fists, it was the only way to keep from slapping him. Altby brought out the worst in her.

"Your lack of cooperation."

Charie chose silence, leveling a contemptuous gaze.

He wasn't at all affected by her disdain. In fact, he smirked.

She ended her silence. "I have no intention of cooperating with you or your employer. Now, if you would leave—"

"Anapol Chervenkof is not a man to accept failure.

You are aware of his relationship with your mother?"

Charie swallowed a lump, once more choosing silence.

"Of course, you are." There was that infuriating smirk and a chuckle.

A foreboding chill slithered down her spine.

"There are certain facts, if made public, which would end her career and yours. Though you are young and naïve, you must have some understanding."

Terror gripped Charie. Had her mother conveniently forgotten to disclose everything? What could her mother have done? Surely she hadn't been intimate with Chervenkof. What was Altby trying to say? Worse, what wasn't he saying?

"Why don't you stop playing this twisted game and tell me?"

"Because *Monsieur* Chervenkof thinks the matter can be resolved without embarrassing your mother. Or you."

"It's time that you left, *Monsieur* Altby. We have nothing to discuss."

"But we do. Your father would part with a great sum of money to keep scandal from tainting *Madame* Marin and you."

"You've known all along about my father."

Altby shrugged. "*Monsieur* Chervenkof always gathers his facts."

"Why does he need money? I thought he was extremely wealthy."

"Let's just say, in his business, the more money, the more success. He is involved in several partnerships that require capital quickly, and many of his assets are encumbered. Hence the need to resort to—how do I phrase this—creative methods."

"Charice?"

Turning away from Altby, Charie nearly cried in relief when she recognized Fitz on the stoop of the house as though preparing to leave.

"Fitz," she gasped as she opened the door and hopped out, nearly slipping on the ice. The man hurried forward, and she nearly fell into his arms.

Altby scrambled out on the opposite side.

"I'm so glad to see you."

"Was that the man who works for Chervenkof?"

"Oh, yes. And he was making the most awful threats. Is *Maman* here?"

"I just left her. What sort of threats?" As Charie met Fitz's gaze, the urge to unburden her load lessened. She wanted to speak to her mother first. And Olar. It was incomprehensible that her mother would have compromised her morals. And what were these "partnerships" Chervenkof had formed?

"Chervenkof is still angry because *Maman* left him. He thinks he can make things difficult."

"That's what Altby said?" Fitz's question led her to believe the answer she'd given wasn't the one he expected.

Did he know something more about this nightmare than he'd shared?

"I must go in, Fitz. I'm about to freeze." Charie intentionally avoided answering. She needed time to sort through Altby's insinuations.

"Of course. Allow me to escort you to the door."

Nodding, she accepted his arm.

As they walked up the freshly shoveled walk, she noticed that Fitz turned his head. Was he hoping to catch sight of the obnoxious Altby? If so, why?

Dance Of Life

12

Novgorod, Russia
Late December

Cold, biting sleet slashed Domitri's face as he knelt before the tomb of the Stanislov family, one marker noting that a Stanislov ancestor had been laid to rest here as far back as 1483. The most recent interment, nearly eight years ago, was that of his wife, Sophia Nadina Stanislovna Auberchon.

Doves, etched into the marble of her marker, soared as majestically as she had when she'd danced. But for all her beauty and all the magic she'd created on the stage, there'd been very little of either in her heart. Sophia had never fully embraced the saving grace of Christ. And her life had reflected that, from her selfish willfulness to her insensitivity.

Had he not been so determined to prevent her attendance at a weekend affair devoted to gaming and revelry, they would not have been on that train. And Sophia would still be alive. He would still be married. Would Sophia be a different woman, now? Or would he be a different man?

But that was the past, and on this day, two days after Christmas, which Domitri had spent with his parents in St. Petersburg, he was at Sophia's grave, praying for her. Telling her goodbye. He knew it was time to let go.

Falling in love with Charice Marin had opened his eyes to so many things. And even though there would never be anything more between him and Charie than brief, sweet memories, Charie had unknowingly freed his heart. And for that, he would be ever grateful.

Placing the lilies before Sophia's marker, Domitri came to his feet. If he hurried, he could make the afternoon train back to St. Petersburg even though he'd told his parents he might stay in the country overnight.

In two weeks, he'd be leaving for Paris, just in time for classes to resume at the academy following the celebration of the New Year. A sudden coldness clung to his cheek, and he realized he was crying. Hastily, he wiped away the moisture with a gloved finger.

"Were you going to come and go without so much as a word?"

Startled, Domitri turned to see Olar standing a few feet away, his gloved hands overlapping the top of his walking stick. The sleet attached itself to his black cloak, forming fantastic patterns.

"I didn't know you were in residence at the palace."

Sophia had always laughingly referred to her home as "the palace," never failing to add it was a huge, drafty cavern that she abhorred.

"Matilda and I thought that Charice might want to meet some of her Russian relatives and see the ancestral home. We finally convinced her to come. I believe she has enjoyed the visit thus far. I haven't had a chance to thank you."

"Thank me?" Domitri asked in surprise. "For what?"

"For keeping her and Petrov off the streets that night after the last performance of *Long Ago In*

Bethlehem.

Matilda's housekeeper told us where she'd gone, and I feared Petrov would believe it his duty to try to make it home. Charice explained how you arranged with the sisters to permit them to stay the night."

"I didn't want anything to happen to her—or to Petrov," Domitri quickly added. "I attended the performance that evening."

"And what did you think?" Olar prodded.

"That Charie was wonderful, and Ullavich's performance was flawless if somewhat lacking in emotion."

Olar chuckled. "Spoken like a man who wishes he'd been dancing the role. We were fortunate that Ullavich's commitment altered, allowing him to take the part of Joseph. Aren't you curious as to how things went with *Giselle?*"

Domitri still had no idea who'd taken his place as Albrecht for the final weeks of the ballet's run. "I am," he admitted.

"Rubenevski located Valmiere, who'd been dismissed from another role for throwing a tantrum."

Domitri almost smiled at that.

"He agreed to come back with a huge increase in pay. Things turned out beautifully and every performance sold out. I sent you several messages and an invitation to join me for one of the performances."

Again guilt assailed him as he recalled throwing those missives into the fire unread. "I wasn't in the mood for socializing. But I thank you for thinking of me."

"Come with me to the house. There's going to be a grand dinner for my brother will be joining us. It's rare that Jakob leaves the peaceful confines of the monastery."

"I planned to take the afternoon train to St. Petersburg. I've been with my parents since Christmas Eve."

"I would certainly enjoy having you spend some time with us. Why don't you stay overnight and leave in the morning?"

"I brought very little with me."

"I think I can provide whatever you don't have. Domitri, I fear we parted on bad terms, and that isn't right. Something urged me to come out here today. I believe God is providing a way for us to heal our wounds."

"There's only one way to find out," Domitri said and managed a smile, though his face felt frozen. "You've convinced me to stay."

****

Charie never tired of the gallery, filled with the faces of countless Stanislov ancestors, some of the men possessing an uncanny resemblance to the count—her father—she mentally corrected. Or was it that her father possessed an uncanny resemblance to his male ancestors?

She usually spent afternoons walking along the stone paved hall while her mother napped before tea. Her walk always ended at the small chapel overlooking the garden, now blanketed in snow. The stone walls were adorned with centuries old Russian icons depicting events in the life of Christ, from his birth to his resurrection. Painted in that style in which the figure was in no way realistic, the images surprisingly inspired and instilled peace.

As she slipped within, she was stunned to see a man kneeling before the stained glass, his head bowed. She nearly turned around until something about the set of the man's broad shoulders struck a chord of painful familiarity. Domitri?

As though he sensed someone's presence, he stood and turned.

Waves of hot and cold swept her, weakening her knees. Wrapping her arms around her, she hoped to still her violent trembling. How could he be here? Was her mind and eyes playing some terrible trick?

"Charice," Domitri said softy, his stance statue-like.

Charie remained motionless. "I didn't know you were here."

"Olar found me half frozen in the family cemetery. He invited me to dinner and to stay the night."

"What were you doing in the cemetery?" Ah—Sophia, she silently answered her own question.

"I brought flowers to Sophia. I didn't know you and your mother planned to spend Christmas with Olar."

"They both thought it would be good for me to meet the Russian half of the family." She gave him a wobbly smile. "Have you seen your family?"

"I arrived in St. Petersburg on Christmas Eve to visit my parents. I decided to travel here before returning to Paris. I have two more weeks before classes resume."

"I didn't mean to interrupt," she offered apologetically. "I like to come here—it's peaceful and comforting. I'll be on my way."

"I was about to leave myself so there's no need for you to go. I'll see you at dinner." She nodded as he passed.

He paused at the door and looked back. "I apologize for my inexcusable behavior the morning after our stay at the hospital. I behaved boorishly and selfishly. I know that you had nothing to do with the fact that Olar withheld the truth of his relationship to you. Yet, you suffered my anger."

Charie wanted to tell him how badly he'd hurt her, but she remained silent.

"I can forgive you for everything except the fact that Antoine Valmiere was so distracted during one performance, he trod upon my toes. They still ache."

Domitri smiled ruefully. "I trust the burn on your leg has healed?"

"Completely."

"I'm relieved to hear that." His eyes conveyed genuine concern.

She was touched. "That night at the hospital when you asked me to stay and talk—"

Domitri interrupted, "You told me you had nothing to say to me."

She almost stopped him so that she could finish her sentence — *I was as rude and unfeeling as I've accused you of being*. Something in his eyes—aloofness; dismissal—halted her words.

He continued. "It appears that our emotions ruled our conduct that evening. I would hope it would not be that way with us now and in the future."

That comment surprised Charie.

"Was Chervenkof ever linked to your mishap?"

"The count—my father—says no." She paused wondering how much she should tell him. What could it hurt? "Something else happened the same day after my visit with you. When Petrov delivered me to the townhouse, Ernest Altby was waiting for me. He made more threats."

Domitri's eyes darkened with emotion. "What do you mean?"

"He hinted that *Maman* had done something—questionable." It was difficult to say the word. She still hadn't spoken to her mother of the incident. Though she wanted to know the truth, she was terrified of discovering more secrets. Her world was already up-ended. Yet, she couldn't avoid the matter forever.

"But I'm hoping he'll leave us alone." Domitri frowned as though he didn't believe that would happen.

"*Monsieur* Robert assures me that my mishap was just an unfortunate incident, for there are buckets of water scattered throughout the theatre in the event of fire. Someone could have unknowingly knocked one over."

"Perhaps," Domitri said, his gaze still disbelieving.

Charie swallowed back the fear that threatened to consume. Only recently had she been able to bring herself to dance near that part of the stage where the gaslights were positioned. She now required that her skirts not be so full or quite so long. When she and her mother returned to Paris, rehearsals would begin for the spring production of *The Pearls of Esther*. She hoped to be completely recovered by then—emotionally.

"I wish I'd partnered you for the Christmas ballet," he added softly.

"I wish you had, too." Embarrassed by her honesty, she hurried forward and knelt before the altar, clasping her hands tightly in prayer while Domitri slipped out of the chapel. *Lord, in Heaven, help me*, she silently pleaded as Domitri's steps faded down the hall. *I'm in love with my sister's husband.*

****

Domitri came upon Yuri, Olar's personal valet, in his guest room, brushing off a coat that looked vaguely familiar. He could have almost sworn it was his own.

Yuri answered his unspoken question. "The count had your things moved from the room you once shared with *gospoja* Sophia. Will this coat be acceptable for dinner this evening?"

"Of course. I'd forgotten I'd left clothing here. But my late wife was always shopping for me, trying to polish my appearance." The joke was lost on Yuri, who continued to brush the garment.

Domitri noticed that the man had also laid out trousers, shirt, vest, and cravat on the bed. He was going to look the dandy—as the Americans called fashionable dressers—tonight with his gold brocade coat, buff trousers, paisley vest of hunter green and dark blue ruffled shirt, and cream cravat. He wondered if the ladies present would realize his garments dated back ten years.

After soaking in a wonderfully hot bath, also provided by Yuri, Domitri turned his attention to dressing and within an hour, presented himself downstairs. He was early, so after receiving directions from the Russian butler—Jules was still in Paris with *Madame* Orenska—he joined Olar in his study.

His former father-in-law looked out a large window that revealed the wintry gardens, a frosted fairyland of snow and ice. Olar turned at the sound of his approach.

"You   should   dress   up   more   often,"   Olar

commented wryly. "You cut a very dashing figure."

Domitri chuckled. "I suppose I should thank you for holding on to my things. I'd forgotten they were here. Who knew I'd need them?"

"That's the beauty of a large home. Plenty of places to stash and store things. The ladies will join us shortly. I asked Enriv to send you to me for I have some matters I'd like to discuss."

"And I with you." Noting the dismay in Olar's eyes, he quickly shook his head. "No, I'm not going to ask you why you didn't tell me Charice was your daughter and Sophia's sister. I understand why you did what you did, though I don't agree with your reasoning. That's over. But I spoke with Charie in the chapel, and she told me her accident is still a mystery.

"You know very well that someone dumped the water exactly at that spot so that she would fall towards the gas lamps. Or fall into the orchestra pit and break her neck. If Chervenkof is seeking revenge upon Matilda, that would have been a devastating blow for the woman."

"Which seems logical." Olar said. "I have men watching Matilda and Charie at all times, day and night. There's been no further communication from Chervenkof. Matters most likely transpired exactly as you say, but there's no way to prove it."

Domitri had a brief flashback to that moment when he realized water was on the stage and how the outside curtain had swayed as though someone had been hiding behind it. There was the guilt gnawing at him again. Could he have investigated and prevented the catastrophe?

He should have worked with Olar to find the one responsible for Charie's near brush with death. What if something worse had happened? *Lord, thank you for protecting her, and please forgive me for allowing my anger to rule my heart and mind. I was acting as though I was the one suffering when actually I was only angry with myself for falling in love again. Falling in love with my own wife's sister.*

"It's all right, you know," Olar spoke softly, as though reading Domitri's mind. "You had a right to be upset. As did Charie."

"If I had paid attention to the things I saw, I would have known Charie was your child. You were so protective and nurturing. And there's her nose and that stubborn chin that is a feminine version of yours. I should have seen the connection long before that moment on the stage. When I look back, I feel like a fool because I couldn't see what was right before my eyes."

"Then rejoin the company. Robert and I are still searching for the perfect Ahasuerus. Ullavich wants the part. He did well enough as Joseph in *Bethlehem*, but he's not a powerful enough presence to fill the role of the king. And he is far too full of himself."

"I hardly think I'm the one for the part. I'm sure Charie wouldn't want me, and I can't blame her."

"Charie is a woman of quiet, but strong faith. Why don't you let her decide?"

"It would be difficult for me to dance with her again and conduct myself professionally. I'm," Domitri hesitated, wondering if he should confess to his wife's father, "emotionally involved."

"Forgive yourself, Domitri. I know you suffer guilt over Sophia's death. Sometimes we humans have a hard time forgetting or forgiving, but, fortunately, we have a Savior who does that when we ask, without question or reservation."

"Olar, I don't know if I should tell you this. I know how important Sophia was to you—how much you loved her." He sighed then continued. "I was deeply in love with her, but Sophia was never happy with me. After the newly wedded bliss faded, I fear she realized she married beneath her station. She loved the attention and adulation, and was verbally resentful whenever I received accolades.

"I attributed it to an unavoidable competitiveness, but more and more she'd go out in the evenings and after performances with a new set she claimed as 'friends.' I often returned to the hotel alone. Sophia was drinking heavily, and I blamed myself for that.

"I'm sorry, Olar. I have often thought that if I had spoken to you, together we might have helped her. Perhaps I should have given her a divorce, but when I made my vows to her, I made a commitment for a lifetime. I'm sorry."

Olar remained silent, lowering his head as though pondering the enormity of what Domitri had just shared. When he raised his head, his eyes glistened with tears. "I knew she was willful and spoiled. I suspected she was not living her life as a woman of faith. But I loved her and I hoped for the best. I thought you would be good for her—solid and dependable and possessed of a great love for our Lord. The past cannot be changed, Domitri. Do not withhold yourself from a chance at happiness. We can only hope that Sophia has now found the peace she sought in life."

Silence slipped between them broken only by the hiss and pop of the wood burning in the hearth, each man absorbed by his memories of Sophia.

It was then Enriv entered, informing Olar that his

brother had arrived.

Olar hurried out with the butler to meet his brother.

Domitri turned back towards the fire, aware that it was the beautiful visage of Charie who danced among the flames.

****

Charie hoped no one noticed how she stared at Domitri when they gathered for dinner. At first, she didn't realize he was in the parlor as introductions were made to Jakob Stanislov, her uncle and Olar's brother.

Jakob was about the same height as Olar, but his eyes were blue, and twinkled merrily. He was a bit thick through the waist, but given his loose fitting garments, it didn't appear to be a problem. Once he moved past the shock of discovering a niece, he was eager to hear all about the ballet.

When Jakob directed his attention to Matilda, Charie spotted Domitri lurking in the shadows, as though unwilling to intrude upon the reunion.

Drawing a deep breath for courage, she walked towards him, and then stopped. Handsome and dashing in a coat of gold brocade, her breaths shortened. She was reminded of how she'd felt the first time they'd met at the theatre. Charie feared she presented a drab sight in her gown of gray.

"You look lovely tonight," he said softly, and she blushed.

The gown was fairly new; the bodice sweeping off her shoulders but modestly cut and flowing out into a billowing skirt.

"And you look most dashing." She hoped her comment came across as teasing banter, even though her heart was in her throat. "Who would have guessed you to be so cosmopolite when not leaping about the stage?"

"There are many sides to me you have yet to know," he rejoined.

"Come meet my uncle. He is quite clever and very funny even though he spends all his days and nights behind the walls of a monastery."

"I met him earlier, before you and Matilda came down. I like him—he's much like Olar and is devoted to serving the Lord."

"I don't know if I could give up everything as he has for his faith. He could have been the count. After all, he was the eldest son."

"But he followed his heart, as we all should. May I escort you into dinner? I see Enriv hovering at the door."

"I'd like that," she said and smiled, laying her hand upon his proffered arm. Happy warmth stole over her as they headed towards the others who were chatting lively while following the attentive butler.

****

It was nearly midnight when Olar and his brother announced they were calling it a night, leaving Domitri alone in Olar's study.

Restless and not ready for sleep, even though he'd be up early to make his train, he aimlessly strolled halls and corridors. Passing the parlor, he noticed someone seated near the ceiling-high Christmas tree.

The woman read by the light of a single lamp, and

there was no mistaking Charie. Clad in a velvet dressing gown, her glorious hair spilled over her shoulders.

"Charie?"

She quickly put the Bible in her lap and looked up.

"What are you reading?" Domitri took a seat adjacent to hers.

"Verses in Romans. Shall I read aloud?"

"Please."

"'Therefore being justified by faith, we have peace with God through our Lord Jesus Christ: By whom also we have access by faith into this grace wherein we stand, and rejoice in hope of the glory of God. And not only so, but we glory in tribulations also: knowing that tribulation worketh patience; And patience, experience; and experience, hope: And hope maketh not ashamed; because the love of God is shed abroad in our hearts by the Holy Ghost which is given unto us.

"For when we were yet without strength, in due time Christ died for the ungodly…But God commendeth His love towards us, in that, while we were yet sinners, Christ died for us. For the wages of sin is death; but the gift of God is eternal life through Jesus Christ our Lord,'" Domitri added softly, quoting a much—loved verse also from Romans. "Makes one rethink the important things in life."

"Domitri, may I ask you something—something personal?"

He looked at her, aware that he could deny her nothing.

"Certainly."

"Tell me about Sophia." There was a deep silence as Domitri warred with his emotions—should he give her the sweet version or the truth? Something within him told him to be honest no matter how painful.

"We first met when she joined the Imperial Ballet as a member of the corp. I had been the *danseur noble* for two years.

"Sophia was very good, but not necessarily better than some of the other female dancers. But when she danced, she conveyed this magnetism that drew the audience. Call it charisma, presence, drama—she lured those who watched her into her world, and those she snared were eager to stay.

"I was one of that number. And when she openly returned my admiration, I fell in love. We married three months after I met her. But it was only then that I learned her father was a count and that she descended from centuries of aristocratic Russians. I feared that her father would call me out, but Olar accepted and welcomed me.

"As I grew closer to Olar, Sophia seemed to distance herself. By then she was the principal female dancer for the Imperial Ballet.

"With fame, Sophia's competitiveness escalated until we were at war with each other. She began to drink, assembling a group of friends whose morals and behavior I questioned.

"When I mentioned as much, she laughed at me and spent more time with them. I suggested we seek God's path for our lives, which also amused her.

"Sophia threatened to leave me, but we worked through the discord. Late one night after a performance in London, I found her packing. When I asked her where she was going, she told me she'd been invited to a weekend house party by one of her new acquaintances.

"Angry, I told her she wasn't going; we were going to spend the weekend together and that we would both be on the midnight train out of London—bound for Cornwall. The ballet master had previously offered use of a family cottage in the area whenever we needed some time away. I had turned down the offer until I made that impulsive decision.

"My temper placed us on that train, which wrecked. You know the rest." Domitri pressed his thumb and index finger to the bridge of his nose, fighting back tears.

"How sad," Charie whispered, "for both of you. "Olar rarely mentions Sophia, and I assumed it was because the memories are too painful. He must have ached over her choices."

"He wasn't aware of everything. I didn't want to burden him. I failed Sophia."

"How can you say that?" Charie asked as she reached out and grasped his arm. "It was an accident. You didn't fail her."

Silence slipped between them—not uncomfortable, but one that allowed them both time to make sense of their thoughts.

Finally, Charie spoke. "When you look at me, do you see her?" There was a catch in her voice, which told him it was paramount that he answer truthfully.

"I see a hint of her smile in yours, in the way your eyes light up when you dance. You have her grace and élan. But when I watch you perform, there is no comparison. You dance for the love of it and it shows. Sophia danced to garner acclaim and adulation. That makes all the difference."

"Do you visit her grave often?" Her words were practically whispered, her eyes shimmering with unshed tears.

"I loved her. A part of me still does and always

will. But I realize I married her without asking God for his guidance in my choice of a mate. Had I done so, I would have seen that she did not possess her father's faith, nor did she have any desire to. I pray that with time my heart will heal; that God will keep me strong and help me to move forward. I know I shouldn't blame myself for something I was powerless to prevent. I long for the day I can put that behind me. Next time I will allow Him to guide me to the woman I should wed."

"There will be a next time?" Charie gave him a hesitant smile.

He laid his hand atop of hers. "Before I answer, what of you and the baron?"

"I told you—we are friends. Nothing more. I've seen a different side to him since he's been working with *Maman*. He's very knowledgeable in matters of the theatre. He will travel to Frankfurt with *Maman* the first of February to begin rehearsals for her new play. She's been practicing her German so that she can perform *Das Fraulein ein der Berg* in the country's language."

"The Miss of the Mountain," Domitri correctly interpreted. "And what is the play about?"

"A young heiress wishes to avoid an arranged marriage with a young nobleman whom she's never met and flees to the Alps to live as a simple peasant girl. She falls in love with whom she believes to be an unpretentious mountain man, who turns out to be a prince who's fled from an arranged marriage. You can imagine the problems that ensue when they realize they are running away from each other."

"Your mother should be perfect for the part. But back to Bauerhausen—he has much to offer a woman."

"I don't love him." Her gaze met his, her eyes a shimmering, pale violet that touched something deep and vital within him.

Relief wrapped about his heart.

"I, too, am praying that God will help me find the one with whom I should spend the rest of my earthly life."

Her words gave Domitri hope.

The moment, charged with unspoken desires and dreams, created a companionable silence that apparently, neither wished to break.

Charie shifted her gaze to the windows, and she gave a cry of delight. "It's snowing again. Doesn't it look like sugar drifting from Heaven?" Coming to her feet, Charie hurried over to the long windows.

Domitri followed and stood behind her. The last thing he wanted to do was ruin the sweetness of the moment by succumbing to his desire to kiss her, so he kept his distance and offered up a prayer thanking God for His grace and mercy.

13

Charie knew her actions were brazen and forward, but having spent such pleasurable time with Domitri the night before, she wanted to at least see him off on the train. So rising long before dawn, she dressed on her own, choosing a wool gown of cinnamon edged in bands of copper velvet.

Slipping on her new, pearl gray cloak lined and trimmed in white fox, a gift from Olar, she couldn't resist a quick pirouette before the cheval mirror, and then picked up the matching muff. Noiselessly, she left her chamber, hoping not to arouse her mother who was installed in the suite of rooms just on the other side of hers.

Swiftly descending the stairs, she made her way to the enormous kitchen, finding Domitri breakfasting alone as the head cook, a plump, cheery woman by the name of Freya, fussed over him. She was pouring him another cup of steaming coffee.

Upon sighting her, Domitri stood quickly, his smile warm and inviting.

"Good morning, *gospoja* Charice," Freya greeted. "Where are you bound so early in the morning?"

Charie had no trouble understanding the woman's Russian. "I am going with *Monsieur* Auberchon to the train station, if he doesn't mind?" Charie looked hopefully at him and his smile widened.

"'He doesn't mind. But I fear I must leave

immediately, and you've not had anything to eat," Domitri said.

"I will pack you muffins, cheese, and goat's milk. You can eat and drink on the way," Freya suggested.

"That's perfect. Please tell my mother and the count I'll return as soon as the train leaves for St. Petersburg."

The woman nodded as she pulled a basket off a shelf in preparation of filling it with the promised items.

Within minutes, Charie was seated in the impressive Stanislov coach, a huge gold crest painted on both doors. Charie felt like a princess as she ran her hand over the purple velvet seat.

Domitri placed his small valise on the floor as he took the seat opposite hers.

They were soon on the road to the village, the freshly fallen snow coating cottages and churches with a lovely layer of pristine white.

Charie marveled at how crisp and clear the air was in the country, so different from the large cities in which she'd spent most of her life.

"I have to admit I'm surprised, but pleasantly. What made you rise so early to join me?"

"I thought you might like the company." Charie placed the basket Freya had packed on her lap, eager to sample the contents. "Have a muffin?"

He shook his head. "I couldn't eat another bite. I am appreciative of your company. Olar and I said our goodbyes last night. But I couldn't bring myself to tell you goodbye."

"Rehearsals begin for *The Pearls of Esther* in just a few weeks. Rubenevski is in his usual state because the principal male *danseur*'s role is unfilled. I know things went badly the last time we partnered, but *Monsieur* Phillipe thought we danced well together."

Domitri's brows furrowed as though something she'd said bothered him.

"I wondered if we could try again."

"Olar put you up to this."

Charie was startled by his vehemence.

"He tried to convince me of the same before dinner last night. I should have known there was some reason for your unexpected cordiality."

"My presence has nothing to do with that." Appalled by his assumption, she was no longer hungry and placed the basket beside her. "Your arrogance is exceeded only by your faulty logic. Do you really think I woke up before dawn, dressed in the dark, and ventured out in freezing temperatures just to ask you to take the role of Ahasuerus? You, sir, are sadly mistaken."

"Am I?" Domitri's voice was rough with anger. "I know how badly you and Olar want this ballet to be the most successful of the season."

"I am not Sophia. I am not seeking fame and glory. I do not need to be lauded or honored. I want to dance a role that holds special meaning for me. I've always admired Esther's courage when the odds were against her. I truly believe you and I could do this."

"That's an opinion we'll never share." Domitri's voice was harsh. "When I return to Paris, I'll be teaching just as I planned. I have no desire to perform on the stage. With you, or anyone else."

"Which is just as well, for apparently, you are better suited to instructing inattentive boys how to *plié* and *relevé* while you selfishly hide yourself away in your studio."

"That's a fine thing to say given the fact you've spent your entire life coddled and cosseted. Now, you are a princess, and you believe a man should kiss your hand and be eternally grateful that you have graced him with your presence. Maybe you're more like Sophia than I realized."

"If we continue this discussion, we will say something regretful," Charie said, burning with indignation. The nerve of him to suggest she was manipulating him. She'd rather perform with one of those preening jackanapes who erroneously considered themselves *danseurs*.

"You're right. If we were not so far along, I would take you back to your palace. As it is, I'm not about to miss my train, so you're coming along."

It was a tense, silent drive into the village.

Charie was relieved to see the train was already there, belching smoke and steam as it neared departure.

Once the coach stopped, Petrov came around to open the door.

Domitri didn't so much as glance at her as he took up his small bag. He swung down easily, but once his booted feet were planted on the snowy ground, he retained his hold on the edge of the door. His eyes focused on something or someone in the distance.

"Well, are you going?"

He remained silent, and then to her surprise, he climbed back into the coach.

"What are you doing?"

"Was your mother expecting Fitz at the estate?"

"No. Why do you ask?" His question and manner were puzzling, and she didn't have the patience for whatever game he was playing.

"Because he just disembarked from the train. And his companion is none other than Anapol Chervenkof."

"That makes absolutely no sense." Her impatience was mounting by the minute. "If you don't hurry, you'll miss the train."

"I can't leave you alone with only Petrov for protection. You'll have to come with me."

"I'll do nothing of the sort. I'm returning to the count's home as soon as you leave."

"That's not possible. There's no plausible reason for Chervenkof to be here. And it is less than reassuring to know your mother's agent is in his company. I'm taking you to St. Petersburg."

Before she could utter a protest, he'd reopened the door and was dragging her with him. He quickly explained to a startled Petrov that the count's daughter had decided to accompany him on his trip and that he should tell the count she was well and in no harm.

The dumbfounded man simply shook his head in bewildered agreement while Charie ineffectually attempted to pull away.

She immediately ceased her struggles when she saw Fitz and Chervenkof speaking with several men, Chervenkof's man, Altby, among them. Fear shook Charie as she met Domitri's steely gaze.

"What if they intend my mother harm? We should return with all haste."

"You and I will be in much greater danger if we try to outrace them to Olar's. Besides, there's no way to know their destination. The count has enough servants and guards to dissuade Chervenkof from intruding where he's not wanted. Don't forget the palace was actually once a fortress. Come along. The train is about to leave."

"Domitri, I have to go back. Chervenkof and his men haven't seen me."

Something in his face made her look over her shoulder, and to her horror, she saw that Chervenkof was walking towards them. "Hurry," she cried, panic quickly changing her mind as she clasped Domitri's hand and rushed forward, slipping and sliding on the snow and ice.

When they reached the train, Domitri lifted her and placed her on the top step, leaping up behind her just as the wheels of the train began to move.

Chervenkof began to run, and with a small leap, grasped the handrail in an attempt to pull himself up.

Domitri shoved him back with his booted foot and losing his balance, Chervenkof fell into the snow.

Charie clasped Domitri's arm as they watched the man recede to a small blur. Yet, there was no doubt in Charie's mind that they would encounter him again.

And the next time they might not be as fortunate.

****

St. Petersburg was a hive of noise and activity when Domitri helped Charie from the train, giving her a first look at the centuries' old city, home of the Russian Tsars. It was nearly impossible to take it all in as Domitri led her forward at a rapid pace.

An older man with salt and pepper hair and beard approached, waving energetically at Domitri.

Domitri's hold on her relaxed somewhat— apparently, this man was a friend. Domitri had been grim, tense, and uncommunicative during the entire train ride.

Charie had succumbed to her weariness, falling

asleep and awaking to find her head on Domitri's shoulder. Concern for her mother's safety dulled the edges of her embarrassment.

"*Monsieur* Domitri," the robust man called out in French. "You are here at last."

"I apologize if you came to the station last night," Domitri said. "I told *Maman* I might stay overnight."

"She remembered, but still she sent me. I managed not to freeze."

Charie could tell the man was teasing.

"And who is your companion?" he asked with pleasant curiosity.

"This is Sophia's sister. She, too, is a ballerina. Rukov, please meet *Mademoiselle* Charice Marin."

"It is indeed a pleasure," Rukov said as he bowed. "I hope that you will enjoy your stay in St. Petersburg."

"Thank you." Charie didn't plan on making her stay very long for she needed to return to her mother and Olar as soon as possible. Domitri couldn't keep her against her wishes. "I'm certain that I will."

Rukov assisted Charie into the wagon, seating her on the plank, which formed a second seat, then tucked several blankets about her legs.

Domitri rode beside Rukov, the two conversing easily in a mix of Russian and French.

The ride was short, and the wagon and horses were halted before a towering residence of some four stories, the exterior of off-white stone with rows of long, wavy-paned windows stretching across each floor. A high, wrought iron gate encircled the home and snowy lawn, which sparkled beneath the light of the sun.

Domitri helped her down and followed her gaze as she leaned her head back to see the roof of the residence. "The first two floors are the dance studio and kitchen. The top two are living quarters. Don't be misled—the Auberchons are not wealthy. We have Rukov who maintains our stable, livestock, and our wagon. Inside you will find only Olga, who serves as cook and housekeeper. Without the pupils, we would have none of this."

"It's beautiful," Charie said and smiled. "There's nothing to apologize for."

"It in no way compares to Olar's home, or that of the Baron Bauerhausen's Paris residence. I wanted you to be forewarned."

"I've been duly warned," she returned dryly.

Domitri arched a brow, as though mildly amused.

It disappeared so quickly, Charie wondered if she'd imagined it. Taking hold of her arm, he led her forward, opening the gate and propelling her towards the massive front door. It opened before he ever grasped the latch and a plump, silver-streaked, raven-haired woman took hold of his arm and pulled him in, chattering rapidly in Russian.

Charie didn't so much as attempt to keep up with the conversation as she tried to take in all that she saw—a large parlor that apparently was now a reception and waiting area where several tutu clad girls gathered in a group giggling.

On the other side were doors, some open, some closed, those open filled with children practicing a variety of ballet steps. As they started up the main staircase, a dozen boys ranging in age from six to early adolescence bounded down, some leaping as though they were still in dance class.

Upon reaching the second floor, the woman, who'd never stopped talking, led Domitri to another door and threw it wide.

Charie peered around his broad back in order to see. There in the middle of the floor, in an enormous room that had perhaps been a ballroom in another time, and lined with floor to ceiling mirrors, was a woman of rare beauty. From her ebony hair to her flawless complexion to her intricate execution of a series of *pas de ciseaux*, Charie was amazed.

Six girls, perhaps ten and five or six in age, stood in a corner watching, just as spellbound as Charie.

When the woman was done, she started to address the girls until she noticed those standing at the door. With a happy cry, she flew over to where they stood, the woman enveloping Domitri in a motherly hug and bestowing a kiss on his cheek. Undoubtedly, this was Domitri's mother, and at that precise moment eyes just a bit greener than Domitri's focused on her.

She spoke in French. "Domitri! How naughty of you not to let me know you planned to bring a guest. Who is this lovely young woman?"

"You may have heard of her, *Maman*," Domitri said, and smiled indulgently at his mother. "This is Charice Marin, the *prima danseuse* of the *Ballet Eleganté* in Paris. Charie, this is my mother, Ekaterina Auberchon."

"I suspected as much." Charie held out her hand. *Madame* Auberchon took it and squeezed warmly. "What a pleasure to meet you."

"And a pleasure to meet you. I have heard of you and read of your successes. I know that you are under the protective wing of the Count Stanislov, a very good man. What a joy that Domitri has brought you here."

"You are in the middle of practice, *Maman*, so we will be in the kitchen sampling some of Olga's stew and honey bread. I just wanted to let you know I'd returned."

"And a good thing. We are having your favorite tonight; *kotmis satsivi*, pickled mushrooms, and *kapusta z pomidoramy*. Olga said dessert is to be a surprise. Please have Olga take *Mademoiselle* Marin to the guest chamber so that she can settle in. Has Rukov brought up her trunk?"

"She doesn't have one," Domitri said, and his mother gave him a puzzled look.

"You might say I came with Domitri on the spur of the moment," Charie said and laughed nervously. "I may need to shop for a few things."

Now Ekaterina regarded them suspiciously.

"*Maman*, I will explain everything," Domitri said quickly. "It's a long story, and you must finish your practice. We will talk later."

"Domitri, do not be part of something that is not good. We will talk sooner than later. Now see that our guest is made welcome." With that, they were dismissed, *Madame* Auberchon turning her back upon them with a wave of her graceful hand, to rejoin the girls who were openly staring at Domitri.

Charie looked troubled. "What does she think we've done?"

"Eloped," he answered, and then guided her away from the door before she could set his mother straight.

****

"So you and *Mademoiselle* Marin haven't eloped," his mother repeated.

Domitri glanced over at his father who sat in his favorite, battered leather chair smoking his pipe. His dark head liberally sprinkled with gray, Dominic Auberchon still possessed the lithe grace of a *danseur*. Now, however, he wore the look and manner of a concerned father, and Domitri felt as though he'd been caught stealing from the cookie jar. His uneasiness increased as both parents focused their gazes upon him, and he squirmed a bit in his chair.

"That's exactly what I said," Domitri affirmed. "I brought Charie with me—otherwise she might have been in serious danger. Her mother has made an enemy of Anapol Chervenkof—you both may remember him as Nap Rheyev."

"The last we heard he was in America," Dominic said as he sat up straighter in his armchair. "How is he connected to Charice Marin's mother?"

"Chervenkof courted Matilda Marin, and when she discovered the nature of his 'business,' she ended the relationship. Chervenkof has never taken no for an answer and recently began to make threats against Matilda and Charie. Charie suffered an accident in October that could have killed her. I'm certain it wasn't happenstance. Someone caused the incident, and I should have tried to discover the culprit. Nothing has been linked to Chervenkof. This morning at the station, when I saw Chervenkof with Matilda's agent, I knew something was very wrong. That's why Charie is here."

"So it has nothing to do with the fact you are in love with her?" his mother asked.

"It has everything to do with the fact I'm in love with her." He was terrible at hiding anything from the woman. "I would never have left her at Chervenkof's mercy." He'd already shared the entire story with his parents—how he'd fallen in love with Charice Marin only to learn she was Olar's daughter and Sophia's half-sister; how he'd behaved unprofessionally and ignored all of Christ's teachings.

"Then we will take very good care of her," his mother said in that no nonsense way of hers."

There was a timid knock on the open parlor door, and they all looked around to see Charie standing there.

Domitri and his father came quickly to their feet, Domitri taking note of the lovely frock she wore—a cinnamon colored gown with bands of copper velvet at the collar and cuffs. Gone were any traces of train soot and her hair had been carefully tended.

He walked over to her and took her hand. "Come join us. *Maman*, Papa, may I formally introduce to you Charice Marin, premier ballerina of the *Ballet Eleganté*, daughter of Matilda Marin and Count Olar Stanislov. And Sophia's half-sister," he added softly.

Charie looked up at him, and then just as quickly looked away as she withdrew her hand and approached his parents, dropping into a small curtsy. "It is a pleasure to meet you, *Monsieur* and *Madame* Auberchon," Charie said graciously. "My former ballet teacher, *Madame* Erlaine spoke often of you both, though at the time I never dreamed I would meet you, nor make the acquaintance of your son."

"Dear, dear Erlaine," Ekaterina murmured. "We both trained together at the Imperial Ballet, which is where I met my husband." She looked over at Dominic affectionately. "I hope she is well."

"She was teaching at le *Théâtre de l'Académie Royale de Musique* until she passed away about a year ago."

"I am so sorry to hear that," Ekaterina said sadly. "She was such a good woman."

"I know that my arrival has taken you by surprise, but I thank you for allowing me to stay here."

"You are a friend of Domitri's, which makes you a most welcome guest. Sit here by the fire, and we will chat while we await dinner. Olga is determined that Domitri shall not leave her table in any way other than full."

"She needn't worry," Domitri said and laughed. "I never leave her table any other way. Have a seat here, Charie." He pointed to a low couch on the other side of his father, and she did as he instructed, carefully spreading her skirts, and then clasping her hands in her lap. The fire glinted off the gossamer strands of her hair, picking out the reddish highlights and casting a warm, golden glow over her features. It was with great effort he took a seat some distance from her.

Talk naturally drifted to ballet, Ekaterina very eager to hear the latest gossip on the reigning queens of the ballet—Taglioni, Elssler, Grissi, and Cerrito. As he listened and watched Charie and his parents interact, he was amazed at how easily Charie warmed to them.

Sophia had always been aloof when in the company of his parents, retaining her imagined superiority even when not performing.

But not Charie. She was eager to glean as much as possible from these two as she posed questions on theory and technique. She shared her trials and tribulations experienced during *Giselle* and *Long Ago In Bethlehem* and how she was looking forward to rehearsals for *The Pearls of Esther*.

Domitri remained silent, wrestling with his own guilt and praying God would help him control his tendency to be stubborn and hardheaded.

It wasn't long before Olga summoned them to the meal.

Domitri escorted his mother, and his father led Charie into the dining room.

Olga had outdone herself, Domitri noted as they took their seats. From the *kotmis satsivi*—roasted chicken with walnut sauce—to the *kapusta z pomidoramy*—cabbage with tomatoes, the table was filled with all of Domitri's Russian favorites.

The four of them held hands as Dominic said grace, and then the small group erupted into animated conversation.

His parents' expressions told him they were captivated by Charie, and when his mother asked her to join her on the morrow to assist her with classes, he knew she'd stolen their hearts as surely as she'd stolen his. And all she'd done was be herself—sweet, and open, intelligent and curious.

After dessert, a Russian fruitcake, Ekaterina offered to take Charie downstairs to see the practice studios, leaving Domitri and his father alone.

His father lit his pipe and settled in his favored chair.

"Go ahead and say it," Domitri said, breaking the silence. "I'm a dolt."

"I wasn't going to say that. I was only going to say that if you let her slip away, you would live the rest of your life without the greatest treasure God can give to a man. The love of a good woman."

"She doesn't reciprocate my feelings."

"You won't know unless you ask. Would it not be prudent to find an opportunity to do so?"

"I can't keep her here forever. I know she's eager to return to her mother and Olar."

"Then you should make the most of the time you do have." His father took a long puff, and then blew a ring up into the air, the aroma of the tobacco reminding Domitri of his boyhood and nights spent with his father by the fire.

Even with their demanding schedule, his mother and father had always found time to be his parents. And should he ever be blessed with a child, he would do the same.

Hearing laughter, Domitri's attention focused on the door, his heart singing with gladness when Charie entered with his mother. His father was right. He should make the most of this God-given opportunity.

14

The next morning, Charie found Domitri sitting at the scared kitchen table, the stone floored room lit with winter white sunshine.

Olga hummed and stirred something with a cinnamony scent in a huge pot over the wide hearth, but paused to bid her good morning in Russian.

"Do you think this could be posted," she asked as she extended the letter she'd written last night to her mother and Olar after retiring for the evening. She'd tried to explain the confusing situation and assure them she was safe and well in the home of the Auberchons.

Coming to his feet, Domitri took the letter from her and gave her a smile. "I'll ask Rukov to do so first thing. I trust you slept well?"

"I did." Charie returned his smile. "But I fear I must be directed to a dressmaker today in order to replenish my meager wardrobe."

"Nonsense," came Ekaterina Auberchon's voice as she moved gracefully into the kitchen, bestowing a kiss upon Domitri's cheek, hugging Olga, and then taking hold of Charie's hand. "I have plenty of things from which you could choose. I am a bit thicker about the waist but we are about the same height, are we not?"

"I couldn't possibly impose upon you in such a manner."

"Of course you can. I will turn you into a Russian

gospoja for a few days, and Domitri will lose his heart all over again."

Charie knew she blushed, but she nearly laughed aloud when Domitri colored.

"So we will eat, and then we will dance with the children. Afterward, Domitri will show you about our lovely old city."

It appeared the matter was settled and as Olga was now filling bowls with what looked to Charie to be oatmeal, she took a place at the table.

Monsieur Auberchon soon joined them, and talk turned to plans for the day. It appeared that both *Monsieur* and *Madame* Auberchon would conduct dance classes until early afternoon.

Then *Monsieur* Auberchon was to pay a visit to the Imperial Ballet to work with Christian Johansson on his new ballet.

Charie knew of Johansson, who had once partnered Marie Taglioni, and then chose to remain in Russia. Charie wondered if she dared ask if she could accompany *Monsieur* Auberchon. As though reading her mind, Dominic spoke to her directly.

"Would you and Domitri like to join me? I believe Katra"—Charie knew this was Dominic's pet name for Ekaterina—"said she wanted you to see something of the city, Charie."

"I would love to watch *Monsieur* Johansson rehearse," Charie said eagerly, drawing a dark look from Domitri. Could it be he was jealous? "I've heard he is an amazing *danseur*."

"So they say," Dominic replied, trying hard not to smile. "I'll let you be the judge. Now, I must have one more slice of Olga's wonderful bread, and then I'm due downstairs."

"As am I," Ekaterina said as she hurriedly finished her tea. "Charie, you will join me?"

"Of course. Might I ask to borrow something more appropriate to wear?" She had donned her same wool gown, which would never do for practice.

Ekaterina released a silvery laugh. "Let's see what I can find among my things." Ekaterina stood.

Charie did, as well, excited and amazed that she was actually enjoying this unexpected adventure in the home of such warm and gracious people.

If only Domitri could be so approachable.

****

"Were you as impressed as you expected to be?"

Charie looked over at Domitri, who was driving a borrowed sleigh through the wintry Russian twilight, and considered his question.

They'd just left the theatre, Dominic still working with Christian Johansson whom Charie had found to be charming and technically excellent. But he fell far short of Domitri's intensity. Why did she always find herself comparing other male dancers to Domitri? And found all lacking.

"You saw him—he's competent and conscientious."

"The sort of *danseur* who would make a good Ahasuerus?"

Charie noticed that a muscle twitched in Domitri's jaw as he awaited her response. "My answer would only lead to an argument."

They were passing the Alexander Column, erected in honor of the Russian defeat of Napoleon and positioned in front of the Winter Palace. The monument was surmounted by the angel of peace and also served as the entry to the General Staff building, opposite the palace.

"I have no wish to argue. There's a little daylight left. Why don't I take you to Decembrist's Square?'

"Isn't that where a revolution took place?" Charie asked, trying to recall Russian history lessons from at least eight years earlier when she routinely sent her governess into fits of despair.

"You might say that." Domitri grinned, and then launched into a more detailed explanation about the officers who tried to oppose the accession of Nicholas I to the throne and ended up either executed or banished.

After passing the square, they headed towards the Peter and Paul Fortress, erected to protect the Neva River delta, and the cathedral. Domitri explained how Peter the Great had chosen this site on the Gulf of Finland to erect his grand city; a man who had tried not to be a tsar and often labored alongside his men as they built what became St. Petersburg. As they traveled past his bronze statue, erected by Catherine the Great, darkness descended quickly.

Domitri suggested they return to the theatre to see if his father was ready to leave, and deliver the sleigh Domitri had borrowed from the ballet's director.

Dominic was awaiting them and after turning the sleigh and horse over to a stable boy, they transferred to the Auberchon wagon.

Domitri guided the horses home.

Upon arriving, they found dinner ready and waiting, Ekaterina looking beautiful in native garb; a heavily embroidered blouse covered by an intricately ornamented sarafan. Her dark hair was braided and looped festively.

After exchanging greetings, they took their places at the more formal dining table.

Domitri was asked to say grace before Olga began serving.

Looking about the room, Charie realized it was equivalent to the dining salon in the Paris townhouse she shared with her mother. The furnishings were less ornamental and more practical in construction. Fashioned of heavy, dark wood, the grained surfaces gleamed from polishing. Drapes of burgundy damask, tasseled in silver, hung at the four long windows and the seat coverings were of a burgundy and silver toile.

A small icon of Mary and the infant Jesus was centered over the sideboard and on the opposite wall hung two beautiful paintings of ballerinas, reminding Charie of Mira's talented beau, Pierre.

He had promised to have Mira's painting completed by the first of the year, and Charie could hardly wait to see it.

Matilda had easily persuaded Olar to find better accommodations for the young man, and he now resided in a habitable flat with a good north light not far from the theatre district.

Olar had commissioned him to paint Charie in a costume from *The Pearls of Esther*, and Pierre was beside himself with delight.

As Olga ladled and scooped generous portions into each plate, Charie couldn't help but note how different dining with her mother was, where one course was delivered and eaten, and then another brought out in tedious succession. She much preferred this more informal and unpretentious serving manner. It allowed the diners to begin eating sooner.

"So, what did you think of the classes?" Ekaterina asked, directing her question to Charie.

"Your pupils are very talented," Charie said, and then smiled at Olga, who filled her goblet with cold milk. "I enjoyed working with them."

"Then you must help me again tomorrow. They were much more attentive with you present. Although they've heard of you, they never expected to meet you. I am sure that is all they talked about after class."

"I should like her to help with my classes on the morrow," Dominic said, a mischievous light dancing in his eyes. "Should not the young men have the privilege of dancing with so pretty a partner?"

Charie nearly choked on a bit of cabbage in her soup, and Domitri laughed.

"Those lads would do well to focus on their ballet and not a pretty ballerina," Domitri said. "From what I saw today, many of them need more focus."

"As does Christian Johansson." Dominic sighed. "His head is too full of how wonderful and incomparable he is and how he danced with Taglioni. He could do with a come down to earth."

"If anyone can help him do that, it would be you, Nici," Ekaterina said affectionately.

There was no mistaking the deep love these two shared, and Charie envied them. If only her parents had managed to work through their differences and not divorced. But there was no need to wonder what if—she'd been most blessed by God and had always known how much her mother loved her. And now she knew her father loved her just as much.

"What did you think of him, Charice?" Ekaterina asked, her gaze cutting quickly to Domitri, who was pushing the food about his plate.

"He was most charming upon our introduction, and quite the accomplished *danseur*," Charie admitted. "But he reminds me of a preening bird, his feathers spread to reveal all their glory with little substance behind the display."

"My thoughts, exactly," Ekaterina agreed. "But I am biased because I believe no man can dance as well as Domitri."

"*Maman*, you are truly blinded by your devotion. There are many fine *danseurs*. What of Perrot?" Domitri asked.

"What of him?" Ekaterina scoffed. "He, too, struts and preens. Of course, he's good, and he knows it. Now you, my son, dance from the heart. You should be back on the stage before you are too old."

"Son, she's right," Dominic said, his eyes serious and his brow wrinkled. "You are wasting your talent teaching Russian to those unruly, undisciplined boys who have been indulged and pampered by wealthy parents. You should be sharing your joy of dance with the world."

"You both sound like Olar." Domitri shook his head, the natural curls at his nape brushing his collar. "My recent attempt at a comeback was less than successful. I am more suited to teaching. Let's not speak of this."

Honoring his request, talk turned to other things, but Charie couldn't help but dream of dancing again with Domitri. The few times they'd partnered had been so marvelous it was difficult not to desire the experience. But that was impossible, so she would have to be content with memories of how it had felt to be in Domitri's arms.

****

Ekaterina took Charie into the bedchamber she shared with her husband on the morning of the New Year's Eve and pulled articles of clothing from an old armoire, tossing them upon the bed. "Chose anything you wish. I rarely wear these things."

Bright silk and intricately embroidered linen garments littered the bed's patchwork counterpane, and Charie laughed in delight as she held up first one item, and then another, looking at herself in the long cheval mirror. There were sleeveless jackets of gold and scarlet and sarafans of a variety of colors and patterns. The blouses were festooned with embroidered flowers, hearts, and whimsical doodles.

"This you must wear for the new year," Domitri's mother announced as she drew a blouse, jacket, and sarafan from a silk wrapping. Of an ice blue fabric, the sarafan's bodice and hem were decorated with silver leaves, petals, and vines. The blouse, of white silk, was also trimmed with silver and the jacket was of silver. It looked royal enough for a princess.

"I couldn't possibly," Charie gasped. "What if I mussed it somehow?"

"You will wear this," Ekaterina announced firmly. "And this." She withdrew a headdress from a large box, Charie oohing as Ekaterina placed it on the bed.

Tentatively, Charie reached out to touch the intricate confection of silk, pearls, and ribbons. "This is a *kokoshnik*," Ekaterina explained. "I wore this when my parents announced my betrothal to Nici. Please say you will wear this tomorrow night."

"I don't think I can refuse," Charie said and laughed. "This is like waking up one morning and discovering you are a princess." Braver now, she took up the *kokoshnik* and placed it on her head, taking a look at herself in the mirror.

"You are," Ekaterina said softly. "Has not Olar told you that his blood is mixed with that of Tsar Ivan III and that Stanislovs have been rewarded and honored in countless ways by many Russian rulers?"

Charie turned to the woman in surprise. "I knew that the Stanislovs were of the nobility, though I wasn't sure in what way. But that doesn't change who I am."

"That is because you have a sense of direction and purpose and a deep love for our God and Savior in Heaven. Always hold on to that, no matter what. Now, it is time to go down to the studio and welcome our little girls. Change here and I'll be waiting for you downstairs." Ekaterina kissed her cheek then let herself out of the spacious room.

Charie couldn't resist another look at herself, and then uttered a low, girlish squeal of pure delight.

****

Ekaterina left Charie alone to finish up a class that was running longer than its scheduled time while she moved on to the next class, directly across the hall.

Charie enjoyed working with these girls whose dream was to one day be chosen by the Imperial Ballet.

Most were the daughters of middle class parents with fathers who were merchants or professors or attorneys able to afford the lessons. A few were daughters of lesser nobles and one was the child of a third or fourth cousin of Tsar Nicholas I.

They all seemed eager to learn and improve, and as Charie watched the last two slip from the practice studio, she couldn't help but recall her first days of training with *Madame* Erlaine.

A small smile crept across her face as she turned away and glided across the floor. The more she danced, the more she lost herself in the joy of the movements, slipping solo into the *pas de deux* from *Giselle*. Unexpectedly, she felt a presence behind her and when a firm, roughened hand grasped hers, she knew it was Domitri.

Neither spoke, moving in harmony with each other, perfectly mirroring the concentration and intensity the steps required. Charie soared among the angels and clouds, swept along on a wave of bliss. How much more wonderful was the *pas de deux* with Domitri than it had been with Antoine Valmiere. With Antoine, she had merely gone through the motions. With Domitri, each step brought her closer to a majestic peak from which she hoped never to descend.

Then, the end was upon them and just at that moment when they would have separated in the performance, Domitri lifted her in his arms and circled the room, bringing them both to a slow, gradual stop. Dropping to one knee, he still held her in his arms, his lips so close to hers she could feel the warmth of his breath brushing her skin.

Pulling out of his arms, she came up on one knee, facing him eye to eye, nervous anticipation curling inside her as she wondered if he would kiss her.

Gently, he cupped her face and tilted her head, her heart pounding frantically. Could this be—?

"Here you are," Dominic Auberchon called out far too cheerily. "Charice, I want to present you to my young men."

Charie and Domitri leapt to their feet, Charie self-consciously pushing back loosened tendrils.

"Yes, of course. It would be a pleasure." Charie hurried towards the door, but paused momentarily to look back at Domitri.

He was smiling—that sort of smile that passes between a man and woman when they realize they have found their one true love.

And that made her smile.

****

"You are wearing the look of a man besotted," Dominic commented from his worn chair by the fire while rings of smoke curled up from his pipe, the rich aroma permeating the air. "I hope I didn't interrupt anything too terribly important earlier today?" There was a teasing note in his father's voice.

Domitri forced his attention from the door to Dominic. Why did it take women so long to dress? He inwardly fumed. He'd been hoping that Charie would appear for what seemed like hours.

"You interrupted nothing other than a marriage proposal," he said, causing his father's brows to rise. "I was going to ask Charie to marry me."

"You are a smart man. You'll have another chance."

"The moment was right—" Domitri's words trailed off.

"And your inconsiderate father interrupted. I hope you will forgive me."

"There's nothing to forgive. Perhaps, the time wasn't as right as I believed it to be. Charie may still be uncomfortable with the fact I was married to her half-sister. When I learned Charie was Olar's daughter, I struggled with a sense of wrongness—that it was a sin for me to be attracted to Sophia's sister; to love her more than I loved Sophia."

Silence slipped between them, Domitri focusing his gaze on the flames in the hearth.

"You know that isn't so."

Domitri nodded. "I'm praying that God will help me let go of Sophia. I want to know His will for me."

"Perhaps He has placed Charice in your life for a reason."

"I don't know. I want to believe He has. I've sensed a change in Charie since coming here."

"She has confessed her love?"

"No. But I'm sure she cares."

"Have you told her how you feel?"

"Not exactly. But surely she knows."

"What is the saying, Domitri—the Americans use it often—don't count your hens before they hatch?"

"It's 'chickens,' Papa," Domitri corrected. "Not hens. Is this not the New Year when amazing things can happen? I will trust that God will open her heart to me."

At that very moment, Charie and Ekaterina chose to enter the parlor, and though his mother was lovely in her sarafan of purple and gold, Charie robbed him of all thought and reason, a regal princess in her pale blue and silver.

Domitri came to his feet and met her, taking her hand and lifting it to his lips. "You are beautiful." He was breathless.

She smiled and blushed.

"You look quite the Russian," she said, smoothing her hand over his silk shirt of brilliant blue.

"So we are at last ready to go to the cathedral?"

Dominic asked as he stood. "If the two of you had tarried any longer, we would not be able to find a seat." He spoke gruffly, but his manner was teasing.

"Hush, Nici. We have plenty of time, and we will find a place to sit. Come, get your cloaks and hats. I'm sure Rukov is ready."

They complied and a few minutes later, with Rukov driving and Olga seated beside him, the group set off for the cathedral in the Peter and Paul Fortress.

****

Charie wanted to giggle at the contraption on Domitri's head, a fur hat of some sort with flaps that covered his ears.

As though he sensed her close perusal, he turned towards her.

"You don't like my *ushanka*?" he asked in feigned hurt. "I'll have you know this is the latest in Russian men's fashion."

"I see." Charie shoved her hands further into her muff. "Well, if it's keeping your ears warm, that's all that matters."

"Actually, just having you beside me warms me."

Charie blushed.

Fortunately, they had reached the cathedral so she was spared a response to Domitri's comment. Lamps and lanterns illuminated the soaring spire of the cathedral, which was topped with an angel holding a cross.

Charie tilted her head back so she could see to the very top of the spire. She almost lost her balance, but Domitri's steadying arm saved her a spill and she smiled gratefully.

Even though most of Russia had already celebrated the New Year several days earlier in accordance with the Julian calendar, the church was filled to capacity.

Charie had never been inside any building as amazing as the Peter and Paul Cathedral, the final resting place of Russian tsars and their families; gold and gilt in abundance, a lofty interior that made one instinctively raise their eyes and lifted their spirits. She was speechless for the first few minutes after they took seats in a pew located at the rear of the cathedral, until Domitri whispered in her ear.

"You're behaving like an American tourist."

That brought her back to the moment at hand. "I am an American tourist. So I have every right to gawk and stare. I noticed that you did a bit of the same when we first entered."

"I can't help it. Every time I enter, I am struck anew by the architectural marvels. This place is amazing, but I feel a communion with the Lord in any house of worship."

"So do I. But how amazing and unexpected to usher in the new year with you and your parents. I just hope *Maman* has gotten my note by now so that she won't worry and will have a wonderful New Year with the count."

"I'm sure she has, and I'm positive they will both have a marvelous celebration."

Charie slipped her arm through his, and snuggled a little closer, willing to forget for the moment that Domitri had once been her sister's husband. Could her love for him ever erase that fact?

15

When Domitri and Charie left the church, snow was falling.

Dominic and Ekaterina were speaking with acquaintances while Rukov and Olga headed back to the wagon.

Taking Charie's arm, Domitri led her towards one of the fortress's walls and after helping her climb the steps, guided her to a high ledge providing a snowy vista of the Neva River.

"It's so beautiful," Charie whispered. "Like a scene in a ballet. Here I am surrounded by snowflakes high above the kingdom with my devoted—" She abruptly fell silent and turned her face away.

Gently, Domitri took hold of her chin and forced her to look at him. He suspected she was crying, but couldn't be sure. "Your devoted admirer?" he suggested lightly.

"Are you, Domitri? What of Sophia? Can you separate the two of us?"

"You're nothing like Sophia."

"But I fear—" Charie suddenly stopped and walked away, her attention fixed upon something in the distance. "Over there, in the light of that courtyard," she pointed to a lone woman who stood with arms wrapped about her, a small valise tucked under her arm. "That woman is wearing an ermine cloak much like *Maman*'s. If I didn't know better, I would say it is—"

"Chervenkof," Domitri uttered in disbelief as a tall man joined the woman. "What is he doing here? And could that truly be Matilda?"

"I'm positive. Domitri," Charie clutched his arm. "What should we do?"

"I pay them a visit." He spoke with more assurance than he felt, but the last thing he wanted was for Charie to be alarmed. He prayed for guidance, but at the moment, confronting the two seemed to be his only choice. Undoubtedly, Chervenkof was threatening Matilda in some way. Where was Olar?

"You're not going alone. If it is Chervenkof, that could only mean something bad has happened. I'm certain that's *Maman*. I'm going with you."

"Charie, please…"

"I'm going." She stomped her boot clad foot.

Looking up to the heavens, the snow still drifting lightly, Domitri wondered if he might see some sort of sign, but none was forthcoming. Time was wasting so he made a decision. "We'll go together. But you must do exactly as I say."

Charie nodded.

Taking her hand, he hurried across the wall and descended the steps closest to where Matilda and Chervenkof stood.

A man stepped out of the shadows and shouted at them—a man whose voice sounded very much like Olar's.

Halting, Domitri looked directly at the man, aware that Charie clutched his arm. Before he could positively identify the new arrival, three more men ran towards them. "Run, Charie. Now!"

To his relief, she complied and lowering his head,

he plunged into the advancing men. Two fell back, sprawling in the snow, but the third kept his footing and slammed his fist into Domitri's midsection.

A woman screamed as he stumbled, but regaining his balance, he launched an attack at his still upright adversary. As his fist shot out, he sent the man reeling, but one of the two who had fallen earlier had regained his feet.

Domitri rushed him and landed a solid blow to the man's bearded jaw. The man slipped, skidded, and then dropped on his bottom, yowling as though he'd twisted or broken a limb. Turning back to the other two, Domitri considered his options, aware he couldn't continue to fight two brawny men alone. God would simply have to show him what to do.

Then he thought of his hat, the one that had given Charie so much amusement. Whipping it off, he flung it, smacking the man closest to him, catching him by surprise. The attacker stumbled and tripped over the yelping man who clutched his leg. The two hopelessly entangled, but Domitri ignored them as the light from the streetlamp glinted off a knife wielded by his third attacker.

A threat of this nature hadn't confronted him since those days of his youth when he'd been forced to defend himself against members of Chervenkof's old gang. But the instinct to survive pulsed strongly—he had every reason to want to live, to marry Charie, and spend his remaining days, however many that might be, loving her.

The man swiped at him, and Domitri jumped aside. But the jump cost him his footing, and he hit the snow and ice hard, his arm aching from the severe jar. Before he could recover, the knife swiped far too close to his throat and he rolled over. Leaping up, he twisted around, his fist shooting out as he did so, knocking the man's arm aside. The hit loosened the man's grip on the weapon, and it flew through the air. Domitri employed one of his ballet leaps and kicked, striking the man hard on his shin. Sinking to his knees, the man grasped the injured area.

Whirling about, Domitri suddenly stopped, face to face with Chervenkof, who held a pistol.

Beside him stood Ernest Altby, holding tightly to Matilda.

Matilda was deathly pale, and her lips moved as though she was praying.

"How fortunate that you and Charice decided to join us this evening," Chervenkof said. "It allows me to tie up loose ends."

"What are...you doing?" Domitri managed between harsh breaths.

"Something I should have done years ago when my mother and I lived in an apartment with no heat, and you lived in a grand house wearing tights."

A sob drew Domitri's attention.

"We received a note stating he was holding you and Charie hostage," Matilda spoke through her tears. "Olar and I brought the money he demanded."

"I told Petrov to let you know Cherie was with me," Domitri uttered hoarsely.

"He was stopped on the return home and given Chervenkof's note with instructions to bring it to us. Petrov was so distraught we couldn't make sense of his tale."

"What of Charie's letter?"

Matilda looked bewildered.

Domitri focused his glare on Chervenkof. "I

suppose you needed a lot of money quickly so you lied and frightened Matilda to obtain it?" He made no attempt to keep the disgust from his voice.

"It worked. Come now, Auberchon; don't cause problems. You've seriously injured three of my best men, and I wouldn't be surprised if they seek retaliation. We can join Charice, who I believe is keeping company with my employees you've yet to mangle."

Domitri knew he had no choice so he walked forward, all the while his mind furiously searching for a way out of this nightmare.

It came quickly and unexpectedly. Six guards from the Winter Palace—Domitri recognized their uniforms—converged. Domitri grabbed Matilda and shoved her down in the snow, and then turned on Chervenkof, thrusting the man's arm up in the air in hopes of dislodging the pistol from his grip. The two wrestled for control of the weapon, and then it exploded.

A painful fire raced through Domitri's upper arm, and he knew he'd been shot.

Chervenkof reached into the waistband of his trousers to remove another pistol, surely primed and loaded, when another shot echoed in the night that was no longer still or quiet.

Wild shouts and yelling filled the air and voices babbled in several different languages.

Unexpectedly, Chervenkof dropped to the snow, his second pistol now falling from his hand as he clasped his upper thigh, the gun discharging as it hit the snow.

Not sure who'd come to his rescue, Domitri snapped his head around.

Olar, his valet, Yuri, and two palace guards headed towards him as rapidly as the snow and ice would permit.

Olar reached him first.

"Charie?" Domitri asked raggedly.

"She's fine and so is Matilda. We thought you and Charice were Chervenkof's hostages."

"That's what Matilda said." Domitri clasped his injured arm tightly.

"Let's get away from here. This isn't the way to start the New Year."

"Considering the fact I'm alive, I think it's a wonderful way to begin the New Year," Domitri said even though cold seeped into his bones and his teeth chattered. He managed to remain upright as he walked with Olar and the two guards.

As they neared a group huddled in shadow, a figure broke away and ran to him.

"Domitri," Charie cried and flung herself into his arms. He winced and she quickly stepped back. "You've been hurt. Oh, Domitri." Charie's voice broke and clasping his face in her hands, she kissed him.

His head felt too heavy to hold up and his legs too weak to support him. Suddenly, he pitched forward, robbed of the opportunity to savor Charie's kiss.

****

"*Maman*, stop fussing over me." Domitri issued his complaint from bed, confined to it for the past three days. He hated feeling helpless and weak, and as long as he lay in the bed, he couldn't feel any other way. "I am not a child."

"You are acting like one," his mother pronounced,

planting her hands on her hips. "You are worse than your father whenever he is unwell. And that is terrible."

"I want to be up."

"The doctor said four to five days of rest. Domitri, you were shot. You need to give yourself time to heal."

"Aren't you needed downstairs?" he asked irritably, ignoring her comment.

"Charice is doing quite well with the classes, as she has for several days now."

"You're keeping her from me. You do realize I intend to make her my wife?"

His mother arched one finely shaped brow. "She has agreed?"

"I haven't formally proposed. Chervenkof interrupted me before I had a chance. And I haven't had a moment alone with her since."

Every time Charie came to see him, she was always with someone—his mother, his father, her mother, or Olar. He was beginning to wonder if she did so intentionally. But she'd kissed him that night he'd been shot as though she would never let him go. Then he'd fainted.

"Don't fret, Domitri. I'm sure you'll get your chance." His mother leaned over and kissed him on the forehead. "Olar sent word earlier that he and Matilda are coming by to visit. Do try to be sociable and not a grumpy bear when they arrive." His mother left, and he soon drifted to sleep.

A knock on the open door roused him.

Olar and Matilda were standing there.

"Your housekeeper said to come up, but if you need to rest," Olar began.

Domitri shook his head emphatically. "If I rest any

more, I shall turn into a worthless lump. Please come in and keep me awake and functioning. I wish the doctor had never said I was to have complete bed rest. I was only shot in the arm."

"I thank God you are doing as well as you are." Olar smiled as he took a seat in the chair nearest the bed.

Matilda seated herself on an old settle that had once graced the parlor when he was a child, still bearing traces of his scuffs and spills. "Chervenkof, on the other hand is not faring as well. I believe he is suffering complications from his wound, and he doesn't have the best accommodations."

"My only hope is that while in prison he will rethink his life's direction." Domitri spoke sincerely. Perhaps this was God's way of giving Chervenkof another chance. "Olar, I was in such pain the first two days, I'm not sure I have the story straight. You said Chervenkof sent you a note asking for money in exchange for Charie's and my safe return."

"The morning you left, Freya told us Charie accompanied you to the station. It was several hours later when Petrov delivered Chervenkof's note to us," Olar said. "He was so terrified, we couldn't make sense of anything he said. Then Markham arrived. He'd been threatened by Chervenkof, who forced him to leave Paris and take him to Matilda. According to Fitz, when they reached the station, you and Charice had just arrived in the carriage. Chervenkof recognized the crest, and then saw the two of you. Fitz managed to slip away from Chervenkof and found another way here."

Matilda picked up the story. "Chervenkof wrote that he would hold you and Charice until Olar provided a sum equal to two hundred and fifty thousand American dollars. He wanted me to deliver it to St. Petersburg, depositing it outside the gates of the Peter and Paul Fortress at midnight of the New Year— the Gregorian new year. The two of you would then be released."

"You hadn't received Charie's letter, so you couldn't know she was safe," Domitri said, and then pressed his lips tightly as he pondered Chervenkof's cunning. The man had a cruel knack of manipulating one's insecurities to his advantage.

Olar spoke. "According to those who have questioned Chervenkof, one of his arms suppliers changed his mind about selling him the guns. However, Chervenkof had already been paid for his brokerage services. When the supplier failed to fulfill his end of the arrangement, the buyers wanted their money back. Hence Chervenkof's desperation. He knew I'd give him any amount of money to protect the two of you. Chervenkof knew I was Charice's father when he courted Matilda."

"I can't recall letting that information slip," Matilda said. "But my maid, Lizzie, knew about Olar and so did Fitz. Olar told Ludwig Bauerhausen when the baron announced his intentions to court Charie."

Domitri physically winced at that revelation.

"Anapol could have easily overheard a conversation I had with any of them when I wasn't aware he was listening. I've sadly discovered Anapol routinely woos wealthy women, flattering them into parting with large amounts of money to finance his illegal activities. This is my fault. I'm so sorry you were shot."

"I've been told I'll live," he said and grinned

ruefully. "Although my shoulder aches as though I've lifted five ballerinas at one time."

"Take care of that shoulder so that you can lift at least one in another month."

"Olar, I'm not taking the role of Ahasuerus. I don't want to mix my professional life with my personal life. Charie and I shouldn't spend every moment of every day and night together."

"What do you mean?" Matilda asked, confused.

Olar gave a low chuckle. "I think he's trying to tell us he plans to marry our daughter. But I fear she's unaware of his intentions." Olar leveled Domitri a piercing gaze. "Have you proposed?"

"I haven't had time. My every attempt has gone awry. I would ask her this minute if you'd allow me to sneak out of here and not tell my mother or Olga."

"Don't rush anything, Domitri." Olar's look was troubled. "Charice is still unsettled by Chervenkof's extortion attempt, and I fear she's never completely recovered from the fire. We're returning to the estate tomorrow."

"Tomorrow?" Dismay filled Domitri. "Is Charie leaving with you?"

"She is," Matilda replied softly. "When your doctor releases you from his care, come to Olar's. We can spend time together and return to Paris on the same train."

"I was hoping—" His voice faded. Perhaps somehow this was God's will, too. Olar was right—Charie had been through a difficult time, and perhaps it wasn't appropriate to ask her to marry him now. He would be patient and wait. "I'd like that if Olar doesn't mind having me under foot."

Olar laughed. "You know you're more than

welcome in my home. Once you're declared fit, you'll have your chance to court."

Olar's words reassured until Domitri faced Charie's departure the next day. He shamelessly bullied Rukov into sneaking him to the station, managing to reach it just as the Stanislov contingent headed towards one of the passenger cars.

Charie saw him, and leaving her parents, ran to him as quickly as the snow would permit. "I can't believe your mother allowed you to leave the house." Pleasure was written on her beautiful face. "I thought our goodbye last night was all we'd have."

"It wasn't much of a goodbye. I wasn't able to do this." Domitri kissed her with all the longing and promise that filled his heart, overjoyed when she responded with equal enthusiasm. If there was ever a reason for him to hurry his recovery, he was holding it in his arms.

"*Ya lublu tebya*, Domitri Auberchon," she whispered in Russian, and then kissed his cheek. Pulling away, Charie hurried back to Olar and Matilda, Yuri, and Markham Fitzhugh.

They all waved, but then quickly boarded the train, which gave every indication it was about to pull away.

Domitri stood there and smiled like a silly schoolboy, watching until the train was a distant speck and his face was practically frozen.

She told me she loves me.

****

Charie wasn't sure what prompted her to visit the Stanislov cemetery, the final resting place of her ancestors. As her feet crunched on the ice crusted snow, she read the names aloud. According to Olar, most of them left honorable legacies. Some, such as Sophia, shined in the glow of fame fleetingly and unhappily. Passing between elaborate markers and opulent mausoleums, she finally located the one she sought. Frozen lilies lay atop the stone, and Charie knew Domitri had left them there. Had it been a week since she'd left him in St. Petersburg? It felt like years.

Thrusting her hands deeper into her muff, she gazed upon the tomb of her half-sister. It was difficult to remember what the woman had looked like, but Charie would never forget the way she danced; the way Sophia and Domitri moved as one.

"Am I wrong to love him, Lord?" Charie's voice echoed around her, the only other sound that of the wind weaving among the icy limbs. She had never known greater terror than when she realized Domitri had been shot. Shot because he'd involved himself in her and her mother's problems with Anapol Chervenkof. What if he'd been killed and it was his grave she now stood before?

Hearing footsteps, she quickly turned. She didn't recognize the approaching man, and planned to move on until he looked up.

Ernest Altby.

Her heart raced and her body shook. She should never have come so far from the house alone. Freya had suggested she take someone with her. Now, it was too late. It would never do for Altby to sense her fear.

"Why are you here?"

"To complete our unfinished business."

"How did you elude the authorities in St. Petersburg?"

"They weren't interested in me; only in Chervenkof."

"My father might have something to say about that." Charie hoped her words conveyed assurance.

Altby laughed.

Apparently not.

"We are the only ones here. This time you will listen to me. Do not think that Chervenkof's current detainment will be permanent."

"If this is about money—"

"It is always about money." Altby snarled as he closed the distance between them.

Charie tamped down the urge to flee. She'd never outdistance him in the snow even though he was overweight, encumbered as she was with heavy boots, layers of petticoats, a wool gown, and her fur-lined cloak.

"My father isn't going to pay Chervenkof."

"Perhaps it is as you say. But there is another who would."

Instantly, she thought of Domitri. Though he would do anything to help her and her mother, Domitri wasn't wealthy.

"The Baron Bauerhausen."

"What?" Charie wanted to laugh at the absurdity of Altby's statement.

"You heard me. The baron is backing your mother in her newest endeavor. Should the public suddenly discover Matilda Marin is not what she seems, he stands to lose a lot. If no one attends her play, the baron will not recoup his investment."

"What could my mother have done that you would use against her? There's no crime in ending an engagement with a criminal."

"Miss Marin, you may not realize this, but there is no legal recordation of your birth. Inquiries have revealed your mother journeyed back to the states while she awaited your arrival, hiding out in a small country town." *Her hometown in Virginia.*

Charie knew this part of the story. "No doctor attended the birth, and no father was documented on anything legal." The words struck terror. Still, she had to appear strong.

"My mother had recently divorced the count and for personal reasons, didn't want him to know of my birth. The count has now claimed me as his daughter."

"Not legally or publicly. Should it come to light that your mother engaged in an illicit affair; a child resulting from the union, she would be positioned most unfavorably."

How many times had she and her mother been shunned by women of society because their professions—actress and ballerina—made them unacceptable? Matilda had always told her to hold her head high and be proud of God's gift. Now Ernest Altby threatened to destroy her carefully nurtured self-esteem. Worse, he threatened to ruin her mother with lies. What if there was some truth to his words? Secret marriage—secret birth—

"But you needn't worry. It's a well-known fact Baron Bauerhausen holds you in the highest regard. Should you ask, I'm sure he would provide the funds to keep your mother's tawdry secret undiscovered and protect your pristine image. It's rumored he is enamored of you, which you could use to your advantage."

"I will do nothing of the sort. I want you to leave. Now." If only Domitri was here—

"I will give you a few weeks to consider my suggestion. If you don't, the Paris newspapers will have all of the details, and then some concerning your questionable parentage and subsequent secretive birth. I daresay in light of these revelations, even Count Stanislov might reconsider parting with some of his ancient gold."

"Neither I nor my mother will tolerate your threats. The authorities will deal with you just as they've dealt with your employer."

"Don't delude yourself, Miss Marin. Men such as Chervenkof succeed because they operate outside of the law. I've warned you. Now it's up to you to do something. Soon."

Having uttered that one dreaded word, Altby turned and walked away.

Shaking uncontrollably, Charie attempted to move. But her legs lacked strength, and with her first step, she stumbled, falling against her sister's crypt. Staring down at her name, tears seeped from Charie's eyes and dripped upon the marble, freezing in the process. Charie feared her heart and soul were just as frozen.

****

After what seemed like hours praying in the chapel, Charie found the courage to seek her parents. Coming upon Yuri, she learned that the count and her mother were in the library. After thanking him, she hurried towards the room, afraid she would lose her nerve before unburdening herself of the terrible weight she carried.

The door was partially open, and their voices came

clearly to her ears. Unwilling to intrude, she hesitated. Words of personal regret tumbled from them both.

"I am so sorry, Olar." Matilda's voice was tearful and uncertain. Gone was the clear, precise speaking voice of the actress. "I can't imagine what I was thinking—encouraging Anapol as I did. I was lonely; afraid of the future. Charie would have her own life. I have made a mess of things."

"No more than I. In these last few days, all of my mistakes have surfaced, taunting me. I indulged Sophia, who needed a strong, guiding hand. I divorced you. I hid the truth from Charice. In all of the important matters of my life, I never once sought God's direction. Faced with the possibility of losing Charie, I fell to my knees and cried out to the Lord. And He answered my prayer."

"And He has answered mine. But this is far from over, Olar. I am so afraid—" Her mother's voice faded.

Olar lowered his voice. "Hush, my love. We will work through this together. With God's help. We are powerless to do anything without Him. I am no longer a threat to you or Charie. I am here to help you. To help us."

"You were never a threat, and I was so wrong to keep you from Charie. I thought you might try to take her from me, especially after Sophia's death. Deep inside, I never stopped loving you." There was a long pause.

Then Olar cleared his throat. "Matilda Marin, I love you more now than I did in those long ago days. I will do anything in my power to protect you and our daughter. But I have a feeling our little girl has another fierce protector. Domitri loves Charice, Matilda."

"I know," Matilda replied softly. "He is a good

man even though I tried to discourage Charie's admiration. I once thought she should accept Lugwig's attentions." Matilda laughed sadly. "I didn't want her to fade into Sophia's shadow. I know now it's not that way with Domitri. Olar, I've been thinking about the new play."

"What about it?"

"When it ends, I'm giving up the stage. I'm two score and two. When I'm on a stage, I can pretend I am the ingénue. But up close—"

"You are a beautiful woman—"

"But it's time to bow out. Gracefully. I'm thinking of returning home."

"Home to Virginia?" Olar's tone conveyed his distress.

"That is my home."

"I can think of another."

Her father's voice dropped lower and sensing her parents needed complete privacy, she quickly turned away. This was not the time or place to tell them of Altby's lewd threats and insinuations. Did the circumstances of her birth matter? God knew the truth. Was her primary concern for her mother? Or was she more worried that her reputation would be shredded by the revelation? What of Domitri? She couldn't drag him into this sordid situation. The embarrassment—the shame. Why would he want to be linked to a ballerina labeled a—

Charie couldn't bring herself to say the word. Tears filled her eyes and she hurried down the hall through the gallery, not giving so much as a glance at her noble ancestors. So far as the world was concerned, they weren't her ancestors, nor was she the daughter of Count Olar Stanislov. She was just a dancer—and everyone knew how dancers were.

Her head down and eyes flooded, it was no wonder she ran into something.

Someone—tall, firm of chest and smelling of sandalwood. And a hint of pine-rosin?

She raised her head. "Domitri?"

He laughed, looking rested and recovered, the only evidence of his wound the sling that cradled his arm. Slipping his unhindered arm around her waist, he drew her close as though to kiss her.

Pushing back, she broke the embrace.

His brows lifted in surprise.

"Why are you here?" The words escaped her lips before she could think what to say.

"Olar invited me. Charie, what's wrong?" His surprise had been replaced by concern.

"Nothing. I'm glad to see you."

"You don't seem glad. You seem—troubled."

"I've been thinking about Chervenkof and my mother. I can't allow him to hurt her."

"Olar won't permit that."

"The count can't control everyone or everything. He's not invincible."

"I'm here for you, too. There's so much I wanted to say to you in St. Petersburg, but never had the chance. I've wasted more than seven years blaming myself for Sophia's death. I cannot say I was happily married. I loved Sophia. I would not have left her, for I believe marriage vows should be honored. But God chose otherwise. And I see things so much clearer. I know that I love—"

"No, Domitri." Charie shook her head emphatically, the tears returning. "You've no idea what's happened—what will happen. I don't want you to be hurt any more than you have been. What is between us—it can't go any further. Not until—"

Domitri's eyes reflected a suspicious glassiness. "You told me you loved me."

"I shouldn't have. Not that I don't. But things have changed. And I don't want you involved. This isn't your concern."

"Anything that concerns you is my concern." His words were rough and angry. He caught her arm and pulled her against him. "Tell me what's happened."

"I can't." Wrenching her arm free at painful cost, she fled, determined to stay the course. This was a problem she'd handle on her own. She'd find some way to satisfy Chervenkof and preserve both her and her mother's reputation.

16

Bewildered and angered by Charie's reaction to his arrival, Domitri considered leaving. His empty apartment in Paris held decidedly more appeal at the moment than Olar's lavish home where he was certain to encounter one very beautiful, but infuriating woman.

Yet, if he stayed, perhaps he could wear down Charie's resistance. He would convince her of his love and that there was nothing she couldn't tell him. It was a matter of earning her trust—making sure she understood Sophia's memory would never come between them. Then, he would ask her to marry him.

As Domitri unpacked with Yuri's help—not that he had much to unpack—he decided to visit the chapel before seeking Charie. He hadn't spent much time in prayer of late, and he had much to be thankful for—Charie, his life, his rapid healing, Olar.

And in a strange way, Anapol Chervenkof. Had he not chosen this time to reappear, Domitri might have remained tangled in regret and self-pity. As it was, the threats the man made to Charice and Matilda forced him from his carefully constructed cocoon. God had brought him and those he loved safely through a terrifying situation and in the process helped him realize how important it was to have love in his life.

Domitri recalled the verses he'd read just that morning from Colossians, "*And above all these things put on charity, which is the bond of perfectness. And let the peace of God rule in your hearts, to which also ye are called in one body; and be ye thankful."*

What if God didn't intend for him to wed Charie? Was he patient enough to await His plans for him? Contemplating a life without Charie was painful, but if he'd learned anything through Sophia's death, it was to trust and have faith that God would guide him in life's choices.

After sending Yuri off, he headed towards the chapel, pausing in his journey to look at the portraits that lined the gallery, amazed at the facial similarities of many of the Stanislov males, including Olar. They all possessed that same determined chin and clear-eyed gaze that bespoke of fortitude and courage. And though Charie more closely resembled her mother, he could see the same determination within her. He'd experienced it firsthand.

"Charice, my *liebchen*."

The words came through the open door of a small sitting room, which overlooked the garden, clothed in wintry white.

Domitri turned and walked to the room. Peering within, he was stunned and dismayed to see none other than Ludwig Bauerhausen with Charie.

She had apparently thrown off her cloak of sadness, for she was smiling up at him from her comfortable seat by the fire. She held a book.

"Ludwig, this is a surprise. I didn't know you were planning to visit."

"My visit is admittedly spontaneous. I found myself missing you during the holidays, and I realized I've become more than fond of you. I simply couldn't await your return to tell you."

Domitri's heart plummeted. So the baron was resuming his courtship. He, an impoverished instructor and *danseur* had very little to offer Charie. The awful truth was that the baron was actually likeable and would undoubtedly see that Charie was pampered and cosseted as she deserved. Domitri still didn't like him.

"I am truly flattered. It is good to see you—"

"But you didn't miss me as much as I missed you," Bauerhausen said and shook his head. "It appears I've conducted my relationships in a far too haphazard manner and am now beginning to reap unpleasant rewards. I've been reading the Bible—" he paused when her mouth dropped open.

If Domitri hadn't been so despairing, he might have laughed at Charie's reaction.

"There are many verses in the Book that point out all the things I've done wrong."

"Recognizing that means you're that much closer to finding the Savior," Charie said. "We've all done things 'wrong' at one time or the other."

"I've committed many deeds and entertained thoughts for which I need to ask forgiveness."

"And God is just waiting for you to ask. It won't hurt—I do it all the time. And you never stop doing things or thinking things that require forgiveness. His mercy is always available and endless. But once Christ comes into our lives, we want to live differently and honor Him." Charie bestowed one of her glorious smiles upon the baron.

Domitri's heart twisted and tore. He couldn't best a reformed rake who obviously adored Charie and would do anything for her. Who could afford to do anything for her and would see her elevated to unequaled status in the world of ballet. Bauerhausen had eliminated the one thing that would have kept Charie from ever seriously considering his suit—his indifference to Christianity. With that chasm bridged, it would be easy for Charie to fall in love with a man equal to her own newly elevated social status. She was no longer just an American ballerina—she was distantly related to the Russian tsar, and her father was a count.

Moving away, Domitri continued to the chapel. Once within, he dropped to his knees before the rail, so overwhelmed and disheartened he didn't know where to begin. "Help me, Lord. Please help me."

In the stillness of the moment, words returned to him spoken by Olar shortly after Sophia's death.

"You must never give up," he'd insisted. "No matter how impossible it seems, you must push forward. It is the Lord's admonition to us. To fight the good fight, to stay the course, and to keep the faith. I believe in you, Domitri. This is not the end."

Standing, Domitri drew a deep breath. He would not give up. He loved Charie, and now was the time to tell her. This was one fight he must win. Leaving the chapel, he retraced his earlier steps. Rather than lurk outside the door and eavesdrop, he entered. He was immediately sorry.

****

"Domitri Auberchon is one very lucky man. I wish you the best, Charice."

"Why do you say that?" Charie swallowed hard as she met Ludwig's amused gaze.

"The man is wildly in love with you even if he

hasn't told you as much."

Charie laid the book aside she'd been reading when the baron had found her. It was just as well he interrupted. She hadn't been able to focus on the words she read, replaying the frustrating minutes spent earlier with Domitri. Wondering where she could obtain the money to make Chervenkof leave them alone. As she looked at Ludwig, she knew she wouldn't encourage him in order to obtain the funds. In her heart, she knew God expected better of her.

"I'm not so sure. But, I'm thrilled you are looking into spiritual matters." Truly heartened by his words, she stood and impulsively hugged him. Just as approaching footsteps echoed on the marble floor. Releasing Ludwig, she looked up, her heart jolting.

It was Domitri, and it was distressingly clear from the look on his face he'd misconstrued what he'd seen.

****

The ache spreading through Domitri as he watched Charie move out of Bauerhausen's embrace was a hundred times more painful than the bullet he'd taken in his shoulder. It required an unimaginable strength to quash the impulse to smash his fist into the baron's face. But that would never do no matter the appeal the act held.

"Domitri, Ludwig surprised us with a visit." Charie's voice was far too merry. Closing the short distance between them, she took his uninjured arm. "He was just telling me he's been reading the Bible. Isn't that wonderful?"

"Yes, it is," Domitri managed, though his jaw tightened in rage. "How fortunate that you've sought the Lord's guidance at this point in your life."

"As the Bible tells us in many places, it is never too late. But now if you'll excuse me, I must look up Matilda. I'm hoping she may resolve some questions the couturier I engaged to design the play's costumes has about a specific gown. I shall see you both at dinner." He bowed in that grandiose manner of his, and then turned sharply, his long stride taking him from the room.

"Domitri, I know what you're thinking." Charie looked up into his face, her expression earnest and open.

What was he thinking? He wasn't even sure. He only knew he wanted to take her in his arms and kiss her. "You don't owe me an explanation, Charie."

Her eyes clouded, and he noticed that her lips trembled as she released his arm.

"I'm not romantically involved with Ludwig."

"Everyone would prefer that you were. He's obviously a suitable marriage prospect—he has a title and wealth; he's cultured and extremely versed in all the arts. He can finance and advance the careers of both you and your mother. And you've turned him into a believer."

"That should make you happy, as well, Domitri. Christians are always happy when another joins the fold."

"If they are doing so for the right reason. I simply can't help but question his motives."

"Then perhaps you need to look within yourself for I wonder about your motives. You seem to believe that the things that were important to Sophia are important to me. They aren't, and if you don't realize that by now, we can't even be friends. I'm almost glad you saw me with Ludwig. It makes me see how closed-minded and obstinate you are."

"Have you shared your 'concerns' with Bauerhausen?" Domitri was pushing, but at the moment the hurt overrode his sense.

"Not that it's any of your business, but no."

"That's the problem. Your concerns are mine. Why can't you understand that?"

"I told you I don't want to entangle you."

"Maybe I want to be. I don't want to be your friend. Whatever it is that has you running away—"

"I'm not running away," she interrupted, tears filming her beautiful eyes. "I'm handling this as best I can."

"Whatever it is that has you running away," he repeated impatiently, "Chervenkof, your parents, your career, I want to help."

"You can't," she cried. "You wouldn't understand."

"You're right—I wouldn't understand. I don't want to understand. I thought I loved you. I loved a dream; an illusion. A perfect princess. You aren't any of those things."

Her tears fell harder and faster.

Turning away, he warred with his conscience—desire—need—God's will.

"You owe Ludwig an apology."

Her words swept away all instincts to make amends and repair the emotional damage. As he walked away, words resounded in his mind. *God, in Heaven, what have I done?*

****

Paris
January — 1846

"I cannot believe you are asking this," Nicolai Rubenevski declared dramatically as he paced his office. His arms lifted above his head, he shook them in emphasis to his words.

Charie sat next to Olar whose aggravation was evident in the twitching of his silver mustache. Charie was actually amused by the unfolding drama—the matter of locating a *danseur* for the role of Ahasuerus.

Normally, Olar allowed Rubenevski, Phillipe, and Robert to haggle over who they wanted for the key roles, but this time he'd decided to invoke his right of final say in filling the principal roles. Declaring all candidates heretofore presented for the role as unsatisfactory—among them Ullavich, Johansson, and Perrot—he now demanded an open audition.

Unheard of, Rubenevski had declared only seconds earlier.

"Well, I am, and the sooner the advertisement is sent out the sooner we can select an appropriate partner for Charice. I have extremely high expectations for this ballet, and I do not want to accept second best for the spring production."

"You are proving very difficult, Count Stanislov," Rubenevski exclaimed. "What does Robert say to this?"

"He says I am paying the salaries so I should have my say. And it is your job to fulfill my request."

"The finest and most talented you have already turned down. Who do you think will respond to this advertisement?"

"The right man," Olar replied, unruffled, and

Charie had to restrain a giggle. He came to his feet, tucking his cane beneath his arm. "I am sure that you will find a way to have the open audition advertised in tomorrow's journal. Now, Charice has an appointment, and I have promised to escort her. Good day, *Monsieur* Rubenevski." Olar gallantly held out his hand to Charie and she took it, rising gracefully.

Once outside of the small office, Charie gave in to her laughter as they walked across the cluttered back stage. "You were magnificent, *Papa*." She had begun calling him such over the holidays, surprised at how natural it slipped off her tongue. "You managed to push *Monsieur* Rubenevski into one of his Russian rages."

"You are actually telling me I was very bad. And I was. But I am not happy with Rubenevski's recommendations."

"Don't you believe God will send us the right man?"

"Of course, I do. But it wouldn't hurt to help Him. That's why we're holding auditions." Olar led her down the rear steps of the theatre, the Stanislov coach awaiting them.

Charie was to have her first portrait sitting at Pierre's new studio and as her mother had left for Germany two days earlier, Olar had insisted on accompanying her.

Mira would meet them, and after the session ended, the four planned to lunch together.

Charie's mood was lighter today than it had been in several weeks. Not that she had put Domitri out of her mind, but she couldn't continue to cry and mourn for the rest of her life. With rehearsals about to begin, she could focus on something other than her parting with Domitri. How could Domitri have misconstrued her hug with Ludwig? His assumptions aggrieved and disappointed. As if she would marry any man because of a title or money. Domitri's insistence that he could solve her problems was insulting; as though she didn't have sense enough to work things through on her own. Not that she had.

Altby's threats were never far from her thoughts. She knew the man would return any day now. And after ceaseless prayer, Charie still had no answer. Perhaps it was time to confide in her parents. But what of the consequences? Niggling deep inside was the knowledge she needed to ask Domitri's forgiveness.

"And that is why," Olar's words drew her back to the present as he settled across from her in the carriage, "we will only settle for the best."

****

The afternoon passed pleasantly, Olar escorting Charie, Mira, and Pierre to an elegant and expensive restaurant with a spectacular view of the Cathedral of Notre Dame and the Seine. The meal and company proved so delightful, it was with reluctance they left the establishment.

Olar instructed Petrov to return Pierre to his atelier, Mira to the apartment she shared with Heidi, Helga, and Vionette, and Charie to the townhouse, now very empty without the presence of Matilda.

Madame Jeaneau met her at the door, the new maid, Brigetta, standing just behind the older woman. Brigetta was Lizzie's niece, recently arrived from Sweden and in search of gainful employment while she pursued her dream of singing in the opera.

Matilda had engaged the girl upon Lizzie's recommendation, and Charie enjoyed Brigetta's company for the two were not so different in age. It was only to be a temporary arrangement until one of two things occurred—Matilda returned or Brigetta was hired to sing in the opera. But for now things were working well.

"*Mademoiselle* Charice, *Monsieur* Fitzhugh is waiting for you in the parlor," the housekeeper informed her.

That was a surprise for Charie believed Fitz to be in Germany with her mother. She hadn't seen him since returning to Paris after the holidays. Fearful something had happened, she tossed her hat, gloves, and reticule on a chair in the hall and hurried to the parlor. Once there, she found Fitz standing by the warming hearth, looking into the flames. He turned at the sound of her entrance and gave her a smile. That reassured her, and she quickly calmed.

"Fitz, aren't you supposed to be in Frankfurt with *Maman*?" Charie asked as she slipped off her cloak.

Fitz, forever the proper gentleman hurried over to assist.

They took seats opposite one another and close to the fire.

"I'll be leaving in a few days. There were some business matters I needed to complete. After doing so, I can devote all my time and energy to Matilda."

"So what brings you here?" Charie had always liked Fitz and enjoyed his company. At one time, he'd given her the impression that he wished to court her, but he was several years older than her mother. Charie had never entertained so much as one romantic thought concerning him, so nothing had come of it.

Whether it was her mother or Olar who had dissuaded him, his overt friendliness had dimmed, though he was always pleasant and professional, just as he was at the moment.

"I wanted to affirm that all was well with you. I know you've been left in the count's capable hands, but Matilda always worries about you. After the accident on the stage—"

His words faded as she recalled that terrifying night, inwardly shuddering. She hadn't thought of it lately, consumed with thoughts of Domitri. But now it rushed back with frightening clarity.

"Well, I wanted to let you know I'd be in the city for a few days more in the event you need anything."

"That's most considerate of you, Fitz. But I'm well and everything is fine. Thank you for your concern."

"Well, it's the least I can do. You know where to find me should you require my assistance. I'm at the same hotel. By the way, I heard that Auberchon refused the part of Ahasuerus."

"My father suggested that he would be good in the role, but Domitri is adamant about continuing his teaching duties at the academy."

"It's probably just as well given his temperament. There you were that night of the first performance of *Giselle*, shocked and terrified by the accident, and all he cared about was the fact you were Sophia Stanislovna's sister. The very nerve of him to march off the stage as though he was the one who's clothing had caught afire. If anyone had a right to throw a tantrum, it was you, dear girl." Fitz shook his head as though deeply saddened.

Yet, something in Fitz's manner struck Charie as insincere. Obviously, he was no admirer of Domitri.

"Did *Maman* tell you about it—the fire?" As she recalled Fitz hadn't been present that evening. Yet, he knew the details. Especially those concerning Domitri.

"Of course. Did they ever discover how the water came to be on the stage?"

"Unfortunately, no. I try not to think about it, especially when I've got to get back up on that same stage very soon."

"I know that you will do splendidly, as always. Remember I'm here if you need me." He rose and Charie did as well, escorting him to the curtained opening of the room. He took her hand and bowed over it. "Hopefully there'll be no mishaps with the new ballet."

"Thank you," she said, oddly troubled by his words.

Madame Jeaneau was waiting for him at the front door and Charie watched him leave. The housekeeper turned to her with a smile.

"How very considerate of him to stop by to see how you are faring. Your *maman* would be most pleased to know he'd done so."

"Yes, she would." Uncertainty hovered at the back of Charie's mind as she wondered if Fitz's visit had been prompted by something else. What that could be, Charie had no idea. It was something she could have asked Domitri were they still speaking.

Turning to the stairs, she made her way up and walked to her room, finding Brigetta within it folding back the coverlet on her bed. The girl gave her a smile and a little curtsy.

"Has the gentleman left?"

Charie nodded as she went over to her vanity and took a seat on the richly upholstered seat. "Have you ever had a feeling something is not as it should be?" Charie asked.

"Many a time when my brothers are up to no good." Brigetta laughed.

"Exactly—when they are up to no good."

"Is something amiss, *Mademoiselle* Charie?"

"I don't know." Charie sighed. "Brigetta, what would you do if you'd hurt someone that you truly cared for and caused that individual to miss out on a wonderful opportunity to do something he loved?" Charie could see Brigetta repeating the question to herself as her lips moved.

"You offended a dear friend, so this friend will not do something that he should do. Is that right?"

"Yes," Charie confirmed, amazed the girl had made sense of her confusing words.

"Then I would go to him and tell him he should not lose this chance because the two of you are angry with one another. And if I was wrong to be angry with him, I would tell him so."

"Thank you, Brigetta," Charie cried happily as she came off her seat and rushed over to the girl, hugging her tightly. "That is exactly what I'll do."

17

Domitri thought it odd that his ballet students were huddled together reading aloud the morning news journal. Entering his studio that Saturday morning so silently no one heard his arrival, he moved up behind his pupils to see what held them enthralled.

The article capturing their attention was an advertisement for a ballet audition. None other than for *The Pearls of Esther*.

Shocked and without thinking through his actions, he reached out and snatched the paper from the boys. He quickly scanned the words, proclaiming dramatically that there was an international search for a *danseur noble* to fill the role of Ahasuerus. What sort of trick was Olar playing, for surely he was behind this?

"*Monsieur* Auberchon," Michal Devone spoke, "may we have our journal back?"

Domitri roused himself enough to realize what he'd done. There were eight questioning faces focused on him. Slightly embarrassed, he handed the newspaper back to Michal. "I'm sorry. I shouldn't have snatched it as I did. But, gentlemen, it is time for class to begin. You can read the paper afterward."

"*Monsieur* Auberchon," another boy spoke up as he took his place with the class. Gerard happened to be the tallest and oldest of the group at ten and five years of age and the most talented. "Do you think any of us would have a chance at this audition?"

"I would never discourage any of you from pursuing such an opportunity," Domitri replied in what he hoped was a tactful manner. "But they may be looking for a *danseur* of a certain age."

"What age would that be?" Michal piped up.

"I really couldn't answer that," Domitri evaded, feeling suddenly a little too warm. And too old.

"Surely not as old as you," Gerard said innocently. "If you weren't old, you wouldn't be teaching."

"I'm teaching because I choose to teach, not because I have to."

"My *maman* says you were once a great *danseur*," another boy commented. "She saw you perform here in Paris with Sophia Stanislovna a long time ago."

It wasn't that long ago, Domitri thought in aggravation. *I've got a lot of dancing left in me.*

Then use it, a voice urged and he looked around for the source.

The boys were staring at him, and he grew warmer. "I am not so old that I can no longer perform."

"Then you should audition," Michal suggested. "You would be dancing with the beautiful Charice Marin. My *granmere* took me to see her in the Christmas ballet. She was wonderful. We would all like to dance with her." There was a unanimous round of shaking heads.

Something akin to jealousy flared within Domitri.

Charie even had schoolboys in love with her.

"I have other things that occupy my time. One of those things is this class, which we must begin immediately. Enough talk of auditioning. If you wish to audition, I give each of you my blessing and my heartiest best wishes." That seemed to force them back to reality and after a small bit of grumbling, he had their attention and class commenced.

The truth of the matter was, Domitri did want to audition, and as he sat at the kitchen table late that evening, after Muzette had tidied up and gone to bed, he reread the advertisement. After his morning class had ended, he'd run out to buy his own copy of the journal and now slowly and carefully perused the announcement.

Why was Olar doing this? Domitri had heard through various gossip channels that Perrot would dance the part of Ahasuerus, but clearly something had happened to change that. How many would audition, and could he seriously compete for such a coveted role?

There would be much younger men vying for the part, each of them aware that securing such a plum role could launch their careers and lift them from obscurity. Rumor had it that an American had taken Europe by storm over the past several months, and it was quite possible he might prove to be Domitri's competition.

Casting the paper aside, he rose from his chair and after meandering through the dark, empty rooms of his apartment made his way downstairs. He ended up in his studio with a single oil lamp burning and he simply stood there, waiting for the voice he'd heard earlier.

No voice spoke, but something powerful spoke to his heart telling him this was something he needed to do. He was in love with Charice Marin, and this could be his last chance to tell her.

Besides, he thought with grim humor, he had yet to tell her he'd apologized to Ludwig Bauerhausen. That hadn't been easy. Even now, he could still taste the bitterness of humbling himself before the amused and conceited baron that morning before he'd left the palace. Even so, the act had allowed him some measure of peace, and taught him to curb his tongue in the future. It was a lesson he would not soon forget.

But the other side of reason shoved to the forefront of his thoughts. He'd refused the role, and he had no right to believe he would be reconsidered even if he auditioned. In all of his years of dance, he'd never before struggled emotionally as he did now.

He'd never walked away from a role no matter his state of mind or degree of agitation, and he'd never declined a role and later changed his mind. What had he allowed himself to become? As temperamental, uncooperative, and egotistical as several of the *danseurs* he'd often dismissed as unprofessional. He would be doing Charie a favor if he never subjected her to his presence again. Her career was destined to soar no matter who partnered her.

Such were his thoughts the following Monday as he stood before his class of irritatingly restless boys, unsure why they were so fractious that morning. Admittedly, mastering Russian was most likely their least favorite task, but they had no choice as long as they were in his class.

Two of the most talkative today were also his dance pupils, one was Michal, his head leaning towards Gerard's as they whispered back and forth.

Domitri rapped his desk sharply with his pointer.

They quickly separated and sat up in their chairs, hands folded upon the scared wooden desks.

"Would you, Michal and Gerard, care to share your conversation with the others? Or were you discussing the review topics for our test tomorrow?"

Both boys looked at one another, and finally Gerard stood and spoke. "We were wondering if you were going to audition for the ballet—you know the one advertised in the journal."

"I was told I'm too old," Domitri reminded him, trying hard not to smile. He insisted on firm discipline in his classes, and it would never do to let one or two boys sidetrack him. "And this is not ballet class. This is Russian class. You will sit down and read the first paragraph on page 160."

Obediently, Gerard took his seat and quickly began to read as instructed.

Domitri followed along in his text until a knock on the door caused Gerard to stop. Wondering who was about to interrupt what had already proven to be an hour of irksome interruptions, Domitri went over to the door and threw it open, certain his expression would tell whoever it was he was greatly displeased. His mouth opened to express his annoyance, and then his lips suddenly and jarringly clamped together.

Charie stood there, attired in a capelet of burgundy and royal blue plaid, and her full skirted gown of blue was trimmed in the same plaid fabric. Her bonnet matched her cape, framed by royal blue ruching. She raised her face to his and managed a smile. "I hope this isn't a bad time."

Domitri glanced around the room, humming with excited whispers.

"But I was afraid you wouldn't see me if I went to your apartment."

Domitri nodded his head, indicating that she move back into the hall. He followed her, pulling the door closed behind him. However, the damage had already been done. He'd never regain order after this for at least two of his pupils knew Charice Marin had just knocked on his door.

"Is something wrong?" Domitri certainly hoped there wasn't, but he couldn't imagine what would have prompted her to come to his place of employment. "Is it Chervenkof?"

"No, nothing of the sort. I asked the headmaster for permission to speak to you. He told me that I was more than welcome to do so."

Of course he did, Domitri thought. No one could refuse Charie anything. Including himself.

"Then tell me what brings you here. I have a room full of fidgety young men who'd like nothing better than to avoid reviewing for their examination."

"Domitri, you don't belong here. You should accept the role in *The Pearls of Esther*. I would truly enjoy working with you."

"Did Olar—?"

She shook her head. "No. He doesn't even know I'm here. You and I parted company on such poor terms, and neither of us should let our feelings keep us from doing what we love and doing it well. Won't you reconsider?"

Domitri wanted to tell her that he would, but what would doing so accomplish? Delay the inevitable. There could never be anything more between them than what they had already experienced. Brief touches and a few kisses. She had made it clear she didn't want him involved in her personal affairs. If anything, his presence might adversely affect Charie's career.

After all, at his age, most *danseurs* had moved into the role of choreographer or owned a dance academy. The leaps and jumps eventually took a toll on the knees. And he was only human.

Grasping her hands, he brought them together, giving her a bittersweet smile. "I thank you for asking me, but the answer is still no."

"Won't you at least think about it? You possess such a marvelous gift. Not only are you a true master of the dance, but you bring such passion and emotion to whatever role you take. If you don't dance with me, dance with someone else. Don't waste what you have." She lifted up on her toes and pressed a quick kiss to his cheek, then dropped down, her smile shy.

Releasing her hands, Domitri allowed her to move away from him. He almost followed her as she started down the hall, but that silly pride of his won the battle and kept him rooted to the spot. He still had students to teach, and an examination to prepare, and essays to review, and classes to teach—

"Enough with the excuses," he thundered aloud in the empty hall. "Enough! God, if it is Your will for me to audition, then I will. All I ask is that I do Your will, not mine."

****

Charie actually looked forward to the auditions, surprising given the fact that Domitri had refused to reconsider. She was certain this would be a day filled with the unexpected, and now that it was here, she was at the theatre early. Dressed in a practice tutu, she prayerfully awaited the first candidate, hoping that God would send them just the right man for the role of Ahasuerus.

Charie imagined herself the princess in an old tale her mother used to tell her as a child. This princess was ordered by her father to choose a husband from a number of "acceptable" men who paraded by for her inspection. After rejecting them all, she fled to the forest and found the man she wanted for her husband there, a lowly peasant boy with a heart of gold.

But by late afternoon, Charie had yet to find the lad with a heart of gold and superior ballet skills. Discouragement and disappointment sapped her spirit.

Rubenevski and Phillipe sat in a corner arguing— Rubenevski favoring a young Russian man by the name of Daliv Bolshev all of eighteen years, but competent, and a rather good, but arrogant American by the name of Alan Tresdale who claimed to have trained with Arthur Saint-Léon.

Olar sat in his seat, chin on the back of his hand, deep in contemplation.

Charie sat on the floor of the stage massaging the foot that one would-be Ahasuerus had painfully trod.

Slipper clad footsteps moved across the carpeted floor of the theatre, and Charie looked up, stunned to see Domitri approaching attired as though he planned to dance. Her heart lurched and her breath caught in her throat.

Rubenevski and Phillipe ceased their heated discussion, and Olar rose from his seat in the auditorium.

"Am I too late to audition?" Domitri's voice rang through the cavernous theatre.

No one moved or spoke.

"Why did you come, Domitri?" Olar asked. "You've told me several times you are done with performing. Do not waste your time or mine if you do not intend this to be a serious undertaking."

"I was wrong to leave *Giselle* as I did. I owe an apology to all of you." His gaze rested upon Olar, and then on Rubenevski and Phillipe. And lastly, he gave a lingering look to Charie.

By now, she had managed to gain her feet, uncertain and confused, but willing to allow God to work His will. If only her heart would stop racing.

"And I am taking this audition very seriously."

"What say you, Charie?" Olar asked.

"We've given every man who has walked in here today a chance. It's the least we can do for Domitri."

Domitri gave her a slight bow as an indication of his thanks. Then he looked back at Olar.

"Phillipe," Olar said, "review the steps of the *pas de deux* with Domitri. Then we will see what happens. Domitri, I make you no promises. We have seen others today that are very good."

"I understand. It will work out as God wills." Domitri squared his broad, muscled shoulders, and then closed the distance between him and the stage. After mounting the steps two at a time, he walked directly to Charie.

"Thank you for bringing me to my senses," he whispered to her.

Rubenevski and Phillipe were speechless for the first time during the course of that long day. That in and of itself was a miracle.

****

Charie, seated before her vanity, wondered why Domitri had asked her to dine with him. She was trying very hard not to attach any significance to the invitation, but she was excited. After Domitri's audition two weeks ago, dancing spectacularly, there had been no doubt Rubenevski and Phillipe would select him for the role of Ahasuerus.

That announcement had been formally made last week. After Domitri resigned from the academy, rehearsals with the rest of the *corp de ballet* had commenced.

Things had gone well; none of the tension and mistrust she'd feared surfaced, and their working relationship to date had been friendly and professional.

The only unsettling event had been an unexpected visit by Ludwig two days ago that had caused Domitri's brows to lower and his lips to pull tight.

But even something good had come out of that— Ludwig had told her that Domitri had apologized to him for the incident at Olar's before Domitri had left Novgorod.

The news lifted her heart and filled it with such unspeakable joy, all she could do was send silent praise to God. No matter what happened between her and Domitri, she knew that he would always be her friend in Christ. But his dinner invitation, extended after rehearsal had ended that afternoon, had taken her by surprise.

"You seem in good spirits this evening," Brigetta observed as she carefully positioned a curl so that it would drape artfully over Charie's shoulder.

"I am, Brigetta," Charie admitted as she took up her bottle of French perfume that she only used on rare, important occasions. Carefully, she dabbed a bit behind her ears. "What do you think of this gown?" Charie worried that the one she'd selected was somehow wrong for the evening's event.

"I think it is lovely and you will surely impress *Monsieur* Auberchon. He cannot help but be captivated."

"Please don't think this evening is to be romantic in any way. We are simply friends, and we're working together."

"If you say so," Brigetta agreed, although as Charie glanced in the mirror, she could see that the girl suppressed a smile.

A knock sounded on the door and *Madame* Jeaneau called out. "*Monsieur* Domitri has arrived. I asked him to have a seat in the parlor."

"Oh my." Charie came quickly to her feet, taking a final look in the mirror, pinching her cheeks to give them color. She rarely wore cosmetics other than when she was performing, but occasionally added a bit of color to her lips.

Brigetta went over to the bed and took up her cloak.

Charie cast a doubtful eye over her gown, hoping the embroidered pale pink satin wasn't too elaborate for dinner. But it was one of her favorites.

Hurrying from her room, she ran down the stairs. She consciously slowed herself to a more ladylike pace as she neared the bottom while Brigetta followed with her cloak over her arm. Walking sedately towards the parlor, she willed her pulse to slow and her breathing to resume a natural rhythm. As she entered, Domitri stood, and she was glad she'd dressed as she had.

Domitri was dashingly elegant in what appeared to be a new black suit, cream-colored cravat, and silk waistcoat of a cream, blue, and gold print. His black hair gleamed with bluish highlights and the stark whiteness of his high shirt collar accentuated the natural bronze tone of his skin.

Without thinking, she pressed her hand above her heart, literally speechless.

"Charie, is something amiss?"

"No, not at all. It's just that you—your suit—you look wonderful."

"Thank you," he said and gave her a little bow. "And may I say you look extraordinarily lovely, as well."

She knew that she blushed, but Domitri simply pretended not to notice. Instead, he joined her by the door and relieved the hovering Brigetta of her cloak. Domitri settled it around Charie's shoulders and with his hand resting at the small of her back, smiled down. "Are you ready?"

"Most certainly." Charie returned his smile. She truly hoped they would have a wonderful evening. They'd spent far too much time at cross-purposes. If only God would help them work through those things that kept them apart. She couldn't help but wonder what it would be like to allow Domitri to share her fears.

****

Domitri almost forgot his clothing was borrowed from Olar until he realized, as he sat in the dining room of the restaurant Olar had recommended for the evening, that every other man present was wearing his own clothing. Domitri was nothing more than a former schoolteacher, making just enough to survive, and a *danseur* who'd wasted his time and talent mourning a lost dream.

Yet, he had much to be thankful for. His arm had healed, he was dancing again, and he was dining with a woman whose worth was far above rubies. This time he would let God take him where he should be. And if that was with Charie, he would praise God the remainder of his days. If it wasn't, he asked for the faith and belief he would need to stick to God's plan for his life, whatever that might be.

"And where might your thoughts be, *Monsieur* Auberchon?" Charie gently teased. Her lovely violet-gray eyes reflected the light of the candles on the table, bathing them in an amber glow.

"My thoughts were on those in this restaurant, apparently all of a certain social and financial standing I will never know. And amazingly, I can say I don't care."

"And I'm glad you don't. Because I don't, either. I'd rather be poor and happy and content."

"I doubt that you will ever be poor." Domitri took a sip of water from a crystal goblet.

"Does that bother you?"

He admired Charie's directness and honesty. She wasn't afraid to speak what was on her mind. "No. But there are men who could afford to bring you to a place like this without thinking anything of it."

"I'm having dinner with you because I want to be with you. And if you're referring to Ludwig—"

He held up his hand to stem the flow of her words, aware of the combative light in her eyes.

She obediently silenced.

Domitri continued. "Not only was I thinking about those dining here; I was also thinking about you and wondering what plans God has in store for us."

"What plans has He in store for us?" Charie asked as she met his gaze.

How he longed to press his lips to hers once more, to hold her, to love her as a husband. The awareness of desire jolted him, and he momentarily lowered his gaze until he could rein in his emotions. He somehow managed a reply. "We need to be open to His will and though I'm not sure what that might be, He will reveal it to us when He's ready."

"I believe the same." Charie gave him a heart-stopping smile. "We're actually in agreement."

"We've been most agreeable since the first day of rehearsal. Surely, I've done something to set your teeth on edge by now?"

"Not that I can think of," she teased back.

The pleasant camaraderie was so enjoyable, Domitri wished the night would never end. He reached across the table and took hold of her gloved hand, bringing it up to his lips.

The moment might have proven to be a turning point had not the attentive waiters delivered their meals.

Sighing, Domitri released her hand, but there was no mistaking the light dancing in her eyes.

****

"Why don't you join me for church tomorrow morning," Charie suggested as the hired hackney cab stopped before the townhouse. Lights proclaimed the fact that either *Madame* Jeaneau or Brigetta awaited her return. She eagerly awaited Domitri's answer.

"I would enjoy that. Shall I come by for you?"

"No, don't go out of your way. Brigetta and I will meet you there."

"How goes her search for employment?"

Charie had told him over dinner about the arrangement with Lizzie's niece.

"Acquiring a role in an opera is nearly as daunting

as obtaining a place in the *corp de ballet*. I've heard Brigetta sing, and she has a strong soprano. But it can be so discouraging when you leave your home to follow a dream and it doesn't materialize right away."

"And what were your dreams when you were admitted to the *Académie*?"

"To dance. That is all I've ever wanted. I dance for the sheer joy of it. From the first moment I saw a ballerina on stage—in fact, it was Sophia, when the two of you performed in New York—I knew that was what I wanted to do. But even so, I know there is more to life than being a ballerina. There is family and home and living one's life in accordance with God's purpose—there is love and marriage—"

Her voice faded as Domitri cupped her chin and brought her face close to his. Seconds later her lips were warmed by his, and never had she known a more perfect moment. Wrapping his strong arms about her, he held her close, and the beat of her heart matched his perfectly just as their steps did when they danced together. Chervenkof and Altby were forgotten as amazement replaced all thoughts and emotions.

"Domitri," she managed to whisper when he lifted his mouth from hers.

"Charie, my love." Groaning, he pressed his face against her hair.

A loud pop, like the explosion of a firecracker, resounded in the still, cold air and the driver, uttering a fearful cry tumbled from his seat. The horse reared, nearly upsetting the hack.

Charie knew they were in terrible danger if the frantic animal bolted, and, Domitri, aware of the same possibility scrambled up to the driver's vacated seat in an attempt to grab the reins. But the terrified horse reared again, and this time the hack tilted precariously.

Charie screamed.

"Get out!" Domitri yelled as the carriage righted. "Hurry!" Crawling on hands and knees, she nearly fell when her heel caught on the hem of her gown, but somehow, she managed to jump to the ground.

The horse reared again and this time, the hack flipped over.

Domitri leapt from the seat as the conveyance crashed and splintered into several pieces. Now free of his burden, the frightened animal trotted a few feet away and began to nibble at the grass as though it hadn't been wild with terror a few seconds earlier.

That was when Charie noticed a closed carriage across the street and the driver urging the horse forward. A head partially leaned out the window and though the light provided by the gas lamps was not the best, she was certain she recognized the man. But her immediate concern was for Domitri, and she hurried over to him, relieved to see him on his feet and brushing off his ruined coat.

The driver was wailing and wringing his hands as he surveyed what had once been his livelihood.

"Thank God you weren't hurt." Clutching Domitri's arm, the earlier warmth spread through her once more as he folded his hand over hers and drew her close in a comforting embrace.

"Did you notice that carriage?" he asked. There was no mistaking the anger in Domitri's voice and in his rigid stance.

Though the carriage was gone, Charie knew whose face she'd seen.

"Yes, I glimpsed it just before it moved. Domitri, I'm certain I saw Fitz."

18

Domitri refused to leave Charie at her home even though she believed it unnecessary, and after notifying the Marin servants, he escorted her to Olar, rousing the man and his servants from bed as the time was well past midnight.

Olar praised Domitri for bringing Charie to him and suggested he stay as well, given the lateness of the hour.

Domitri demurred and after asking Charie once more if she was all right—he'd already asked her the same a dozen times or more—he kissed her on the top of her head and bade them both goodnight. Though it was very late, he had one more stop to make before he returned to his home.

The hotel Morroc was one of the finest in Paris with its mosque-like towers and Moorish décor. Charie told him Markham Fitzhugh had resided there during his stay in Paris. Given Charie's certainty she'd seen Fitzhugh in the mysterious carriage, Domitri wanted to visit the man. There were questions he needed to ask. And he didn't care if he interrupted the man's sleep, if he happened to be abed, which Domitri doubted.

The drowsy eyed front-desk clerk managed to drag himself from his stool and pull out the guest registry. Yes, he knew of Markham Fitzhugh, but couldn't recall seeing him about lately. The records indicated that Fitzhugh had checked out over a week earlier, bound for Frankfurt.

Domitri knew Fitzhugh planned to join Matilda in the city where her new play was set to open the first of March. He'd visited Charie a few days earlier announcing his imminent departure. What was Fitzhugh up to?

There were no answers forthcoming, so resigning himself to disappointment, Domitri headed home, his body now suffering the effects of his wild leap from the crashing hack.

Sleep was elusive, but he was up, dressed, and walking to the small protestant church that Matilda and Charie attended early the next morning. He was a little stiff and his shin was bruised, but other than that, he was none the worse for the previous night's experience. There was no doubt someone had intentionally spooked the horse in the hopes of injuring the occupants of the cab. Or, which possibility he feared the most, one of the occupants—Charie. He still believed Anapol Chervenkof had been behind the stage accident. But if not, the real culprit was still determined to hurt Charie. Why, Domitri couldn't begin to guess.

Petrov assisted Charie from Olar's carriage when Domitri reached the chapel, Olar alighting behind her.

He immediately went to Charie, who looked lovely in a gown of brilliant amethyst. She seemed unaffected by the previous night's drama and gave him a warm smile as he took her hands.

"How did you sleep?"

"Not well. I was so worried about you even though Papa assured me you could take care of yourself."

"I didn't sleep well either, not because of an

injury," he quickly assured her, "but because I kept sorting all the pieces to this puzzle in my head. I'd like to talk to you and Olar after services. Something about this situation doesn't make any sense."

"Of course we'll talk. We can all go to Papa's. He doesn't want me to return to the townhouse just yet. I'll say something to him."

A feminine voice called out a greeting, and looking to his side, Domitri recognized Mira and her beau, Pierre Gouneau, approaching.

Once they'd joined the group. they filtered into the church and found a pew together.

Domitri managed to seat himself beside Charie and discreetly took her hand in his while savoring her lovely smile.

****

"You're right, this doesn't make sense," Olar agreed as Jules placed a bowl of steaming white bean and celery soup before him, the first course of their lunch now being served, following Olar's blessing.

Charie watched her father run his spoon through the liquid in an effort to cool it before tasting it just as she often did.

He'd invited Domitri, Mira, and Pierre to join them for luncheon after church and now they sat at the long table in the beautiful dining room, its walls covered with fifteenth century Flemish tapestries.

Charie noticed how Mira's wide eyes roamed the room as though she couldn't believe where she was.

Domitri remained quiet while the soup was served, apparently lost in his own reflections of last night's near disaster. "I wish that you had found

Fitzhugh."

"The hotel records indicate he left for Frankfurt more than a week ago," Domitri said. "And he stopped to see Charie before—supposedly—leaving."

"I know it was Fitz. I wish there was a way for us to contact *Maman* quickly."

"It's a shame Bréguet's new telegraph doesn't reach Germany. As slow as communication currently is, it would be quicker for us to send a message by carrier pigeon." Domitri's lips curved upward in grim humor. "And at the moment it would be nearly impossible for any of us to travel to Frankfurt."

"I can," Pierre said.

Charie was glad to see that the young man was gaining weight and wearing clothes without patches and holes.

Olar had spread the word among those in his circle that Pierre was quite talented, and already the young man had received several commissions in addition to Olar's.

Charie wondered how she would ever find the time to sit for her unfinished portrait now that rehearsals for *Esther* had begun.

"Baron Bauerhausen has asked me to do a portrait of his mother as a gift to her on her birthday. As Mademoiselle Marin will be limited in the time she can spend with me over the next few months, I could travel to Frankfurt and begin the painting of the dowager baroness. Of course, my primary objective would be to update *Madame* Marin as to the happenings here and discover *Monsieur* Fitzhugh's whereabouts."

"That might not be a bad idea," Olar said as he stroked his bearded chin. "I would send Yuri with you, and he could bring back the information while you remain to complete your commission. Yet, if Matilda can vouch for Fitzhugh's presence, that leaves us with nothing. Chervenkof couldn't be behind this latest accident even if he had something to do with the water on the stage. At present, he is still residing in a St. Petersburg prison."

"Until we receive word from Pierre, we have to be careful," Domitri pointed out. "I would suggest that Charie remain with you, Olar."

"As should you. We don't know the target of last night's incident," Olar reminded Domitri.

"That's out of the question. I have my afternoon and Saturday classes. I am also tutoring two of my worst former students who happen to be my two best dancers. And I wouldn't want to leave Muzette alone."

"Domitri, you don't need the money. You are being paid handsomely to dance the role of Ahasuerus." There was no mistaking Olar's bad humor.

"That's not the issue. I enjoy instructing. And one day I will teach dance to make a living just as my parents do now. I can't perform forever."

"I'm sure you have a few good years left," Mira piped up brightly, believing she'd just complimented Domitri. His scowl wiped the smile off her face. "Did I say something wrong?"

"No, Mira, you said nothing wrong," Charie assured her friend, trying hard not to smile. "But Papa, I don't want to be forced from my home. Aren't we overreacting?"

"Charie, how could we be overreacting to the fact we were both nearly crushed?" Domitri exploded. "I agree with Olar."

"And I insist that both of you should remain under

my roof until such time we can resolve this matter. It's not as if I don't have the room. Neither event was an accident. And I want to keep an eye on you both. Have Muzette come here, Domitri, if you are uncomfortable leaving her alone. Renska will welcome the company."

Charie silently wondered how a woman who spoke only Russian and a woman who spoke only French could possibly provide one another company, but she kept her thoughts to herself.

Olar was determined.

Which meant Charie and Domitri had no choice in the matter. After luncheon they were sent off together in the Stanislov coach to visit their respective residences to pick up whatever personal items and clothing they would need and to make arrangements with their servants.

As night fell, Charie and Domitri returned to Olar's home with both Muzette and Brigetta.

Madame Orenska took Charie and Brigetta to a guest suite larger and more spacious than her room at the townhouse.

Domitri was installed in a guestroom just a few doors down from hers, and Muzette would be using a spare room in the servants' wing.

Given the elaborateness of the accommodations, Charie decided she shouldn't complain and simply enjoy the opportunity to spend more time with her father. As for being under the same roof as Domitri, it was impossible to repress a tiny thrill of excitement. God knew how much she loved Domitri and perhaps her elation was only a natural reaction.

As Charie settled in the large poster bed, bordering on sleep, a terrifying memory resurfaced. She was surrounded by marble and granite crypts, cloaked in snow and ice. Sophia's name was engraved on one, the top covered with frozen lilies. And Charie was not alone. Ernest Altby was there—threatening; warning.

Sitting up, she drew a deep, ragged breath to steady her nerves. She hadn't come up with the money Altby demanded. Had the accident been arranged by Chervenkof's man to frighten her into compliance? What would Altby do next to make sure she produced the funds? Would he release the damaging information he'd promised to spread? But it was Fitz she'd seen in the carriage. She was sure of it. And Fitz wouldn't try to hurt the daughter of his employer. Or would he?

Charie hadn't considered the fact Fitz might in some way be connected to Chervenkof and Anapol. If that was so, what did Fitz have to gain?

No answers came to mind, so she lay there replaying all the events, unable to put them in order. She couldn't tell anyone about Altby's threats, not yet. His implications were demeaning and tawdry. But if she didn't do something soon, the resulting scandal might force her and her mother to retire sooner than they'd planned. Neither of them would ever be able to hold their heads high.

*****

Pierre left the next morning with Yuri, bound for Frankfurt and Matilda.

Charie prayed for their safe arrival and hoped whatever Pierre discovered from her mother would shed some light on the mystery unfolding in Paris. Consequently, she was distracted during rehearsal, earning a severe rebuke from Rubenevski and puzzled frowns from Domitri. Resolving to put her mind to her practice, she forced out all thoughts of the carriage accident and managed to finish the day with a nod of satisfaction from Rubenevski.

Much later that evening, long after her father's household had retired for the evening, Charie donned her dressing gown and ventured downstairs to Olar's library. Finding a volume of Shakespeare's sonnets, she opened it and began to read, hoping that she would grow sleepy.

"Can't sleep?" Looking up with a slight start, she saw Domitri lounging by the open door, still clad in breeches, boots, and a white shirt open at the throat. She tried hard not to stare overlong at that exposed portion of his chest.

"No. I wish Yuri would return with word from *Maman* about Fitz."

"Don't let this worry you." Domitri entered the room with its towering cases of books, world maps, and globes and seemed perfectly suited to the surroundings. She'd never stopped to consider how well-educated and knowledgeable he was.

"You're much safer here."

"I suppose so." Charie gave him a rueful smile. "I have two bodyguards—I should be very safe indeed."

"Olar is understandably concerned with your welfare, Charie. There is no doubt the man loves you."

"And I, him. What's so amazing is that I loved him like a father before I found out he was. Perhaps, somehow, I always sensed a deeper connection between us."

"I saw that connection, but being the blind idiot I am, I wasn't able to grasp the obvious. Just as I've struggled with the obvious since the first day we met."

"What do you mean?" Her words came out breathlessly, the book in her lap now forgotten.

Domitri knelt by the chair in which she sat and took her hand. "I am in love with you, Charice Marin. And I wish, very much, for you to become my wife. Before you give me an answer, you should know that I admire and cherish you because you are you; not because you are Sophia Stanislovna's sister. I ask God to allow me the privilege of loving you, protecting you, and making a home with you. I wish to dance with you, in spirit, soul, and body until that moment I draw my dying breath, and then my greatest hope is that we will do the same when we are united in Heaven. I can't offer you wealth or luxury, but I can offer comfort and security and a love deeper than the wells of eternity."

Silence slipped around them as his words floated upon the chilly air, but inwardly, Charie burned with the fire of a love the likes of which she'd never thought to experience. What should she say—what could she say? She should say what her heart was telling her.

But what if the scandal changed Domitri's feelings? He'd endured such pain and loss when Sophia died. His first marriage had fallen apart long before the train accident claimed Sophia's life. Could she subject him to the ridicule and speculation when the details of her mother's unorthodox conduct became public—the questions—the secretiveness of her birth—the absence of a father? What if Chervenkof twisted the facts of his relationship with her mother, presenting her mother as an immoral, unprincipled woman?

"I," she swallowed painfully, "I can't give you an answer."

Domitri tightened his hold on her hand. "What's in your heart, Charie?"

"Love," she gasped. "I do love you. But things are so uncertain."

"They don't have to be." He was insistent, wearing away her resistance.

Her gaze fixed on his, those green eyes urging her to confess it all and cast her worries on his broad, muscled shoulders…her traitorous heart was about to lead her where she knew she shouldn't be. "Not now. I can't do this now. Don't press me, Domitri. I don't want to anger you—"

"I'm not angry." His tone was surprisingly gentle, his eyes conveying the love he'd just professed.

Charie felt horrible. How could he be so compassionate, so understanding? She didn't deserve his love.

"I can wait. I will wait until you're ready to share your love. If your heart leads you elsewhere, I won't be happy, but I'll accept your decision."

"You are amazing," Charie whispered as she raised her other hand, and then traced his scar with her fingertips. "Patient and giving. And loving."

Domitri grasped her fingers, and then kissed each one, slowly and softly.

Charie nearly choked on the sob his touch evoked.

Releasing her, he stood, smiled, and then walked away.

She wanted to stop him, to call him back, but she couldn't. Dropping her face in her hands, she allowed the tears to fall freely.

****

"Someone didn't sleep well last night," Olar observed on the ride to the theatre the next morning.

Domitri shifted his gaze to Charie, who sat beside Olar, her eyes shadowed and troubled. If only she would open up to him.

Charie straightened in her seat and pasted on a smile.

Domitri shrugged. "I passed a fairly good night." Not exactly the truth, but he'd made peace with himself, determined to wait as long as necessary. Until God clearly showed him there could be no future with Charie. "What of you, Olar?"

"I slept very well, thank you," he replied, his gaze moving from Charie to Domitri as though silently probing for what wasn't being said, "knowing that the two of you were beneath my roof. And by the way, I know that both of you were in the library for a while."

Charie's face paled, and Domitri felt as though he'd swallowed a rock, his collar suddenly too tight.

"Papa, Domitri and I were just talking."

"Is there anything you'd like to share?" Domitri looked at Charie and she shook her head slightly.

"Not...yet."

"Why the hesitancy?"

Charie squirmed and averted her eyes, pretending to look out the window.

"The two of us have confessed a fondness for one another." Domitri spoke, eliminating the need for Charie to answer.

Olar's brows shot up. "I see." Olar feigned a gravity his eyes belied. "I'll have to be patient."

So will I, Domitri added.

Having reached the theatre, they were stunned and dismayed to see several *gendarmes* outside guarding the door.

Domitri was out of the coach first, Charie and Olar

directly behind him.

The guards barred his entrance.

"No one is allowed inside," the officer informed him curtly.

"I am supposed to be here for rehearsal."

"An investigation is being conducted, and no one is to go in."

"What sort of investigation?" Olar demanded, having now come up beside Domitri. "I am Count Olar Stanislov and my ballet company, under the direction of François Robert, rehearses and performs in this theatre. Now, I ask that you permit me to enter, along with my daughter and *Monsieur* Auberchon."

Charie trembled.

Reaching for her gloved hand, Domitri squeezed it reassuringly.

"Then you're the one we've sent some of our men to find—please go in. The captain has questions for you."

"Tell me what has happened?" Olar requested in such a way the officer immediately answered.

"A man was found by *Monsieur* Nicolai Rubenevski behind the stage, severely beaten and near death. Even now we can't be sure he will survive although he has been taken to the public hospital."

"Have you identified the man?" Domitri asked tersely while tightening his hold on Charie's hand.

"He was able to give us his name before he lost consciousness—he is *Anglais*—an Englishman. The name is Fitzhugh, *Monsieur* Markham Fitzhugh."

****

Charie was certain this nightmarish day would

never end as she restlessly paced the somber, dark halls of the forbidding public hospital, silently praying that she never become so ill or hurt so badly she had to be taken here.

Nurses walked up and down the halls, their expressions mirroring the grimness and joylessness of their profession. Surely, a hospital didn't have to be like this—why couldn't there be sunshine and smiles even if those within the walls were ill? Just being in a pleasant environment could help one to heal. She thought of the children's hospital, and though it was old and in need of many repairs, the kind, compassionate nuns made all the difference.

But at the moment, Charie was cold and despondent, having been left alone when Olar and Domitri were admitted to the ward where Fitz had been placed. A nurse informed them that Fitz had regained consciousness. The two men refused to take her with them, telling her it was not a place for her to be.

But she had questions to ask the man—specifically why would Fitz want to hurt her and Domitri? Matilda had always depended upon Fitz to handle all the irritating, time consuming details of her career so that she could devote herself to rehearsals and performances. He'd always been professional, courteous, and most congenial. What changed him?

She knew now she could no longer delay telling her father and Domitri of her encounter with Altby in Novgorod. The man would never give her peace until he'd either frightened or blackmailed her into meeting his demands. Charie found herself wringing her hands. *Oh Lord, I'm so afraid.*

Having walked to the furthest end of the long,

gray corridor, Charie noticed a stairway that led to the lower floors. She was about to turn around when she froze in terror.

Emerging from the shadows was Ernest Altby, looking hale and hearty and far too pleased with himself. Immediately she lifted her skirts in preparation of running from the man, but he was surprisingly quick. Grabbing her arm, he thrust her against the cold wall. Placing his hand over her mouth, he pressed the barrel of a pistol against her cheek, speaking roughly into her ear.

"If you thought I wasn't serious the last time we spoke, you made a mistake. This time I am going to finish what I planned. And if you scream, I'll simply finish it more swiftly than I intended." With strength she never would have imagined he possessed, he wrapped his arm about her waist and hauled her towards the stairs, her heart hammering while she weighed the consequences of attempting escape. He would kill her if given provocation, so she remained silent, praying that someone would see them downstairs.

Such was not to be for the stairs ended at what appeared to be a servants' entrance, deserted at that moment, when he pulled her through the door.

She struggled when she saw the waiting coach, but hearing the unmistakable cocking of the pistol, she ceased her efforts and walked unsteadily towards the conveyance.

Opening the door, Altby shoved her within, yelled something to the driver in Russian, and then quickly followed, slamming the door. The coach immediately rolled down the snow-covered lane.

Righting herself, Charie looked at Altby, his bulk

filling the small space opposite where she sat.

He still gripped his pistol.

"Why are you doing this?" Charie fought the tears that wanted to spill. "Why would you risk your life and your freedom for Anapol Chervenkof?" To her amazement, Altby laughed.

"Poor, ignorant child. I don't work for Chervenkof. He works for me. He has failed to accomplish his task. Now, it's up to me to take care of things. I am the one you should fear. Allow me to introduce myself—Ivan Nikitin, at your service."

19

As Domitri gazed down at Markham Fitzhugh, his face a mass of reddened blotches and purple bruises making him nearly unrecognizable, he didn't know if he was sorrowed or disgusted. Fury kept him silent as Olar calmly questioned the man.

The Englishman had already confessed he'd been drawn into the Russian arms scheme after meeting Chervenkof during that time when the man courted Matilda. Jealousy had driven Fitzhugh to reveal Chervenkof's criminal side to Matilda, earning the Russian's disfavor.

But the two men put aside their personal rivalry when they discovered a mutual need and greed. Now Fitzhugh's involvement had led to a beating so severe, if he survived he'd most likely be crippled for life. Fitz coughed.

Olar helped him sip water and waited for the liquid to ease his throat.

"Why has Charice been targeted, Markham?"

With his eyes swollen shut, Fitz turned his head towards the sound of Olar's voice. "The money." Fitz rasped.

"Charie has no money. Her earnings are held in trust until she reaches twenty-three years of age or she marries."

That was news to Domitri, not that the knowledge made any difference in his desire to marry her. Those funds belonged to her.

"The insurance I obtained." Fitz coughed again but it subsided quickly.

Olar persisted. "What insurance?"

"With Lloyd's...of London...on Charice—in the event—" He faltered and began to cough.

Olar helped him drink from the glass once more. "In the event of what?" Olar resumed his questioning.

"Couldn't—couldn't dance."

Horror spread through Domitri as the enormity of Markham's words registered.

"Chervenkof had you do this?"

"No. I did so some time ago. Wanted to make sure I'd have something to fall back on if Matilda released me from her employ."

Even if it meant crippling Charie? What sort of man had Markham hid behind his polished façade? Domitri wondered.

"I told Chervenkof what I'd done in a moment of drunken bravado. Then, just before *Giselle* opened, he informed me he needed funds immediately and that now would be," he paused to draw a labored breath, "a good time for an accident to occur. It was either help him or he'd 'help' Matilda discover what I'd done."

Domitri's blood chilled, and he clenched his fists to keep from adding to the man's physical misery. He was instantly contrite and silently prayed for forgiveness for the uncharitable thought.

Markham had already suffered enough because of his greed.

"So when the fire didn't injure Charie," Domitri spoke, "you arranged other accidents. You had something to do with the incident in St. Petersburg at Christmas and most recently, spooking the cabby's horse. What did Chervenkof promise you?"

"Not Chervenkof." Fitz attempted to open one eye, but had no success. "Altby—he's behind everything."

"Altby?" Olar and Domitri spoke in unison.

"I thought he worked for Chervenkof," Domitri said.

Markham moved his head back and forth in an attempt to convey no. "His name…is Nikitin—Ivan. He runs the organization—Chervenkof was merely his public mouthpiece. It's Nikitin who needs the money. He was here earlier, and then slipped away when the nurse brought you in. He's going to ki—ki…" Another fit of coughing racked Markham's body and blood bubbled out upon his lips.

Olar compassionately wiped it away.

"Kill Charice." Markham went limp as though he'd fainted.

Domitri turned and ran from the ward even though Olar called out to him to wait.

When he entered the corridor, Charie was nowhere to be seen. Taking the central stairs with a series of leaps, he prayed he'd find her on the lower level. A frenzied search earned him strange looks, but no Charice. Rushing outside, there was still no sign of her. Running past startled hospital staff and visitors, he halted at the rear of the unwelcoming facility just as he glimpsed a short, squat man pushing a woman into a coach about fifty feet from where he stood.

The man turned at that moment. Ernest Altby. Altby yelled to the driver to go and the coach lurched forward.

Domitri knew Charie was with Altby. His heart pounding painfully, he looked around for a way to follow. With no time to waste, he ran towards Olar's carriage.

Petrov was talking to the horses from his seat as though conversing with humans.

"Get down!" Petrov glanced up and seeing Domitri's expression, jumped to the ground. Domitri took his place within seconds, urging the horses to a gallop.

As the carriage barreled forward, Domitri saw Altby's coach on a long, narrow lane that led away from the hospital and, fortunately, wasn't far ahead. He didn't know what he was doing—he could only pray God would help him reach Charie in time.

****

"Ivan Nikitin?" Charie repeated, uncertain she'd heard correctly. What did he mean by saying Chervenkof worked for him? Was he joking?

Altby didn't answer right away, his attention focused outside the window. But then he turned and gave her an unpleasant smile.

"I am Russian by birth—granted I was brought to American when I was two years of age. But by the age of ten, I was an orphan living in the squalor and filth of the New York City you never see. By twelve, I had killed a man for the coins in his pocket. At ten and five, I was the leader of a gang composed of the most fearless men that lawlessly roamed the city. The more fear we instilled, the greater grew our power.

"Though I was the leader, the one with the ideas, the plans, and the means of execution, I had inherited my sire's lack of height and consequently, lacked the physical presence of a man who invoked admiration and loyalty. Instead, I invoked ridicule and contempt.

"I needed someone to play the part of the leader, yet follow my instructions. That someone was Anapol Chervenkof—Nap Rheyev—recently arrived from Russia, filled with impossible dreams of using American money to fund a revolution and become wealthy in the process. He exuded charm and confidence and was exactly the man I needed.

"Things went very well—I remained in the background, posing as Chervenkof's aide while I accumulated my fortune. Chervenkof was most successful at courting wealthy women, convincing them to part with huge portions of their bank assets. He grew greedy and decided he wanted a larger share of the earnings.

"Unknown to me, he secretly struck out on his own, arranging deals with his old Russian friends who were ready to arm themselves and their compatriots for one of the numerous 'revolutions' that were forever plotted but rarely implemented. I could have told Chervenkof it wouldn't work." Altby—Nikitin—fell silent.

Charie was frightfully aware of how fast the coach was moving along the snowy road. The driver had the horses at a reckless gallop, and she was bounced with bruising force even though she grasped an overhead strap to steady herself. She feared her teeth might be shaken loose. "I suppose you were angered when you discovered Chervenkof had gone into business for himself," Charie managed through teeth that rattled.

"Naturally. By this time, Matilda was his target—famous, beautiful, and rich, not to mention the mother of an incredibly promising ballerina with enormous earning potential. And it didn't hurt that her father was one of the richest men in all of Russia."

"How did Chervenkof discover that Olar Stanislov was my father?"

"He overheard a discussion between your mother and Markham Fitzhugh, who was involved in a bit of financial creativity himself. He wanted to insure his lavish lifestyle continued in the event Matilda Marin reached a point where she no longer required his services. He was worried she would marry Chervenkof or, even worse, return to her former husband, Stanislov, and would no longer need an agent to handle her affairs.

"So, without your mother's knowledge, Fitzhugh took out an insurance policy on you through the Society of Lloyd's at London's Royal Exchange that would pay him should you become unable to perform."

A fierce chill swept Charie, and she bit down so hard on her lower lip, she tasted blood.

How could Fitz have done such a thing? Charming, sophisticated Fitz?

Altby—Nikitin—was telling her that Fitz, without compunction, would have hurt her in some way to obtain the insurance money if the need had arisen, setting him up nicely for the remainder of his life. With startling, horrifying clarity, Charie realized it was Fitz who'd sloshed the water on the stage. But there were still so many pieces that didn't quite fit.

"What does Fitz have to do with Chervenkof's dealings with the Russians? My mother hasn't released him from employment. What does he have to gain?"

"Chervenkof was displeased when Fitzhugh dredged up enough of his wrong doings to turn Matilda against him. Because of Fitzhugh's nosing about, your mother severed the relationship with Chervenkof. He'd spent the sum delivered to him by the Russians intended for me, and hoped your mother would provide enough money to replace the funds I expected. And the Russians still awaited the delivery of their guns. Chervenkof went into hiding when he was unable to deliver my money and produce the promised weapons. When Fitzhugh bragged to Chervenkof about the insurance he'd obtained on you, Chervenkof used the information to blackmail Fitzhugh.

"Not one to overlook mismanagement of my funds, I set out to find Chervenkof. When I finally located him last summer, I made it very clear who was in charge. I took care of his angry clients, and then considered what you and your mother could add to the pot. Knowing who your father was, aware of the insurance, and certain your mother would do just about anything to keep you safe, the makings of a very lucrative exchange had been placed in my hands."

"But my accident at the theatre, and the faked kidnapping in St. Petersburg...the carriage mishap just a few nights ago—"

Altby chuckled, which angered her. In that moment she decided that being angry was better than weeping in fear.

"Fitzhugh was behind the first event—although he thought he could stage the accident, file the claim for the insurance, and then disappear before Chervenkof could find him. But as you know, that didn't work, and I threatened to reveal his duplicity unless he helped me. You can imagine how agreeable he became when faced with the prospect of his own demise.

"He failed again in St. Petersburg—not entirely his

fault, and was warned not to make another mistake. But he did—the carriage didn't tip over and cripple you as intended, so I had no alternative but to mete out the punishment Fitzhugh, by now, so richly deserved. Hence, his residence in the hospital. With Chervenkof rotting in a St. Petersburg prison, I'm going to handle matters—I've already sent another missive to the count demanding money for your release. Only this time, after I receive the money, I won't be handing you over to anyone.

"I'm going to kill you because you have made what should have been easy very difficult. I have unhappy Russians who are decidedly distrustful. I don't plan to suffer the same fate as Fitzhugh."

Charie could scarcely believe what she was hearing. "You're going to kill me because your minions couldn't carry out your orders? Are you serious?"

"Of course I am. I saw you dance in *Giselle*—you are indeed a marvel. It's very sad that your star will dim as quickly as your sister's did. The count will be inconsolable with grief."

The racing coach tilted precariously as it careened around a bend in the road on two wheels.

"He should slow down," Charie insisted aloud. She was almost glad that Altby was visibly shaken. "If he keeps up this pace, he'll kill us both before you get your chance to kill me. And you'll never get your money."

Altby poked his head out his window and to her horror, he aimed his pistol out of it. "Your misguided lover has decided to follow us. You can thank him if we tip over." He took aim, and frantic that he would harm Domitri, Charie grabbed Altby's arm and jerked with all her might.

Hurling vile curses, Altby shoved her.

Charie fell hard against the squabs, hitting her head on the edge of the opposite window. Pain darted behind her eyes as she struggled to sit upright, and then tried to grab Altby once more. Before she could grasp his coat sleeve, the door nearest Altby crashed open.

Domitri swung within, like a trapeze artist she had once seen in a circus. Using his booted feet, he forced Altby against the opposite door.

Charie pulled herself into a tight ball in an attempt to keep out of the way. But Altby still had his pistol, and she knew he would use it.

The coach rocked dangerously, the driver increasing the breakneck pace.

Charie knew they would crash. It hardly mattered that Domitri had come to her rescue if they both perished, and she feverishly repeated the Lord's Prayer.

****

Domitri's fist shot out, catching Altby hard in the jaw.

Altby's head snapped back, and blood spurted from the corner of the man's lips, inflaming his already uncontrollable fury. Roaring, he swung at Domitri.

A scream ripped from Charie's throat, terrified that Altby's punch would send Domitri out the opening. Suddenly, the coach lurched oddly, the wheels on the left side leaving the ground.

Domitri grabbed her arm and hauled her against him, wrapping his other arm about her waist.

No longer hindered by Domitri's grip, Altby

aimed the pistol at them both.

But to Charie's shock, Domitri—one arm still tight around her—used his other arm and grasped the doorframe with his free hand. Hauling them out of the coach, Domitri held on to the shattered door, and then used his legs to catapult them away from the coach. They hit an area of deep snow and tumbled several feet through what felt like tufted grass, rolling to a stop in an icy stream.

A terrifying shriek rent the air followed by a horrendous crash and suddenly, everything was quiet and still.

Charie pushed herself up, soaking wet and teeth chattering from cold and fright.

Domitri was already moving towards her. Taking hold of her arms, he pulled her up, enfolding her.

Charie sobbed brokenly as she clutched his torn coat, burying her face into his chest. Domitri held her so tightly, she wondered if her ribs were crushed but it hardly mattered. God had brought them through this terrible ordeal, and no one would ever separate them again. No mortal one.

"I have to see what happened, my love." His hoarse whisper brushed her ear. "There's a possibility someone is hurt and needs help. You must stay here. Will you be all right if I leave you?"

Charie managed a nod, but no words would pass through her frozen lips.

Releasing her, he made his way up the snowy bank, and then moved out of her range of vision.

Charie paced, rubbing her arms for warmth, sending up thanks to God for protecting them during such a ghastly ordeal.

A shot rang out in the cold air, and forgetting all

about Domitri's request that she remain by the stream, Charie managed the arduous climb up the embankment in spite of sodden skirts and petticoats.

After reaching the road, she broke into a run, the biting cold making her lungs ache. Reaching the scene of the accident, she covered her mouth with her gloved hands.

Altby's coach looked worse than the cab had the other night after it tipped over.

The horses had broken free before the crash for they were nowhere to be seen and had most likely galloped down the road. The driver was propped against a tree, his left leg twisted at an odd angle, the man in obvious pain.

There was no sign of Domitri. Her heart thumped erratically. "Domitri! Domitri!"

Had Altby survived the crash and shot Domitri?

No, no, I mustn't even consider that. Looking about, she had no idea where to search. Then she saw them, Domitri carrying Altby over his shoulder as though he was a very large sack of potatoes. Hurrying forward, Charie halted a few paces away as he dropped Altby on the ground, the man unconscious, bearing a multitude of cuts and bruises, but still breathing.

"I heard a shot." Her words came out breathlessly.

"Fortunately, Altby's aim isn't very good."

Charie almost smiled at his attempt at humor.

"I chased him into the forest before he stumbled and I could catch him."

"I can't believe either man survived the wreck. What do we do now?"

"Wait. I'm sure Olar isn't far behind. Are you hurt?"

"Just a bump on my head. And you?"

"That dratted bullet wound in my shoulder is aching, but other than that, I'm well. Fitzhugh was working with Chervenkof and Altby."

"I know. The most unbelievable part is that Altby was behind everything."

"Fitzhugh told most of the story when Olar and I spoke to him in the hospital. As soon as he let it slip that Altby had just visited him before our arrival, I knew you were in danger. I looked for you and realized you were no longer in the hospital. Then I saw Altby shoving you into a coach."

"Thank God you followed, but Domitri, how did you follow?" He gave her a tired grin.

"I 'borrowed' Olar's coach. I'm sure the horses had enough sense to stop once I hopped off."

"What you did was dangerous, risky, and reckless, and," here she paused to draw a breath, "so very brave." Flinging herself against him, she hugged him as though she would never let him go.

Domitri hugged her just as fiercely.

When the shrill neighs of approaching horses reached her ears, Charie turned her head, relieved to see her father and six Paris *gendarme*s.

Petrov, now reinstated as driver, guided the previously abandoned Stanislov coach at a rapid pace. Releasing a deep sigh, she sagged against Domitri. Could it be the nightmare was finally at an end?

"Domitri, I must tell you the real reason I declined your marriage proposal." Pushing back tumbled curls and snarled tresses, Domitri smiled down at her.

"Not now, Charie. There's plenty of time for explanations." He pressed a kiss to the top of her head, and she shut her eyes, drawing strength from his arms, feeling safe and protected.

****

Domitri found the serenity of the small church most welcome given the tumult of the past several days, and he was glad to find the doors open. As he settled in a pew near the front, his eyes rested on the lovely stained glass window depicting Jesus delivering the Sermon on the Mount. The pieces of glass were so intricately and realistically arranged, Domitri almost imagined he could reach out and touch his Savior. And though he couldn't in the literal sense of the word, he could do so through his heart and mind. And they were both sorely troubled.

Shutting his eyes, he allowed himself to recall that harrowing day when Altby abducted Charie. Having heard Fitzhugh's confession at the hospital and Charie filling in the missing pieces with what Altby told her, Domitri could only shake his head in wonder and amazement.

What a miracle God had enabled him to bring Charie safely through the near catastrophe, and Domitri had offered up his heartfelt thanks and praise. But as he'd held her in those moments before Olar's arrival, he realized he would have lost all will to go on had something happened to her—that allowing her to move forward without him would be better for them both. He'd thought his world irreparably shattered when Sophia died.

To be separated from Charie would leave him but a sad shell of a man—a man who could be of no use to anyone and certainly not to God. If he caved in to his desires and earthly needs, he would marry Charie, ill-prepared to meet the realities of life. Sadly, death often intruded upon happy ever after.

Dropping to his knees, he clasped his hands and rested his forehead upon them. Searching his heart, he struggled for the words—for a way to express his fears and longings and why he was afraid to embrace love.

"Oh, Lord, I'm lost and confused. I thank you for protecting Charie and for allowing me to bring her to safety. Yet, I fear that pursuing the dreams of my heart could only cause more pain. I'm not sure I could survive losing Charie. Even though You have revealed through the resurrection of Your Son that death is not the end, how could I remain on this earth without Charie? I may die before her, but there is always the possibility...I want to be free of this doubt.

"I know that I should simply turn things over to You and allow You to guide my steps. Wouldn't it be better for me to end things now with Charie, and make it through life alone? You've given me back the ballet. Surely, that should be enough. Oh Lord, help me— allow me a glimpse of hope."

He fell silent as he struggled to contain his tears, an occurrence that always left him unsettled. Hearing footsteps, he looked up, recognizing the reverend. The man smiled at him as he came to his feet.

"I've seen you with *Mademoiselle* Marin on Sundays," the man said in French. "You are the *danseur*, Domitri Auberchon, are you not?"

"I am. The door was open, and I came in to pray. I hope that was all right."

"The house of God is open to all. I did not mean to eavesdrop, but you were speaking aloud to our Father, and I couldn't help but hear. I surely do not have all the answers, but I have one question to ask. Is it not better to spend a day with one beloved than spend a lifetime unhappy? Is that not what our Lord wishes for each of us? That is a question you must answer for yourself. Rest assured, my son, you have God's love and grace. We've done nothing to deserve it, but it is there for us without fail."

Tears clouded Domitri's vision. He wasn't convinced that marrying Charie was the right thing, but he knew denying what was in his heart was the wrong thing.

"Go in peace," the man offered, and then continued towards the altar.

Domitri drew a deep breath, aware that his load had already lightened.

****

"*Maman!*" Charie cried excitedly, jumping from her chair and flinging herself into the arms of the woman who now stood at the door of her dressing room.

"My dear, dear, Charie," Matilda murmured, tightening her hold. "You are well and safe. I thank the Lord above for protecting you and for giving you two very brave men to watch over you."

"You know, *Maman*?" Charie asked uncertainly as she pulled back and met her mother's tearful gaze. "About Fitz and Chervenkof and Altby?"

"I know everything, Charie. And I am so saddened that Fitz died. When Pierre and Yuri arrived with their bizarre story, I refused to remain in Frankfurt wondering what was happening here. Ludwig worked things out so that I could leave. Yuri, Lizbet, and I took the first train we could and arrived in Paris about two hours ago.

"At the townhouse. *Madame* Jeaneau informed me that you'd been staying with Olar. When I reached Olar's, I was told that the two of you had already left for the theatre. I found Olar with *Monsieur* Rubenevski, and, well—I know more than I want to and all I can say is praise God you are well and safe." The two hugged again.

As they separated, Charie brushed at her eyes.

"You are all right, aren't you?" Her mother's eyes were filled with love and concern.

"I wasn't injured, *Maman*, but Domitri—" Her voice faded as she recalled the past few days since the coach overturned. A disturbing distance had slipped between her and Domitri, something she couldn't quite define, as though he was keeping her at arm's length. They hadn't had so much as five minutes alone, and he and Muzette had returned to their home now that Altby and Chervenkof were no longer a threat. Had he somehow learned of Altby's accusations, altering his feelings for her?

"The two of you haven't worked things out? What are you waiting for?" A note of exasperation heightened her mother's voice.

"Weren't you the one who thought Ludwig would make a more suitable husband?" Charie gently teased, her tears now evaporated.

"I was wrong. Besides, it appears Ludwig is now enamored with the daughter of a Prussian nobleman— a beautiful, but quiet girl who is most devoted to her family and to her faith. You did make a difference in Ludwig's life. His priorities have changed."

"I hope he finds happiness. You're the one who made me see him in a different light. But Domitri—it's almost as though he now fears what he feels for me. I truly believed he was over Sophia."

"Perhaps his fear is in losing you, which he nearly did. Sometimes it's harder to love and risk losing that love than to deny love and never face that possibility."

"If he would just talk to me—"

"Charie," Mira called out and popped into the dressing room, "they are ready to—Madame Marin! You are here—this is wonderful. You will stay until opening night?"

"I plan to. Charie, we'll talk later. I don't want to delay you. I'll be sitting with Olar." She kissed Charie's cheek then swept past Mira.

Mira looked questioningly at Charie. "Is everything all right?"

"I hope so," Charie managed and gave her friend a tremulous smile.

20

It had been nearly a week since Domitri's encounter with the minister of Charie's church, a week that had found him reading the Bible and fervently seeking God's will in his life. Now, he was mere hours away from the opening performance of *The Pearls of Esther*, and as he sat in the empty theatre, he opened his Bible to the book of Esther and began to read.

After he finished, he realized how courageous Esther had been in asking the king to save her people when she could have easily been banished or killed. How like Charie with her loyal heart, her great beauty, her indomitable spirit, and her God—given gifts. Flipping back a few chapters, he read aloud.

"'*And the king loved Esther above all women, and she obtained grace and favour in his sight more than all the virgins; so that he set the royal crown upon her head, and made her queen...*'"

Charie was the queen of his heart, now and forever, and just as the minister had said, was it not preferable to have but a short time with one who is loved than to face a lifetime without that one?

Shutting the Bible, he sat there and gazed upon the stage, now decorated as Ahasuerus' palace garden, resplendent with faux marble columns, hangings of purple linen, silver, and gold; the imitation paving tiles of black and white marble covering the floor of the stage. Had the real Ahasuerus not found Esther, what happiness would his wealth have brought him?

There would be no more pushing Charie away; indeed, he planned to fully embrace and enjoy the love that she had brought into his life. There would be no more uncertainty, no more guilt, no more wondering if he was making the right decision. He would let go and let God take charge. And no matter where life led him and Charie, he would spend every moment of his life loving and treasuring her for the rare woman she was.

In a matter of hours he would be on that stage with Charie, dancing the part of a great king, ruler of lands from India to Ethiopia, with hundreds of men and women at his beck and call. A man who possessed a power unmatched by few earthly men. Domitri had none of that, nor did he wish for any of Ahasuerus' riches. He only desired the love of one woman. And she was all the riches he would ever need.

Coming to his feet, he hurried towards the stage, took the steps and commenced a series of leaps across the stage. He had to draw up quickly when another stepped from behind the curtains, attired simply in a practice tutu and torn leggings, Charie's favored dance attire.

"Shouldn't you be saving some of that energy for tonight?" she asked even as she moved away from him in a series of coquettish *piqué* turns.

He quickly caught up to her and grasping both of her arms, raised them over her head and pivoted her about to face him. Still on her toes, her lips were just a hairsbreadth beneath his. Gently lowering her arms and folding them behind her, he pressed her close to his thudding heart, his gaze fixed upon her.

"I was leaping across the stage because I can no longer contain my joy."

"And why are you filled with such joy?" Her words were softer than a whisper but still he heard.

"Because I love you, and I want nothing more than to marry you. Tell me that you will marry me, Charie."

"I was afraid that," she began, and then stopped as though her emotions wouldn't permit her to continue. "I thought these past few days—" Charie attempted to speak once more and failed again.

"I thought I was being noble and selfless, but I was being ignoble and selfish. I want to spend every second God allows me to live on this earth loving you. I fervently hope that you feel the same about me."

Charie didn't answer him. "Altby came to me in Novgorod," she began uncertainly, her lips trembling and her eyes glassy.

If only he could erase the pain.

"Altby blackmailed me. He made terrible threats, and insinuated *Maman* and Olar—Papa—were never legally wed. He said no record of my birth exists, nor is there anything to prove that Olar is my father. Altby said that unless I gave him the money he demanded, he would see that the information was spread with the intention of ruining *Maman*, and ultimately, me.

"I planned to speak to my parents, but I overheard them talking, and it is obvious they both still care for one another. It didn't seem the right time to burden them with Altby's threats. I thought I could handle the matter. But I couldn't. I didn't want to tell you because I was ashamed and worried some of the story might be true. I was too afraid to find out for sure. And I didn't want you dragged into a scandal. You'd suffered enough…"

Domitri silenced her with a kiss—full of promise, and hope, and certainty. All the things that faith in

God's plan could bring.

"My love, you should know I would never have given any credence to the words of a greedy, grasping, power-seeking bully. I love you, and God made the perfect soul for me when He created you."

"Society frowns upon *Maman* and I because she's an actress and I'm a dancer."

"You are a child of God. You have nothing to be ashamed of. I want to share your cares and your worries. I want to share your love of ballet. I want to share your life."

It was as though the sun appeared there on the stage as a glorious smile lit Charie's face.

"Then, yes. Yes, yes, yes."

****

"Charie, Charie," Mira cried excitedly through the small crack in Charie's dressing room door. "She's here; she's here!"

Coming to her feet, Charie caught up her dressing gown, slipped it on over her costume and threw open the door.

Mira took hold of her hand as they hurried through the labyrinthine maze of the backstage, dodging the scurrying bodies that were making final preparations for this special midday Easter Eve performance of *Esther*.

Just as Charie began to wonder where Mira was taking her, she saw the child.

Suzette was carried by a young man, of average height, but strapping and healthy in appearance. Suzette's cheeks were pink and her eyes sparkled.

"*Mademoiselle* Marin," Suzette cried out happily,

and Charie hurried over to the child who was now placed on her feet. Charie dropped to her knees and hugged the little girl who was holding on to her ballerina doll, the one Charie had given her at Christmas. Now four months later in April, with spring gilding Paris and warming the air, Suzette was well enough to attend the ballet. Such a miracle was this child, Charie thought in wonder as she gently pushed Suzette back to get a good look at her.

"How you've grown," Charie observed.

Suzette giggled. "*Maman* says I eat more than both of my brothers. But everything tastes so wonderful. I don't have to see the doctor nearly so much anymore."

"Well, I am very glad to hear that. I'm so happy that you could come."

"I'm so glad you invited me," she said. "*Maman* made me a new dress." She took a moment to pirouette while holding out her full white organza skirt with the tiny rosebuds embroidered on the sheer fabric. The underskirt was pink satin as was the gigot-sleeved bodice. "Thank you," she replied happily.

Charie offered a silent apology to God for her outburst months back. She had questioned how God could let such a sweet child be so ill. Now, here that child was, growing stronger and healthier every day.

"But I am not nearly so beautiful as you."

"I might have to disagree," Charie teased. "Now, who is this young man with you?"

Awkwardly, but eagerly, the youth came forward, looking to be about sixteen years of age.

"This is *mon frère*," she explained. "Louis."

"It is very nice to meet you," Charie said extending her hand.

Louis quickly took it and pumped it vigorously.

"It is wonderful to at last meet the one who has been so good to my sister. Thank you for inviting us." Before Charie could reply, Suzette burst out joyfully.

"It is *Monsieur* Domitri!"

Domitri laughed as he joined them and scooped Suzette up in his arms.

"*Monsieur* Domitri, this is Louis," she explained, waving at her brother.

"And it is good to meet you, Louis," Domitri said extending a free hand to the young man. "Thank you for bringing Suzette here today."

"She has been so excited. And I am honored to meet you, *Monsieur*. But surely you and *Mademoiselle* Marin have much to do before the curtain rises. We should find our seats."

Domitri handed Suzette over to the open arms of her brother. "Then we shall see you after the performance. Remember, you are to be our guests for luncheon this afternoon."

"*Oui*, your invitation said as much, but we would hate to impose."

"Don't be silly," Charie protested. "We want you to be with us. Meet us here after the final curtain."

Suzette bobbed her head of dark curls, and her brother whisked her away, Suzette chattering excitedly.

Domitri turned to her with a smile. "Nothing is impossible for our Lord," he said and Charie nodded.

"I will not be so quick to doubt in the future," she assured him as she slipped her arm through his. "Shall I give you a kiss for good luck?"

"Let me see." He pretended to think on her offer. "One for luck, one for happiness, one for joy, and one for love. That makes four."

"Be content with one." Charie lifted up on her toes and kissed him on the lips.

Domitri wrapped his arm about her and made the kiss lengthen into the time it would have taken for her to give him four.

When he released her, she was breathless, as though she'd just completed a series of *fouettes* around a room. What was it about this man that so completely rattled her? Whatever it was, her wedding day couldn't arrive soon enough for her to find out.

****

"I think Suzette plans to follow in your footsteps," Domitri commented as he and Charie walked arm in arm in the spring twilight. They had just seen Suzette and her brother off at the station, bound for their country village outside of Paris.

The day had been such a pleasant one—the performance had gone well, and Suzette and her brother had expressed their thorough enjoyment of the ballet and luncheon, taken on the terrace of a café renowned for its simple, but tasty fare.

The conversation during the meal had been most interesting, Suzette revealing to Charie how Domitri had asked her to pray that Charie would marry him when they had visited her in the hospital at Christmas.

Charie found the revelation most charming, and she offered up her own thanks to the Lord that Suzette's Christmas prayer had been answered.

By the time, they'd finished their meal, Suzette's eyelids were drooping, and it was most evident the child's excitement was finally taking its toll.

Domitri had offered to carry Suzette, who fell

asleep on their short walk to the train.

But she did manage to murmur a sleepy goodbye as Domitri handed her over to her effusively grateful brother.

Now Charie and Domitri were on their way home, and Domitri had suggested a walk before the patiently waiting Petrov drove them to their respective residences. He was glad to have this private time with Charie before parting.

"It may be difficult to find a seat so will you meet me early at the church in the morning?" Charie asked, as though Domitri might forget it was Easter on the morrow.

"Yes, I will. And I plan to sit with the loveliest ballerina in Paris—no, make that in the world."

"I've never known you to use such flattery," she returned, a soft smile tilting her lips adorably.

"It's not flattery—it's the truth. It's been a long day. Are you tired?"

"Not really. I'm so filled with the wonder of everything that's happened. I remember months ago asking God to reveal His will, yet my heart was breaking as I did so, for fear you would not be part of His plan for me."

"And I suffered the same. Charie," he said and stopped, turning her so that she faced him. "This isn't going to be easy. I am stubborn, and I can be unreasonable, and I—"

Pressing her gloved fingers to his lips to still them, she looked up at him, giving him a smile.

"Do you love me?" She lowered her hand so he could speak.

"More than I can ever tell you if I live to be a hundred."

"You can start now," she suggested. "And continue doing so for the rest of our lives."

The cooing of two white doves drew their gazes heavenward, and they watched them in fascination as they circled above their heads. Their wings would briefly touch, and then part, as though the doves were engaged in a sort of courtship dance.

A dance of life, Domitri thought as he gazed down at the woman he loved.

Epilogue

June, 1846
Norfolk County, VA

The Marin farm would be a beehive of activity by the time the sun peeked above the horizon on the day of the wedding.

Which prompted Charie to rise just as the first tiny hint of pink pinpointed the location of the soon to rise sun. With the house still quiet, she let herself out and ran barefoot across the meadow to a nearby meandering creek. There she gathered wild roses and Queen Anne's lace, planning to include them in her bridal bouquet.

Returning to the rambling, three-story farmhouse where her mother had been born and raised until her journey to New York City twenty-five years before, Charie found that the other inhabitants had now risen, including her parents, her future in-laws, grandparents, aunts, uncles, cousins, four dogs and three cats.

She noticed that Olar, Domitri, Dominic, and her grandfather were already in the kitchen drinking coffee and conversing in a smattering of English, Russian and French.

She found her female relations gathered in the dining room, debating the arrangement of the cake and sweets table. Dodging them, she hurried upstairs to find her mother, grandmother, Ekaterina, and Mira fussing over Charie's wedding dress of cream and gold satin. She certainly hoped something hadn't happened to the fairytale gown that her father had engaged a Parisian couturier to fashion for her special day.

Upon hearing her entrance, they all looked up.

Mira hurried over to relieve her of her flowers.

"I was about to come looking for you, young lady," Grandmother Marin said, a twinkle in her eyes. "I was wondering if you'd changed your mind and run off."

"No, Grandmother," Charie assured the elderly woman with the snow white hair, "wild horses couldn't drag me away today. I've never been so happy. Why are all of you looking at the gown?"

"We were just saying how beautiful you'll look in it," Matilda answered as she walked over to Charie and hugged her. "You'll look like a princess."

"She is a princess, of sorts," Mira reminded them in halting English. She'd been working very hard to learn the language since discovering she was to travel to America for Charie's wedding.

The two girls had practiced every day for three months.

Pierre returned from Frankfurt a few days before their departure and had proposed to Mira, which she'd joyously accepted. So, upon returning to Paris, there would be two more weddings to plan.

Charie had already agreed to be Mira's matron of honor at her ceremony to be held in the fall at her family's home in the country. And much to Charie's joy, Matilda and Olar planned to remarry on New Year's Day of the next year.

"I will not have any of that princess talk here.

Today I am simply Charice Marin Stanislovna about to wed my beloved and surrounded by all of my family and friends. That's all that matters."

"We're just happy that you decided to come home to get married," Grandmother said, coming over to hug her, too. "This will always be your home, and you know you're welcome whenever you can visit."

"Domitri and I plan to do just that. Papa told us that we may be dancing in New York the first of next year in a new ballet based upon a Mozart opera. We'll be sure to come down then. And I'm glad we decided to be married here, too. Of all the places *Maman* and I have been, this is by far the loveliest and most peaceful."

Hearing numerous footsteps tromping up the stairs, they all hurried to the door to see the female aunts and cousins heading up.

The bedchamber quickly filled with laughter and chatter.

****

Domitri couldn't take his eyes from Charie as she moved among the guests in her grandparents' home, amazed that he'd been her husband for nearly two, marvelous hours. The ceremony at the small, country church had been simple, but meaningful.

Tears of joy rimmed Charie's eyes when he'd kissed her to seal their vows. Never had he seen a lovelier sight than Charie as she'd walked down the aisle with Olar, arrayed in a splendid gown and carrying simple wild roses and Queen Anne's lace.

Never had he wanted anything so badly as to be able to claim Charie's lips as her husband, knowing he had at last, and mercifully, received God's direction. Now, unable to reach his beloved, he could only gaze at her across the crowded parlor of the Marins' home.

"She's your wife, Domitri," a voice spoke over his shoulder, and he knew without turning it was Olar. "You're standing there gazing at her like a love struck schoolboy. I believe Shakespeare once said, 'Faint heart never won fair lady.' Go claim her before the dancing begins outside."

Domitri lost no time following Olar's order, but silently promised himself he wouldn't be so docile with all of Olar's demands. Yet, when he thought of what Olar's prodding had accomplished over the past several months, he couldn't help but wonder if the count had been God's instrument in returning Domitri to life. For he was gloriously and wonderfully alive.

****

Charie saw Domitri striding towards her as though no one could, or would, dare deter him from his purpose. Taking hold of her arm, he led her outside where the fiddlers were already tuning up for the afternoon's festivities. Pausing a moment, he took her face in his hands and kissed her until she was breathless and clutching his arm.

All around them people loudly urged them to move to the platform constructed for the dancing, the musicians having broken out into a tune that made Charie want to tap her foot even though she knew her husband with his French and Russian roots had never heard the likes of before.

"I believe they're playing our song," he whispered as he gazed into her eyes.

"Our song? They're playing *Turkey in the Straw*— it's an American tune."

"Every song they play today is our song. And we shall dance to them all."

"Yes," she agreed softly as she reached up and lightly touched the scar that ran along his jaw, no longer a reminder of his past, but a reminder of how she loved everything about him. "We will dance, just as the doves did that evening in Paris."

Suddenly, Domitri lifted her in his strong arms and whirled her about, Charie laughing in abandon.

She had found happiness that she never thought she'd find, and she silently thanked God for his blessings even as her accomplished *danseur* husband trod on her toes in his attempt to execute the steps to *Turkey in the Straw.*